I0733621

Fate, Coincidence, and Other Curse Words

Fate, Coincidence, and Other Curse Words

Kenneth Creech

BALANCE OF SEVEN
Newport, VT

Fate, Coincidence, and Other Curse Words

Copyright @ 2024 Kenneth Creech
All rights reserved. Printed in the United States.

No part of this book may be used or reproduced in any manner whatsoever without written permission except in the case of brief quotations embodied in critical articles and reviews.

This is a work of fiction. Unless otherwise indicated, all names, characters, businesses, places, events, and incidents in this book are either the product of the author's imagination or used in a fictitious manner. Any resemblance to actual persons, living or dead, or actual events is purely coincidental.

For information, contact:
Balance of Seven
www.balanceofseven.com
info@balanceofseven.com

Cover Art by Laras Putri
lele.ragadipa@gmail.com
Instagram: @_larasputri_

Cover Design by Kenneth Creech

Developmental Editing by Charleigh Brennan

Copyediting, Formatting, and Proofreading by TNT Editing
www.theodoretinker.com/TNTEditing

Publisher's Cataloging-in-Publication Data

Names: Creech, Kenneth, 1982- .
Title: Fate, coincidence, and other curse words / Kenneth Creech.
Description: Newport, VT : Balance of Seven, 2024. | Summary: Reincarnations of the Greek gods of fate and coincidence, seventeen-year-old Destiny and Chance continue their endless debate over which is more powerful. To test their abilities, they try to help their gay friend Jonathan find a boyfriend, but their struggle over eternal bragging rights might just cause everyone to lose.
Identifiers: LCCN 2024946058 | ISBN 9781947012707 (pbk.) | ISBN 9781947012714 (ebook)
Subjects: LCSH: Gods, Greek – Fiction. | Sexual minority youth – Fiction. | Gay high school students – Fiction. | Dating (Social customs) – Fiction. | Fate and fatalism – Fiction. | Coincidence – Fiction. | Illinois – Fiction. | BISAC: YOUNG ADULT FICTION / LGBTQ+ / General. | YOUNG ADULT FICTION / Romance / LGBTQ+. | YOUNG ADULT FICTION / Legends, Myths, Fables / Greek & Roman.
Classification: LCC PS3603.R44 F38 2024 (print) | PS3603.R44 (ebook) | DDC 813 C74--dc23
LC record available at https://lccn.loc.gov/2024946058

28 27 26 25 24   1 2 3 4 5

To those who were with me
on my path to completing this book,
especially those who had a hand in
bringing it to life.
Fate and coincidence played a major role,
but so did all of you.
Thank you!

Contents

Prologue	1
One	11
Two	20
Three	28
Four	37
Five	48
Six	57
Seven	66
Eight	76
Nine	84
Ten	93
Eleven	101
Twelve	108
Thirteen	116
Fourteen	123
Fifteen	132
Sixteen	142
Seventeen	150
Eighteen	160
Nineteen	169

Contents

Twenty   178

Twenty-One   187

Twenty-Two   196

Twenty-Three   205

Twenty-Four   213

Twenty-Five   221

Twenty-Six   230

Twenty-Seven   241

Twenty-Eight   249

Twenty-Nine   256

Thirty   265

Thirty-One   274

Thirty-Two   282

Thirty-Three   289

Thirty-Four   296

Thirty-Five   305

Thirty-Six   312

Acknowledgments   317

About the Author   319

Prologue

Sitting in a coffee shop, Lachesis stared out the window at the passing people, whose cheeks were pink from the cold as they navigated the city sidewalks. A never-ending stream of people flowed through downtown Chicago like the river nearby, and Lachesis loved to watch them. She knew their souls the moment she saw their faces, for she had been the one to measure their lives. No matter their nationalities and backgrounds, she knew everything about them. As if watching her own children play, Lachesis reveled in even the smallest details of the lives they led during their time on this planet.

One man practically yelled into his phone as he strode past, stressed out. He planned to propose to his girlfriend later that evening, and his expression betrayed a war of emotions. He needn't have worried, though. Lachesis could see that she would say yes.

On the corner, a young girl played guitar, her face

hidden behind long, dark hair. She sought her big break in the music industry, which unfortunately would never happen. In a few weeks, though, she would meet someone who would lead her to a new passion.

Heading for a meeting to discuss a big promotion, a frustrated woman pushed a stroller through the crowd. Her husband had forgotten it was his day to take their son to daycare, and she had no idea what she was going to do with the currently sleeping boy while meeting with her associate vice president. Lachesis saw that her son would wake up, and his bright-blue eyes would remind the associate vice president of his own son. She would land the job of her dreams today, but she wouldn't know that for another twenty-three minutes.

Seeing those pathways unfold in people's lives was rewarding. Lachesis smiled whenever she saw the good she brought about. Knowing she was the reason positive things came to pass comforted her when she witnessed the pain that also existed in the world. She never enjoyed that part— the heartache, death, and other great losses—but she knew that with the good must come the bad. Even though the mortals might not understand why, the loss they each experienced was part of their path. Not always fair and rarely understood at the time, both the good and the bad of an individual's path got them where they needed to go.

Watching mortals' paths unfold and guiding them when necessary were both a joy and a burden. Lachesis never liked to admit it, but she would intervene from time to time. However, even she couldn't stop the inevitable.

Stirring her coffee, Lachesis was so engrossed in the images steadily flowing through her mind, she hardly noticed the door of the small shop opening and closing.

Suddenly, her mind went blank, as if someone had

turned off a light inside her. Blinking rapidly, she grabbed the table in front of her to steady herself. Though she could still see the physical world around her, she felt so vulnerable without her additional senses, she might as well have gone blind. Heart racing, she wiped sweat from her brow and looked around for what had changed.

She didn't need to look far; after all, the lack of visions could mean only one thing: *he* had somehow found her again. It had been decades since their last encounter, and she had almost succeeded in forgetting about him entirely.

Caerus was taller than her, though their golden skin was almost identical. His light-brown eyes gleamed with the easy humor of one who had never known guilt. Meanwhile, Lachesis's gaze, though warm with empathy and understanding, bore the weight of death, for she was the one who measured lives and determined the paths they took.

He showed no sign of having noticed her as he flirted with the male barista taking his drink order. The barista blushed and looked away but didn't pass up the chance to slip the flirtatious man a card with his phone number on it. Leaning back in her seat, Lachesis crossed her arms and watched Caerus pick up the card and wink before walking away from the register. Still flushed and struggling to function normally, the barista poured a drink while sneaking glances at the golden-skinned man, who seemed not to notice.

Lachesis had to give it to Caerus; his power gave him a magnetism that worked on all mortals regardless of their sexual orientation, relationship status, or mental state. It wasn't an actual aspect of his power but rather a side effect of who he was and what he could do. People looked at him as they might a winning lottery ticket, amazed good fortune was so close they could touch it.

She felt for the barista, though, who looked embarrassed when he realized he'd made the wrong drink. He quickly made another, visibly concentrating the second time around. When the barista finally placed the drinks on the counter, Caerus picked up both cups and said something softly before turning and walking away.

Even without her visions, Lachesis knew what would happen next and waited for Caerus to notice her. As his gaze locked with hers, his eyes opened wide with surprise and sparkled. He walked over to her table, carefully pulled a chair out with his foot, and set both drinks down.

"Fate, it's been so long!" he greeted, using her age-old nickname. "May I join you?" Without waiting for her approval, he removed his coat, set his bag on the table next to the steaming cups, and sat. "I have to admit, I'm surprised to see you in Chicago. I thought you would still be out west." His smile revealed teeth a brilliant white against his tan skin and short, well-manicured beard. "How have you been? How long has it been? Twenty, thirty years? You don't look a day over twelve hundred." He chuckled.

"I'm well past that, as you well know. Thank you, though, for what I assume was an attempt at a compliment." She met his gaze without a hint of amusement, her arms still crossed. "I do so *enjoy* your flattery, Coincidence."

"I only ever speak the truth." He winked, knowing his flirtation wouldn't have its intended effect on her. Reaching for one of the cups on the table, he slid it over to her. "I feel like you could use a refill."

Lachesis accepted the drink graciously and took a tentative sip. To her surprise, it was delicious, and she savored the sweet warmth enveloping her tongue. "What is this?" she asked, curiosity piqued.

"You know, I have no idea." Caerus tipped his head in the barista's direction. "The young man at the counter accidentally made it and asked if I wanted it since it would go to waste otherwise. Guess it was just a happy accident." He smirked.

Lachesis raised an eyebrow, drawn in by his baiting despite herself. "I think you mean it was meant for me. You know I always get what I want."

She took another small sip. The coffee warmed the chill she had started to develop with his arrival, but it did little to calm her frayed nerves now that they were so close together. Her inability to see people's paths now that he was there made her feel almost defenseless against him. She pulled her coat tighter around her shoulders.

Caerus sat back in his chair, the ghost of his previous smile tracing his lips. Gods were unable to use their powers on each other, so she could never be certain how he felt or what he would do next, but she could imagine the emotions racing through his mind as he squinted and furrowed his brow. "What brings you to the city?" he asked, before taking a sip of his drink.

Shifting in her seat, she pulled her hair over her right shoulder. "A lady never reveals her secrets, you know."

Caerus leaned closer, his eyes focused on the dark-brown waves of her hair. "I thought that was magicians," he said with a smirk. When she laughed, he relaxed back in his chair. "Seriously, what brought you out here? I thought you lived in California now."

"Keeping track of me, I see." She, too, sat back. "I'm here for a visit. I woke up last week and decided to get out of town for a bit. Chicago popped into my head, so here I am."

She didn't bother telling him that a vision of herself in

a different body was the reason for the trip. He wouldn't have believed her anyway. They had been down this road multiple times before, and it never ended as she hoped it might. They had been in opposition since their creation. While she focused on what was to come and what was meant to be, he constantly tried to lure people away from their paths with promises of instant gratification.

Caerus had once compared himself to a spider wandering a world of webs. He could pick and choose which strands to follow and even change entire webs if he wanted. The mortals who followed his influence might find themselves better off or might wind up caught in a web they had no business in at all.

"So you're saying you couldn't stay away from me? That makes sense; most people can't. My easy-going personality and the way things go my way most of the time make me a great guy to be around."

Lachesis knew he couldn't help himself, but it didn't make the exchange less frustrating. Even when they were younger, he'd loved antagonizing her as she sat weaving with her sisters. She would measure lives, knowing every twist and turn their paths would take, and he would whisper to her about free will and choice and how he gave them a chance at something spontaneous, while she doomed them to follow one predetermined path forever.

"Oh, please! Chicago is a big city full of people. The fact that you walked into the coffee shop I was sitting in and got a drink made perfectly to my tastes"—she held up her cup—"proves that there *is* a path, even for us, and you walked right into it!"

The chill in her core spread, and she knew her vision was somehow about to come true. She didn't understand what it meant, though. How could she possibly be a teenager again? She'd stopped aging thousands of years ago and had never heard of an immortal aging backward.

"Besides, I wouldn't have been here if it wasn't meant to be."

Caerus's smile faltered, and she knew her words had stung. He'd always claimed that things were more manageable when one accepted that everything was due to random cosmic alignments that could be manipulated but not controlled. He could nudge things and make circumstances align to his benefit when he wanted to, but everything else was happenstance. While she saw singular paths, he saw thousands. Snow might fall just a little harder than expected overnight and make people late to work, or a shoelace might come undone, leading its owner to find a dollar bill on the ground when they stooped down to tie it.

"These aren't the works of you or any of the other gods. It's just random luck, good or bad. Opportunities are fleeting. If you don't grab them immediately, they may disappear."

His words still lingered in the back of her mind. He'd been the reason she'd left her sisters and gone off on her own to seek the truth about what happened to the mortals she watched.

Lachesis carried the world on her shoulders because she felt she could control things. She believed she could predict every small change and how each would impact people. Every time they met, though, Caerus would question her, making her doubt herself despite the evidence she'd seen to the contrary.

When he wasn't around, she felt empowered and confident. But when they were together, her visions disappeared, and her confidence crumbled. It was part of why she spent so much time on her own.

But avoiding him wasn't always possible, even for her.

Years ago, Caerus had taken a liking to a particular mortal and had altered the patterns of the world to bring the mortal luck and prosperity that wouldn't have been his without Caerus's interference. Caerus had attempted to use the mortal to prove to Lachesis that there was no real plan, but the drastic changes required to bring everything back into balance were worse than Caerus had imagined. Lachesis had had to intervene to save the mortal from an untimely death—which she still hadn't forgiven Caerus for— but he still wouldn't accept that she had known what should have occurred all along.

"It was pure luck I ended up here," Caerus said, though he looked a little uncertain. Just as Lachesis lost her visions around him, Caerus couldn't manipulate her or the people and situations directly around her. However, he never second-guessed his explanations, no matter how powerless he might be around her. "I was nearly run over by a woman with a stroller in her mad dash through the crowd and happened to see this coffee shop when I jumped out of the way. That you were here had nothing to do with it. I didn't even notice you until after I got your drink, so that proves nothing."

Lachesis laughed loudly, then clapped a hand over her mouth, embarrassed. Once the people around them had looked away again, she dropped her hands to her coffee cup and drank the rest of the warm liquid.

"That woman was headed to a critical meeting today, and nearly running you over was what she had to do to get there while her son was still asleep. Your toes would have been a worthwhile sacrifice had she crushed them."

Caerus shrugged. "Well, agree to disagree, I guess. I hope you enjoy your time here in the city, whatever the purpose. I'm afraid I have to be going now. As I said, this was an unintended stop this morning, and I have other appointments." The levity returned to his eyes as he gathered up his bag and stood to put on his coat. "It's always nice to run into you, Fate, especially when it's a happy accident."

"A happy accident? Oh, Coincidence, this was always meant to be!"

As if her words had been the trigger, the chill in Lachesis's core exploded outward, engulfing her and Caerus in a flash of white light. Her mind detached from her physical form, and she seemed to float on the river of people she had watched earlier, their lives and paths leading her toward something she couldn't quite make out.

In the distance, a pinprick of light appeared, growing larger and brighter the closer she came, accompanied by reassuring murmurs and a rhythmic throbbing like a fast heartbeat. Physical sensations returned as she neared the light, and she tried to push herself away from it, unsure what awaited her on the other side.

Everything was happening so quickly, she couldn't process it all. She tried calling out to her sisters and then to Caerus, but her voice wouldn't work. Even the yelling in her mind was drowned out by the continuous beating noise, which had gotten faster.

How could this happen? Gods don't die.

As the light became unbearably bright, her body was squeezed on all sides. Lachesis had no choice but to curl in on herself and close her eyes against the brightness.

Suddenly, the world went silent, though only for a second. As her senses were overwhelmed, she screamed.

Advocate Eureka Hospital
Eureka, IL

"One more push, and she'll be out!" the doctor encouraged. "Come on, big breath in . . . and push!"

Selena Martinez concentrated on pushing with all her might.

"Great job, Selena," the doctor said as she finally pulled the baby free. The nurse took over, working quickly to suction out the baby's nose and mouth.

With sweat pouring down her face, Selena collapsed back against her pillow. Only when she heard the first cries of her miracle baby did she finally take a deep breath. Tears of joy and relief streamed down her face. All the years of heartache and disappointment had finally ended; the baby she had first dreamed about months ago was finally here.

When the nurse carefully placed the baby on Selena's chest, Selena stared into her daughter's face, heart filled to bursting with love. Warm tears slid down her cheeks as she gazed into familiar brown eyes ringed with golden flecks. She felt like she already knew her and was only meeting her in person for the first time.

"I love you," she whispered quietly, repeating it until her daughter looked at her.

"Have you picked out a name yet?" the doctor asked, removing her surgical glasses.

Selena nodded slowly, careful not to disturb her newborn daughter. "Her name is Destiny."

Destiny, hurry up!" Jonathan yelled from the front entryway of the Martinez home. "I'm not waiting around for you again today. My mom'll kill me if I'm late one more time!"

"I'm coming. *Cálmate!*" Destiny yelled back from her bedroom. "We're not going to be late. Trust me, I know what I'm talking about."

Jonathan rolled his eyes. "We *will* be late, and you know I don't know Spanish that well!"

Despite his complaints, he couldn't help but chuckle. Waiting for Destiny to finish getting ready for school had been part of his daily routine since they'd started elementary school. Now as a junior, he knew what to expect. Fortunately, their school was close enough that it only took them a few minutes to walk there.

Jonathan and Destiny had been friends since birth, due mainly to their being born on the same day. Their mothers had met in birthing classes and bonded over their shared due-date month. When Jonathan's mother went into labor early, she'd been happy to discover that Selena had been induced and had given birth that same day.

That had been over seventeen years ago.

Jonathan's earliest memories were of him and Destiny running around their homes, playing hide-and-seek, dress-up, or Destiny's favorite, "What if?" They would watch people and imagine stories about what would happen next in their lives.

Try as he might, Jonathan had always struggled to come up with anything beyond where the people might have been going. He wasn't clever enough to come up with any details about the rest of their day, and he never really had a knack for imagining their histories. Destiny, on the other hand, would watch them for a few moments with her face scrunched up tight and then tell an elaborate story about what she thought would happen to them throughout the rest of the day.

She ended every story with the insistence that she was just guessing. She never explained her obsession with the game, but once in fifth grade, she told Jonathan that some part of her knew she was different from other people.

He hadn't really understood at the time. The following year, though, when he noticed how cute the other boys at school were, he realized he might understand exactly what she meant.

Sometimes, Jonathan would catch Destiny staring at *him* the way she had other people during their "What if?" games, her features tight and her eyes fixed squarely on his face. She wouldn't look away until he said something, at which point she would blink as if coming back to herself and tell him she couldn't see his future. Then she'd laugh, as if it were a joke, and run off to do something else.

On their thirteenth birthday, she announced that she

had decided his future was to be her friend "forever and ever."

They never played the game again.

Jonathan had actually forgotten about the whole thing until last year, when he saw her wearing that same expression at school. Her eyes had been fixed on a group of seniors as they walked out to the parking lot, piled into a car, and sped away to grab lunch. When Jonathan had touched her shoulder, she had looked up at him, her eyes swimming with tears, which she quickly brushed away. She had walked away before he could ask her what was wrong. The following day, the principal had announced that students would no longer be allowed to leave campus for lunch. Rumors had spread quickly, and by the end of the day, everyone had heard about the car accident and the student who hadn't survived.

"Hello? Earth to Jonathan. I said I'm ready."

Startled back to the present, Jonathan blinked up at Destiny, who stared down at him with her head cocked. Her makeup was flawless, as always. When the rest of the girls at school were struggling to apply mascara without clumps, Destiny had already mastered a winged liner so sharp, it looked deadly. Running her fingers through her hair, she seemed to consider piling the mass of waves up into a messy bun, but after a few attempts, she dropped it, allowing it to frame her heart-shaped face.

"Oh, hey. Sorry about that." He laughed. "Sleeping with my eyes open, I guess."

Grabbing his backpack from the floor, he walked out the door, Destiny on his heels. Linking arms, they set off for school.

Unlike Destiny, who was all curves, softness, and dark beauty, Jonathan was tall, thin, and blond. While Destiny had matured into a confident person who spoke her mind without a second thought, he was shy and more likely to go out of his way to avoid confrontation. Together, they were the perfect pair, balancing each other out. She made him bolder and stopped kids from teasing him for being gay, and he occasionally stopped her from direct confrontation when a subtler approach was possible.

They were so perfectly suited that despite liking guys, he'd considered asking her to be his girlfriend in seventh grade. Before he could, she'd told him she was glad they were just friends. He'd taken the hint, and their friendship had remained just that.

Two years later, she had shared with him that she was asexual.

As they walked, they talked about the previous night's homework and speculated about the coming day's gossip. Jonathan swooned over the cute guys who drove past, and Destiny listened patiently as he moaned about how desperately he wanted a boyfriend and a car. He couldn't wait for the day he finally had a way to get out of Eureka, even if only for a few hours.

Just as they stepped off the curb to cross the road in front of the school, a car came out of nowhere, horn blaring. Jolted out of his daydream about escaping the small town, Jonathan lurched back up onto the curb, pulling Destiny with him. The driver didn't bother to slow down or glance back to see if they were okay before turning into the student lot.

"Where the hell did he come from?" Jonathan yelled, heart racing.

A cold burn began to take root in Destiny's stomach as she stared after the car. She'd had no idea it was coming. While she couldn't see Jonathan's future—or her own, for that matter—she would usually get a sense of things like this based on seeing the paths of others.

So why hadn't she seen this?

Pressing a hand to her stomach, Destiny tried to shake off her uneasiness. "Right? What an asshole! Where do kids learn to drive?" She shook her fist in the direction of the parking lot where the car had disappeared.

Laughing, Jonathan shook his head. "That's right. Damn kids don't know what's good for 'em." He grabbed her hand from her stomach, and they crossed the street without another incident.

Once inside the school, they headed for their lockers, where Destiny noticed small groups of students, primarily girls, huddled together and whispering.

"I wonder what's going on," Jonathan said, nodding toward a nearby group.

"Must be especially juicy if it's already spreading this early." Destiny grabbed her math book, a notebook, and a pencil from her backpack and put everything else away.

Suddenly, she froze, her breathing growing shallow. "Something's wrong." She reached blindly for Jonathan as her gaze darted back and forth. The paths surrounding their classmates had begun to fade. She could still see them, but she had to concentrate to keep them visible. She hadn't faced something like this since . . .

The thought was so egregious, she refused to entertain it. *There's no way he'd come here,* she reassured herself, trying to calm down.

Jonathan caught her hand and scanned the hallway. "What do you mean?"

"I'm not sure." She shook her head slowly. "But don't do anything stupid today." She turned and focused sharply on him. "I mean it!" She immediately felt terrible for snapping at him, but the sudden weakening of her abilities had her on edge.

Brow furrowing, Jonathan tilted his head to one side and huffed. "Okay, damn." He held up his hand in a three-finger salute. "I promise, as long as you promise to stop freaking the fuck out. You're starting to scare me, and you know I'm terrible in a crisis."

He squeezed her hand lightly and pulled her into a hug, rubbing her back gently. Taking an unsteady breath, she closed her eyes and leaned into his familiar comfort. Since her birth in a mortal body, her growing powers had occasionally overwhelmed her senses, and Jonathan's support and physical presence always helped her relax. Focusing on just being present in her body, she breathed in through her nose for four seconds and out through her mouth for six.

By the time he let go, her breathing had steadied.

He gripped her shoulder and met her gaze. "You good to go to class?"

Though she still felt anxious, she nodded. Worrying Jonathan over something she couldn't explain would do neither of them any good. "Go on. I'll see you in history."

As Jonathan hurried down the hall toward his first class, Destiny tried to ignore the pain in her stomach and what it meant. But she couldn't keep the egregious idea she had tried to ignore earlier from resurfacing.

What is Coincidence doing in Eureka, and more importantly, why now?

Jonathan had tried to focus as Ms. Halpern explained the central themes of the section from *Romeo and Juliet* the class had been assigned to read, but he had already read ahead and didn't need the review. Instead, he doodled in the margins of his notebook while he waited for her to move on.

He was so engrossed in his drawing that he barely noticed when the door opened and Ms. Halpern stopped her overview. Only when she said, "You can take the desk next to Jonathan," did he look up and notice the new kid who had walked in.

At the front of the class stood a guy who was so classically attractive that calling him a model would have been an insult to just how gorgeous he really was. His skin was tanned to perfection, and his black hair was curly but in a uniform way that suggested he either spent a good amount of time on it or had a whole team of stylists on standby to keep it perfect. His chiseled cheekbones and square jaw were amazing on their own, but paired with the plump-lipped smile they perfectly framed, they were absolutely stunning.

The words *Greek god* sprang to mind, but Jonathan chased those thoughts away as quickly as possible. Glancing up, he realized the new boy's light-brown eyes were locked on him. Jonathan nervously dropped his gaze to his desk and watched out of the corner of his eye as the new kid sat down next to him. Pulling out a notebook and pencil, the new kid silently started taking notes.

Jonathan was careful to keep his eyes on his desk or Ms. Halpern for the rest of class. Even so, he couldn't miss how most of the girls in class turned to look at the new kid before blushing and turning back around. Even some of the guys turned around, but they mostly seemed curious.

When the bell finally rang, Jonathan gathered his stuff quickly, eager to tell Destiny about the new kid before the next class started. In his haste, though, his pencil slipped out of his hand and rolled under the desk beside him. Looking up, Jonathan found that the new kid's eyes were fixed on his face. Jonathan instinctively smiled, and when the new kid smiled in return, Jonathan could have sworn the fluorescent light glinted off the kid's perfect teeth.

Grabbing the pencil from under his desk, the new kid stood and leaned closer to Jonathan, offering him the pencil. "I think you dropped this."

"Thank you," Jonathan replied automatically as he accepted it, unable to pull his gaze away now that they were staring at each other from such a short distance.

Finally realizing what he was doing, Jonathan blinked and maneuvered around the new kid, who stood smirking in the middle of the aisle, refusing to move.

When Jonathan reached the hallway, he heaved in a deep breath. It had felt like all the air had been sucked out of his lungs when they'd been standing so close together.

"Hey!" A hand lightly grabbed Jonathan's shoulder, and he turned to see the new kid staring at him. "Do you think you could point me toward my next class?"

"Oh, sure!" Jonathan squeaked. He cleared his throat. "Do you have your schedule?"

Pulling out his schedule, the new kid handed it over and took a step closer, pressing their shoulders together. Jonathan glanced around to see if anyone was staring, before taking a small step to the side. Reading over the schedule, he realized they had math together later that morning.

"Looks like you have Spanish in the C wing, just down this hall and to the right. You can't miss it." He handed the new kid back his schedule.

"Thank you." The new kid narrowed his eyes, and his gaze turned predatory. Before Jonathan could turn and flee, the new kid offered Jonathan his hand. "It's nice to meet you, by the way. I'm Chance."

Two

Jonathan stared at the outstretched hand as if it were a coiled snake preparing to strike. When nothing happened, he gingerly took Chance's hand and shook it. "Uh, hi, I'm Jonathan."

The corner of Chance's mouth curled up, revealing a dimple in his cheek. Pulling Jonathan closer, he stared into his blue eyes as if searching for something. "What are you?"

"Excuse me?" Jonathan pulled his hand back and retreated to a more comfortable distance. Desperate for a reason to look away, he pulled his phone out of his pocket and checked the time. "Oh shit, I'm late."

As he headed for his next class, Jonathan couldn't shake the feeling that Chance had been flirting with him. Everyone in school knew Jonathan batted for team Alphabet Mafia, but Chance had only just arrived. How had he picked up on it so quickly? Spreading his fingers wide, Jonathan examined his hand as if an answer might appear scrawled across his palm.

When the second bell rang, he picked up the pace. Hurrying into his next class, he saw Destiny in her usual seat and took the desk in front of her so they could talk without their classmates overhearing.

"You won't believe what happened in first period!" he whispered.

Destiny's brow furrowed, and she seemed unusually nervous. "What?"

"There's a new kid in school, and I think he was flirting with me!" Jonathan's heart sped at the possibility of finally having someone interested in him.

"Really? Are you sure he was flirting?"

Destiny's question doused Jonathan's excitement, and doubt crept in.

"Well, no, I'm not sure . . . but when he shook my hand earlier, he didn't let go right away, and he even pulled me closer until our noses were almost touching."

Jonathan faltered, remembering the question Chance had asked. *"What are you?"* Had Chance been making fun of him? It seemed like a strange question to ask a stranger, but he hadn't sounded malicious, just curious.

He continued his explanation, though with less confidence. "He also made eye contact with me and smiled when he first got to class. Which . . . I guess could have just been him being friendly? He is new, after all. Maybe he was trying to make a friend?" He looked at Destiny. "What do you think? You always seem to know what people are going to do."

Before she could respond, Mr. Wright started his daily announcements. Reluctantly, Jonathan turned back around and pretended to pay attention as his mind wandered.

As Mr. Wright moved into a lecture on the election

of 1800, Jonathan couldn't help replaying the interaction with Chance in his mind: How Chance had looked at him. What the look could have meant. How Chance had used the handshake to pull him close before letting go.

Jonathan didn't realize he was grinning until Mr. Wright spoke his name.

"Something amusing, Mr. Daniels?"

Jonathan snapped out of the memory and stared at the now-silent teacher. His cheeks burned as he struggled to respond.

"*Hamilton*," Destiny whispered behind him.

Jonathan could have kissed her for the save. "I was singing a song from *Hamilton* in my head. Sorry."

Nodding, Mr. Wright returned to his lesson, and the rest of the class followed suit. The flush slowly faded from Jonathan's face, and he kept his head down for the rest of the class to avoid additional attention. When the bell rang, he and Destiny gathered their belongings and walked toward their last class before lunch.

"So, what did he look like?" Destiny asked as they made their way through the crowd of students pushing their way through the halls.

"Who?" Jonathan replied without thinking. "Oh! You mean the new kid?"

"Yes, obviously." She laughed and nudged him in the arm. "I already know what everyone else in this school looks like!"

"Sorry, I was so traumatized by Mr. Wright calling me out that I chucked the whole thing with the new guy out of my mind." Jonathan couldn't help but feel excited as he mentioned Chance again.

"Well . . . ?"

"He's about my height, maybe a little taller. He's got

curly black hair, brown eyes, and a great smile. He has these adorable dimples, and he's pretty tan." Looking down at his pale arms, Jonathan wondered what he'd look like with a tan. Unfortunately, he only ever burned and then returned to his normal ghostly white. "He's pretty cute. The way almost everyone else looked at him, I don't think I'm the only one who thinks so either. Even some of the guys in class seemed to be checking him out, but maybe they were sizing up the competition? I dunno. I don't understand straight guys."

"Eh, he just sounds like any other guy to me."

"That's because you"—he poked her in the side—"don't like anyone at school."

"That's not true. I like you." She poked him back and then stepped out of range when he tried to get her again.

"You know what I mean! You, my virtuous friend, make everyone else in school seem like a walking advertisement for teen hormones."

She laughed. As he turned toward his class, she lunged toward him and grabbed his hand, squeezing it. "See you at lunch. And stay away from the new kid!"

"No promises!" He walked off toward math class, a small grin teasing the corners of his lips.

The good mood didn't last long. Math was his least favorite class this year. Not because he didn't like math but because Mr. Davies was incredibly rude. Coach of the freshman football team, he made fun of students in and out of the classroom, bullied quieter kids, and was generally a jerk to anyone who wasn't an athlete. It was the only class in which Jonathan chose to sit at the back of the room, hoping to go unnoticed.

Unfortunately, when Jonathan opened the door of the math classroom, a familiar face sat at his usual desk.

Chance watched Jonathan walk toward him, excited for another opportunity to figure out the enigma before him.

To his surprise, the first words out of Jonathan's mouth were, "You're in my seat." And his tone wasn't deferential or lust-filled, as most people's would have been.

"Oh, sorry about that. I just picked one at random." Standing up, Chance moved one seat over and leaned toward Jonathan, who avoided Chance's gaze.

"Um, that's, uh . . . that's where I usually sit."

Chance glanced up to find another boy standing beside his newest desk. He could tell the boy would normally have been easily influenced, but even faced with Chance's full attention, he just stood there, waiting for him to move.

Sighing, Chance tried a different tactic. "Would you mind if I kept this one? My friend Jonathan is here, and he's the only person I know in this class." He forced as much charisma into his voice as possible and laughed happily when the boy finally nodded and walked away.

"Why'd you do that?" Jonathan sank lower in his seat, as if trying to disappear. "There's an empty seat over there."

He pointed to a desk a few rows over, right in front of Mr. Davies's desk. That it was the only open seat and the boy Chance had displaced was still looking around desperately for another option made it clear it wasn't a place Chance would ever want to be.

"I'm quite happy with this desk. Thanks, though. Besides, that guy just sat there, so now I can't take it."

Glancing over, Jonathan winced. "I guess he did."

"Must be my lucky day, huh?" Chance winked, hoping Jonathan would flirt back.

Unfortunately, Jonathan seemed to be doing his best to ignore Chance, instead focusing on the equations Mr. Davies was reviewing from the previous night's homework. No one else was quite as focused, and only a few minutes passed before Mr. Davies threw a piece of chalk at a girl in the second row who was staring at Chance. She yelped and ducked her head but went right back to staring at Chance almost immediately.

Chance tried not to laugh when he realized the chalk was now stuck in her hair, seemingly forgotten.

Returning his attention to the front of the room, he realized Mr. Davies was staring at him, seemingly surprised to see a new face in his class. "Who the hell are you?"

"My name's Chance. I'm new."

Mr. Davies looked at his attendance sheet for the first time that morning. "Chance what?" he barked.

"Chance Symptosi," he replied. "It's Greek."

"I didn't ask for your life story," Mr. Davies growled. "Just your name."

"Well, that's good. If you had, we'd be here all day!" Chance laughed.

Mr. Davies's lips barely twitched, and Chance's expression faltered. Looking around, Chance realized most of the students weren't paying him as much attention as they had earlier in the day.

"Whatever," Mr. Davies grunted. "Just keep up." He turned back to the board and returned to his lesson.

"That's impressive," Jonathan muttered, looking at Chance for the first time since class had started. "He's never that nice."

Chance leaned closer. "That was him being nice?"

"Trust me, that was him being extremely warm and welcoming. I think he almost cared there for a second; I didn't know he could do that." Jonathan chuckled, and Chance laughed along with him, happy to have made a connection with the enigma seated next to him.

When the bell rang, they walked out into the hall together.

"Where are you headed next?" Chance asked. He'd attempted to use his powers throughout the rest of class, to minimal effect, but Jonathan seemed to be the only person who never felt his pull. Chance planned to follow Jonathan around until he knew exactly who, or what, he was and why he was immune.

"I'm meeting my friend for lunch," Jonathan replied. "How about you?"

"I have lunch now too. Do you think your friend would mind if I joined you?"

"I . . . don't see why she would."

Chance raised an eyebrow. Jonathan obviously wasn't telling the full truth, but Chance couldn't be sure what he was keeping to himself. "She, huh? A girlfriend or a girl friend?"

Jonathan laughed. "A girl who is my friend." Despite his lighthearted response, he dropped his gaze to the floor as he led the way to the cafeteria.

"Well, her loss, then. You seem like a pretty cool guy."

Jonathan glanced at Chance, his face expressionless, though his eyes seemed to roam quickly over Chance. "I think she'd argue that our friendship is better than dating because we tell each other everything and don't have to worry that a breakup would ruin things."

Chance shrugged. "Agree to disagree, I guess. I'd rather love and lose and love again." Smirking, he brushed his hand down Jonathan's arm.

"Jonathan!" called a female voice from across the cafeteria.

"There she is." Jonathan pointed to a girl bathed in a beam of light shining through a second-story window. It was impossible for Chance to see her face, but a strange sense of déjà vu came over him, growing stronger the closer they got to her.

To his surprise, the color drained from her face when her eyes landed on him. Chance frowned. Between her and Jonathan, Chance was beginning to worry that something was wrong with him.

That is, until her eyes narrowed in a familiar way and she crossed her arms. Recognition slammed into him, and he knew exactly why his powers had begun to fail him.

When they reached the table where she stood, Jonathan hurried around it to hug her and gestured back at Chance. "This is the new kid I was telling you about. Chance, this is my friend—"

"Fate."

Three

Jonathan stared at Chance, confused. "Uh, no . . . her name is Destiny. She and I have been friends since birth."

Destiny leaned into Jonathan. "Yes, our friendship was meant to be." Despite her pleasant tone, she glared at Chance.

Meeting the glare with a mild look, Chance offered her his hand. "Nice name. You look like a Destiny."

She took his hand hesitantly. After a quick shake, she dropped it and pressed a hand to her stomach.

"Oh my god, yes," Jonathan said, realizing Destiny was probably just hungry. "I'm starving. Let's jump in line before the rush." He led her and Chance toward the already growing lunch line.

"So, Chance, what brings you to Eureka?" Destiny asked. "It's such a small town, we don't really get a lot of new students. Do you have family here? Or did you move for your parents' job or something?"

Chance glanced at Destiny and shrugged. "My dad

and I just moved here." He turned his head and scanned the cafeteria. "No family or friends, just us."

"Why's that?" Jonathan asked around a bite of French bread pizza.

Chance's jaw tightened, and his distracted gaze suddenly seemed more purposeful. "My mom passed away last year," he said quietly. "We needed a change of scenery to get away from everything that reminded us of her, so a couple of weeks ago, we ended up here."

"Oh god." Jonathan set his pizza down. "I'm sorry to hear that."

"Thanks. It was really hard the first few months." Chance looked down at his food. "It hit my dad harder. He refused to get out of bed most days, and he still hasn't gotten over it." He fell quiet for a moment, before shaking his head and sitting up straight. "I'm hoping that starting over in a new place will help, but only time will tell." Clearing his throat, he lightly scratched under his eye. His finger came away wet.

Destiny jumped in again. "But why Eureka? Did he have a work connection here or something?" Jonathan frowned at her, wondering why she was harping on that, but she didn't even glance at him.

"No, he just took out a map of the US and threw a dart. Eureka was the closest city to where it landed, so we ended up here." Taking a bite of his chicken sandwich, he glanced at her, his lips covered in mayonnaise.

"He threw a dart?" Jonathan asked, shocked by the freedom that statement suggested. "It could have landed anywhere, and he would have just moved you?"

"Yep, pretty much. He's a pretty go-with-the-flow kind of guy, always has been. My parents didn't even decide on a name for me in a traditional way. They just put a bunch of names they liked in a jar while my mom was pregnant and then drew one as they were going to the hospital the night I was born."

"Did they know you'd be a boy at least?" Jonathan asked, nearly finished with his pizza.

"Nope!" As Jonathan gaped at him, Chance laughed. "I could have ended up being called Gwen or been a girl named Patrick. Fortunately, it worked out. Things usually do. My life is based on coincidences and random chance, so the name is perfect." He glanced at Destiny, the glob of mayonnaise still clinging to his lips.

Narrowing her eyes, Destiny threw a napkin at his face. It stuck to the offending sauce, which he wiped away. "My mom knew I'd be a girl before she even got pregnant. Back when she and my biological father were still together, she had dreams about having children, but they were always fuzzy and nondescript, and she couldn't get pregnant, even with IVF. Once they divorced, though, she dreamed about a girl with wavy dark hair and a heart-shaped face. The next day, she got a call from her doctor's office that they'd had a mix-up at their lab and they still had one embryo she could have implanted if she wanted." Her face softened in fond reminiscence. "She named me Destiny because she knew she was destined to have me."

Jonathan stared at her, wide-eyed. "You've never told me that story before." She patted his hand gently. "I don't have any interesting story behind my name. I'm named after my grandpa. That's it."

"Family names are great, though," Destiny said. "They show your family's history and connect you to them and their legacy, which is amazing."

"I agree," Chance said. "Who wants to be a girl named Patrick?"

Jonathan and Chance laughed at the joke. Even Destiny let slip a chuckle, which surprised Jonathan.

The three continued talking until the bell rang, signaling the end of lunch and the beginning of their afternoon classes. As they stood to leave, a group of popular girls approached Chance and pulled him away from the table. Looking back at Jonathan and Destiny over the girls' heads, Chance shrugged, before following the girls down the large hallway toward his next class.

Jonathan watched them disappear into the crowd. "At least they're walking him in the right direction."

Destiny rolled her eyes. "I'm sure he'll be just fine."

Turning to her, Jonathan touched her arm gently, his mouth tight with concern. "How are you feeling? You seem . . ."—he struggled to find the right word—"off, somehow. Is everything okay?"

She nodded. "I just had a weird feeling in my stomach all morning that something terrible was about to happen. That's why I kept telling you to be safe and avoid the new kid. But instead, you,"—she jabbed a finger at his chest—"ran right toward him!" Her tone was serious, but her eyes glinted with affection.

"To be fair, I didn't run toward him. He chased me down." Averting his gaze, Jonathan shrugged. "I just . . . let myself be caught."

She laughed. "I'll bet you did. Do you think he's gay?"

Jonathan shook his head. "Honestly, I don't have the slightest clue. It definitely felt like he was flirting with me, but he seems to flirt with everyone. He also couldn't keep his eyes off you the whole time he was here."

She shrugged. "I didn't notice. Seemed like he was looking around for someone else the whole time."

"Of course you didn't notice; you were too busy worrying about me." Reaching over, he squeezed her hand. "And he only looked at you when you were busy doing something else."

She intertwined their fingers. "Well, he's wasting his time. And you know I can't help but worry about you. It's who I am."

By the end of the school day, Destiny was looking forward to getting away from the other students so she could relax. She'd been aware of her limited abilities all day, and concentrating on the paths while also paying attention in class had been too exhausting to keep up.

How do mortals live like this, not knowing what's coming?

At least she knew the source of the interference, if not why. She just needed to keep her distance from Chance and his father until she could get to the bottom of their sudden arrival. No matter what Chance said, their moving to town couldn't have been random; it smacked of Caerus. And while Chance's influence felt weaker than she was used to from Caerus, Caerus would have had seventeen years to do what he pleased while she was still growing into her own. He could easily have had a son her age, and it would have been just like him to name that son Chance.

Now he was here, ruining everything she'd built for herself.

Fortunately, she wouldn't have to think about it for the rest of the day. She and Jonathan had made plans to spend the afternoon binge-watching the newest season of *The Rainwater Eight Trials*. She might not be able to use her powers on Jonathan, but the scripted drama was predictable, which was soothing.

After today, she needed soothing.

"Hey!" Jonathan fell in step beside her as she headed for the main doors of the school. "How was the rest of your day?"

"Eerily calm." She wished she could share just how true that was. "How was your day?" she asked, hoping to distract herself from her unease.

If her strain came out in her voice, Jonathan didn't seem to notice. "It was terrific. I ran into Chance between sixth and seventh period, and he said he didn't have any plans after school—"

"So he asked if I wanted to come over and watch TV with you guys." Chance fell in on Jonathan's other side. "It was too good an offer to pass up!" Chance offered Destiny a smile. "Hope you don't mind."

"Not at all. It's Jonathan's home, after all. It's not my place to say who can and can't hang out." Destiny was upset, but when she looked at Jonathan, he wore a shy, apologetic expression. She nudged him with her elbow to let him know it was okay.

When they arrived at Jonathan's house, they dropped their backpacks by the door and kicked off their shoes before entering the family room. Destiny took her usual spot on the right side of the couch, and Chance sat on the left, leaving the middle seat as a buffer zone where Jonathan could sit.

Jonathan walked into the small kitchen and opened the refrigerator. "Do you two want anything to drink? We have Coke, Sprite, water, orange juice . . . that's about it." He glanced back at them, waiting.

"Just water," Destiny said at the same time Chance

did. She turned her head to frown at Chance, who did the same.

Jonathan laughed. "Okay, that was creepy. Don't start talking in unison like those twin ghosts from that haunted hotel movie." Pulling down three cups from the cabinet, he filled them with water and grabbed some Goldfish crackers, before joining them on the couch.

"Thanks," Destiny said, just as Chance said the same. She laughed at the annoyed expression on Jonathan's face and then realized Chance had joined in. Taking a deep breath, she felt the tension between her and Chance dissipate slightly.

"No, seriously, stop that!" Jonathan said between bouts of laughter.

"Can't make any promises." Chance's eyes flicked toward Destiny. "We seem to be pretty in sync for some reason."

"Well," she teased, "as I like to say, everything in life happens for a reason."

Chance rolled his eyes. "I think I may have heard something about that in the past."

Destiny narrowed her eyes as Chance turned his attention to the TV. He definitely seemed to know more than he was saying, but how? Had his dad mentioned her and their past together?

Whatever it was, she had no way of asking in front of Jonathan without giving something away.

Jonathan leaned forward and grabbed the remote. "Okay, Chance, this is one of our favorite shows, so you'll have to deal with us talking most of the way through it. And every time one of the guys takes his shirt off, we pause it to admire them." He hesitated, then added, "If you want . . .

we can pause it when the girls do the same, even though you can't see everything."

Chance laughed and sat back, shifting deeper into the cushions. "I can get into that. But if you pause every time something happens, we may be here all night." He laughed as Jonathan's face turned red.

Destiny laid her hand on Jonathan's arm. "Well, some of us have homework, so let's start this party!"

"Right!" He pushed the button to start the episode. When the theme music started playing, he and Destiny sang along, laughing as Chance tried to join in even though he didn't know the words.

Around the halfway point of the first episode, Jonathan paused to make sure Chance was keeping up with the storyline. When he leaned forward to push play again, Chance laid his arm along the back of the couch, shifting closer to Jonathan as he sat back. Destiny frowned disapprovingly at Chance, but he refused to return to his original position. She kept trying to make Chance move by hitting his hand with hers and encouraging Jonathan to sit closer to her, even going so far as to suggest he was crowding Chance at one point. Despite her best efforts, Chance assured Jonathan he was fine and kept his arm around him until the end of the second episode.

When he finally moved it, he rubbed his shoulder. Destiny smirked. *Serves him right.*

Before the third episode could start, Destiny climbed to her feet. "I think I'll have to call it a night early. I have to get caught up on my reading for American government, and I still have some research to do for my English paper."

Jonathan grumbled but agreed that he should probably do his as well. As he did, he shot Destiny a questioning look, flicking his eyes toward Chance as if asking what he should do about him.

She spoke up immediately. "Chance, why don't you come with me? My mom can give you a ride home." The relief on Jonathan's face made her happy.

"Yeah, sure, that'd be great." Chance stood up and shook his arm again before squeezing Jonathan's bicep. "Thanks for the invite, Jonny. I didn't think I'd make new friends so fast."

Destiny rolled her eyes but watched Jonathan to see how he'd react to the nickname. He seemed oblivious as he walked them to the front door.

"Thanks for coming over. It was cool to get to hang out." He waited as they pulled on their shoes and opened the door when they were ready to go. "Call me later," he said to Destiny as she walked by.

She nodded, knowing they'd be talking about Chance. "You know I will."

She led Chance down the driveway toward the sidewalk as Jonathan shut the door behind them. As soon as it was closed, they both spoke.

"We need to talk."

Four

"Who the hell are you?" Destiny demanded once they'd gotten far enough away from Jonathan's front door that he wouldn't be able to hear them. "And what're you doing here?"

"I think you know exactly who I am, Fate."

She narrowed her eyes, studying Chance more closely than she had in Jonathan's presence. Gasping, she stumbled backward. Coincidence wasn't Chance's dad; he was Chance! How had she not seen it before? His face and body might have changed, but she would know that cocky attitude anywhere.

"Where have you been?" she hissed, doing her best to keep from yelling. "It's been seventeen years. Why have you suddenly shown up now?" Since he hadn't shown up when she was younger, Destiny had assumed she'd been the only one reincarnated.

Chance's nostrils flared. "What d'you mean, where have I been? I've been stuck wherever my parents moved me." He ran his hands through the hair along the sides of his head. "The last time we were together, I was reborn, and by the looks of things, so were you. And I told you the truth earlier: my dad threw a dart at a map, and this is where we ended up. I honestly had no idea you'd be here." He leaned closer. "More importantly, I have no idea what happened to land me in a mortal body!" He jabbed his finger into her shoulder. "What the hell did you do to me?"

Her face burned. Trying to calm down, she wrapped her arms around herself and squeezed tightly. Only when her breathing was back under control did she speak again.

"What makes you think this was my fault? It's the same thing that always happens when we get too close: you push too hard trying to control everything, and things go wrong. This time, you messed up, and now"—she threw her arms up in anger—"we're *both* paying for it."

Chance's mouth dropped open, and he spread his arms wide. "Excuse me, what? I didn't do anything." He began to pace. "We ran into each other at the coffee shop—you surprised me there as well—and then you said what you always say about things being 'meant to be.' Next thing I know, I'm being born." He spun around and got in Destiny's face. "Do you know how traumatic it is to suddenly be a baby?"

Destiny gestured at her own body, but Chance didn't seem to notice. Instead, he returned to pacing, eyes wild.

"I could remember everything about the last few thousand years," he ranted, waving his arms dramatically, "but I couldn't even speak! And when I was finally old enough to try using my powers, they weren't there! It took me years to get them back, and even now, they're a fraction of what they were."

He spun back to face Destiny and glared. "And for the record, I don't try to control things. I just encourage them to go the way I want. You're the one who wants to force everything into some predetermined plan."

Planting her hands on her hips, Destiny cocked one hip out to the side, refusing to back down. "I don't force anything," she said, voice low and steady. Her eyes were narrowed so dramatically, she suspected he wouldn't have been able to see them if they hadn't been glowing with power. "I *watch* things happen. I *never* interfere to purposely change paths, even when I wish I could!" Her voice rose as her mind raced through everything she would have changed if she could have, and a chill slid down her spine. "I've dealt with things to the best of my ability."

Taking a step closer, she poked Chance in the chest. "And for your information, I lost my powers, too, when I was reborn! I've worked hard to get them where they are now. Being around Jonathan has helped, so I was clearly sent here for a reason." She took another step toward Chance, who stumbled back. "You need to do your little *thing* and get your dad to move you both somewhere else. Now." Taking a final step closer, she crossed her arms and thrust her chin out stubbornly.

Chance's eyes hardened. "Sorry, but no can do. You know it doesn't work like that. I influence things to go my way, but the chips fall where they may. My mother's death was an accident, and the two of us moving here resulted from the randomness that followed."

"And what did you get out of her death?" Destiny demanded harshly.

Chance recoiled. "What? How could you ask that? She was an amazing woman, and I loved her as much as any child loves their mother. I had nothing to do with her death. If anything, that was your doing!"

The accusation hit Destiny like a fist in the stomach,

and her anger fled, leaving only remorse. Since being reincarnated, she hadn't questioned her abilities or purpose once; losing everything had taught her a valuable lesson about her role in the world. She refused to let him lead her astray again, but that didn't excuse cruelty on her part.

"I'm sorry." She held out a hand, palm up. "I didn't mean that. I just don't understand why you're here and why now."

His face softened. "I wish I knew. But for now, it seems like I'm stuck here, so we'll have to figure out how to play nicely."

"Fine." Dropping her hand, Destiny stepped aside, and they continued down the sidewalk. "But you have to leave Jonathan alone. He's too kind to get caught up in your . . ." She waved her hand in Chance's direction. "Just give him space until we figure out what's going on."

"And how am I supposed to do that? I met him before I knew you were here. I can't just pretend I don't know him now." He smirked. "And I can't help it if he likes me."

Rolling her eyes, Destiny tried not to let the smirk get to her. With her around, Chance would have no power over Jonathan.

"Besides," Chance added, "you weren't exactly following your own rules this afternoon. You were all over him."

Destiny eyed him for a moment. Taking a deep breath, she decided to tell him the truth.

"My ability doesn't work on him." Chance's mouth dropped open, but she rushed on before he could say anything. "It's always been that way. When we were younger, I could see what would happen to the people around us and ensure they stayed on the right path, but whenever I tried to see what was happening to him, it was blank. Not blank, even, because that would at least be something. It was a complete inability to know how to keep him on the right path or what that path looked like, almost as if he weren't there."

Chance perked up. Maybe he could finally prove to her that not everything happened for a reason. Outside what people could control in their immediate environments, the world was a constant chaos of random happenings. She wouldn't accept it without proof—she never had before—but now he had the perfect opportunity to show her how wrong she'd always been.

If he had to use Jonathan to do that, so be it.

He feigned nonchalance. "He seemed to respond to *my* attention, so maybe that's a *you* thing." He tried not to gloat as Destiny's cheeks reddened and her eyes narrowed.

"But did he drool all over himself when you showed up?" she countered, crossing her arms. "I know you must have tried something on him. Otherwise, he would never have invited you to sit with us. Jonathan isn't outgoing enough to immediately make friends with the new kid."

Chance thought back to the first class of the day. Jonathan hadn't acted influenced at all. Attracted, maybe, but not in the way Chance was used to. Destiny hadn't been around then, and everyone else had eventually fallen in line with his whims. His expression darkened. "No, he didn't."

Destiny nodded. "There's something about him. I don't know what it is, but he's impossible to read. And we're just friends. There's nothing now, nor will there ever be, anything romantic between us." She dropped her hands to her hips. "I don't know for sure, but I feel like I'm here to help him, which means I'm going to be his friend forever. Besides, you know I've never been into any-one—mortal or god—romantically or sexually." She looked him up and down, then shrugged. "I'll leave that to you."

Chance laughed, knowing he more than made up for her lack of interest. "What do you suggest, then? I can't ignore him. Besides, if you don't know the right path for him, maybe I'm here to help you find it." He loved using her beliefs against her, even if he disagreed with them.

She scoffed. "You're right, unfortunately. I can't make you leave him alone completely, and until he makes up his mind about you, forcing the issue would be more likely to hurt him than help him. So for now, let's both agree that he's off-limits." She gave him a withering look. "Meaning you agree not to try to make him fall for you."

He groaned, annoyed. There went his best oppor-tunity to prove her wrong. Plus, since Jonathan hadn't immediately fallen for Chance, he was that much more appealing. "Fine," he groused. "I won't make any romantic or emotional advances."

"And nothing physical either!"

Chance scoffed. "I forgot how specific you could be when you want to." He raised his hand as though swearing an oath. "I promise that all advances beyond friendship are off-limits." Lowering his hand, he held it out expectantly. "Happy now?"

Destiny took his hand, sealing the promise. "Oh, I won't be happy until you're long gone from here and Jona-than and I can get back to our lives without your inter-ference. But for now, I'm satisfied with our agreement." Dropping his hand, she turned to the driveway they'd stopped next to and started toward the house.

When he started to follow, she turned back to him and frowned. "What're you doing?"

"You said your mom would give me a ride. I was coming inside to wait for you to ask."

"Are you kidding? I'm not asking her to give you a ride! You're *you.*" She waved a hand to encompass all of him. "Why don't you walk? It would be good for you."

Jonathan and Destiny were walking into school the next morning when Chance joined them. People stared as they passed, and Chance seemed to soak up the attention, head high and smile bright. Jonathan felt a little jealous of the attention Chance was receiving, which was silly when that type of attention made Jonathan want to disappear. He'd been asked to speak at a school assembly once during his freshman year, and despite making it through the speech with no mistakes, he'd been so self-conscious, he'd vowed to never do that kind of thing again.

"You planning to speak to us this morning, Chance, or just walk in silence?"

Destiny's question jarred Jonathan back to the present, and he realized he'd fallen silent when Chance showed up.

Chance leaned around Jonathan to grin at Destiny. "I didn't realize you missed my voice so much. I'd be happy to talk about anything you'd like." Rolling her eyes, Destiny turned her head away. "No? Okay, well, keep me posted if you change your mind. In the meantime,"—he focused on Jonathan—"I thought I might walk with Jonathan to our first class since I'm still learning where everything is."

"No problem," Jonathan said as they stopped at his locker.

"Great." Stepping in between Jonathan and Destiny,

Chance pulled his hand out of his jacket. "I also brought you this."

Jonathan stared at the deep-purple flower Chance held out to him. "Where did you find this?" He reached for the flower, eyes focused on its delicately curled petals.

"I found it on my way to school." Leaning close, Chance wrapped his arm around Jonathan's shoulder and continued in a hushed voice. "It made me think of you. It's a hyacinth, though it's not the more-common variety you find these days. This one is special."

"Hyacinths are my favorite flower! Thanks, Chance." Beaming, Jonathan leaned around Chance to show Destiny the beautiful bloom.

She nodded in acknowledgment but didn't respond, shooting Chance a strange look that Jonathan chose to ignore.

Jonathan carefully pressed the flower in between the pages of one of his books before turning back to Chance. "How was the rest of your night?"

"Great, thanks. I saw those girls from lunch yesterday after we left your house. They were kind enough to offer me a ride back to my car, so Destiny didn't have to ask her mom to do it." He looked over his shoulder at Destiny. "And then I had dinner with my dad, did some homework, and watched a little TV before bed. What about you?"

"More or less the same, though I spent some time on the phone with Destiny." Jonathan cupped a hand over his mouth, hoping to hide his smile.

"Oh, really? What did you two talk about?" Chance turned to Destiny again, but her face remained neutral.

"Nothing specific." Moving around Chance, she stood next to Jonathan. "I just pointed out that you seemed like a guy who always wants things his way, regardless of how it might affect other people." She examined her nails as if bored with the conversation. "But Jonathan thinks we should give you a chance . . . Chance. So don't mess it up."

Turning to Jonathan, she reached up and hugged him before heading off to class. "See you later."

As Jonathan and Chance made their way to their own class, Chance spoke playfully. "Destiny is not a big fan of me, it seems."

Jonathan shrugged. "Honestly, I think she likes everyone. She just doesn't want to get hurt, so she sorta keeps people at arm's length." He hesitated a moment before adding, "Last year, when some kids got in a car accident, she was practically inconsolable, and we weren't even friends with any of them." He smiled fondly. "She has a giant heart. She just doesn't wear it on her sleeve."

They talked all the way to class, where Chance took the seat next to Jonathan again. This didn't go unnoticed by their classmates, who eyed the pair and began to whisper among themselves. Jonathan ducked his head.

While he didn't hide the fact that he was gay, he also didn't outwardly express it in any way that would draw attention from other students. He had joined the Gay-Straight Alliance when he accepted that he would never date a girl, but other than him and Destiny, the club was made up of straight girls and one lesbian. The gay male dating pool in Eureka simply seemed nonexistent, so he'd never had a boyfriend or even kissed another guy—which meant that even though his being gay wasn't a secret, it might as well have been.

Until now, it seemed.

Fortunately, Ms. Halpern walked in just before the final bell and immediately launched into the themes from the previous night's reading assignment. Most students turned their focus up front, but as Jonathan scanned the room, he found one pair of eyes staring back.

Eyes that belonged to the one guy Jonathan never wanted to notice him: Luke Martin.

Luke didn't look away, even after Jonathan caught him staring. Sinking down in his seat, Jonathan refused to look anywhere but the front of the room for the remainder of class. When the bell finally rang, he rushed out, not bothering to wait for Chance.

He and Luke had been friends in elementary school because their dads had worked together and, well, everyone had been friendly back then. As soon as they started middle school, though, Luke met Mike Lawler and his popularity skyrocketed due to his athletic prowess, while Jonathan stayed right where he liked it—just under everyone else's radar. By the time they reached high school, Luke had become even more popular, spending all his time with the baseball team. Their past friendship, however limited, had been forgotten, and Jonathan was often the target of the team's harassment whenever their paths crossed.

Being noticed by Luke for spending time with Chance was sure to end badly, so Jonathan took the easy way out.

Conflict avoidance was his specialty.

Chance was laughing as he caught up with Jonathan. "What happened back there? You practically pushed Ms. Halpern down on your way out of class. Are you having a bathroom emergency?" He made a big show of taking a deep breath and holding his nose. "Do I need to stand guard at the door while you unleash the fury of your insides?"

Jonathan shot Chance a look of disgust. "Gross! No, my insides are just fine, thank you. I just didn't want to be late to class." Not wanting to answer any more questions, he veered toward the nearest restroom. "But now that you mention it, maybe I should stop by the bathroom while I have time. I'll see you later."

Shoving open the restroom door, Jonathan hurried inside, leaving Chance behind.

Five

By the time the afternoon finally rolled around, Jonathan was exhausted. He hadn't done well on a pop quiz in history, and now he was fighting a massive headache. Squinting against the brightness of the hall lights, he massaged his temple as he walked to his next class. When a nearby locker slammed shut just as he passed by, he flinched away from it.

And ran face-first into Luke Martin.

Luke stumbled back a few steps, then surged forward into Jonathan's face. "Watch where you're going, Jonny!"

Jonathan jerked back, surprised. He and Luke hadn't spoken in years.

The surprise didn't last long, not with the headache pounding against his temples. Unfortunately, his sense of self-preservation seemed to slip away with it.

"Shut up, Luke," he snapped. "It was an accident! I certainly wouldn't have run into you on purpose. Maybe if you'd been looking where *you* were going, it wouldn't have happened!"

"Well, someone decided to put his big-boy pants on today," sneered Mike Lawler, captain of the baseball team. He looked around the hall, and Jonathan couldn't help looking with him. They were surrounded by other students, all of whom pretended not to be watching, but Jonathan knew they were. Some even had their phones out, recording the interaction for social media.

When his gaze landed back on Jonathan, Mike added, "Why don't you take your big-boy pants and walk away before your mouth writes a check your ass can't cash."

Luke laughed, even as his face paled. He looked like someone had punched him in the stomach.

Chance suddenly emerged from the crowd to stand beside Jonathan. "Why are you so interested in his mouth and ass, huh? Seems a little sus to me."

"Who's this, Jonny, your little boyfriend?" Despite the taunt, Mike stared at Chance as if he couldn't pull his eyes away. "Is he going to fight your fights for you now?"

Chance wrapped an arm around Jonathan's shoulders. "So what if I am? What're you going to do about it?"

Jonathan hunched his shoulders as his face burned and tears stung his eyes. *What is he doing?* Looking around at the gathered crowd, he struggled to breathe.

"He's not my goddamn boyfriend!" He shrugged off Chance's arm. "And I can fight my own fights!"

Just then, the bell rang, and Mr. Davies stepped out into the hallway. "All right, show's over. You all better get to class. Now!" His voice carried over the hum of the crowd.

"Whatever," Mike said. "You're not worth the detention." He knocked into Jonathan's shoulder as he shoved past. Luke followed, but not before giving Jonathan a strange look. Once they were gone, the crowd thinned.

Stepping out of the departing crowd, Destiny took up a protective position beside Jonathan, touching his side to let him know she was there.

Jonathan's heart pounded, which didn't help with the raging headache. Turning on Chance, he glared at him. "I don't need you to stand up for me, especially not by saying you're my boyfriend! Why the hell would you say that in front of all those people?"

Not waiting for Chance to respond, Jonathan turned, grabbed Destiny's hand, and stalked away. Chance called after him, but Jonathan ignored him.

When he could no longer hear Chance, he slowed his pace and wiped his burning eyes. "I can't believe he just did that in front of everyone. Now everyone's going to make a big deal about me dating the new guy."

Destiny rubbed her thumb softly across his. "I understand why you're upset, and I don't blame you. He's an asshole who only thinks about himself; that much is clear." Pulling Jonathan to the side of the hall, she faced him and peered up into his eyes. "But as much as it pains me to say so, I think he was only trying to help."

Jonathan's head pounded harder. He began to protest, but Destiny cut him off.

"Which is no excuse for what he did, and if you want me to, I will hunt him down and end him." As she spoke, she neither laughed nor broke eye contact, and Jonathan had no doubt she would follow through.

Taking a deep breath, he shook his head and sighed. "I'll spare him your wrath for now. But if he steps out of line again, I may take you up on that." He pressed his lips together gently, feeling drained. "Thank you. I'm glad I have you."

"And you always will."

For some reason, she didn't sound as confident about that as she usually did.

The following day, Jonathan did his best to lie low, hoping to avoid another confrontation, especially with Luke or Chance. Chance had reached out the night before, sending jokes, memes, and sexy photos, but Jonathan had ignored them. He got to first period right as the tardy bell rang to avoid conversation and left as soon as class ended. Chance yelled after him, but Jonathan ignored him, quickly ducking into history.

Unfortunately, Chance followed him in and just stood beside his desk as he busied himself preparing for class.

"Hey! Do you want to see a band play tomorrow night?" Chance held out a colorful flyer.

Reluctantly, Jonathan stopped fiddling with his notebook and accepted the flyer, keeping his head down.

His reluctance disappeared as soon as he got a good look at it. "The Telepathic Tacos are playing?" Snapping his head up, Jonathan gaped up at Chance. "How did you find out about this? I've heard they play local shows, but I only ever hear about them after the fact."

Belatedly, Jonathan realized he was practically shouting in his excitement, and he glanced around as his face heated up.

Chance leaned over, using the story as an excuse to get close. "I was walking out of the burger place on Center when this flew up and hit me in the face. I thought of you and thought it might be something we could do together."

Destiny sat down at the desk behind Jonathan. "What are we doing?"

Jonathan turned around in his chair and showed her

the flyer. "Chance found out the Telepathic Tacos are playing this weekend. We have to go!"

Destiny's face lit up. "Yes!" Staring intently at the information on the page, she added, as if to Chance, "Jonathan and I discovered the band one night while walking past a coffee shop in Peoria. They played a song about pepper kisses and burning tongues, and we were hooked!"

"Great," Chance said, expression blank. "It's a date. A three-way if you will." Laughing, he walked out.

"He's gross," Destiny whispered as Mr. Wright came in and started setting things up for the class discussion.

"I don't know. I think he's funny." Jonathan pulled his textbook out of his backpack and turned to the page written on the whiteboard. "But I agree, the thought of the three of us on a date is pretty gross."

He chuckled as Destiny hit him on the shoulder.

"He wishes he could date us. Trust me."

Once Mr. Wright had started the lesson, she leaned forward and whispered, "So, I take it you've forgiven him for yesterday?"

Jonathan nodded as he started copying notes from the board. "I thought about what you said. If he was trying to help, I should give him a little leeway."

Destiny sighed. "Sometimes, I wish I'd just keep my thoughts to myself."

Unlike the day before, the morning passed quickly. The possibility of seeing the Tacos perform live had significantly improved Jonathan's mood. He could hardly wait for the weekend, and he got so caught up in his thoughts, he missed the lunch bell. Chance had been called out of class just before the end of the period so only the loud exodus of his classmates returned Jonathan to the present.

Shoving his notebook in his bag, he rushed to catch up with the crowd going down the hall.

"Destiny!" he yelled over the noise of the crowd.

Turning, she pointed toward the other side of the hall. She waded through the crowd to wait for him.

"Thanks for waiting," he said once he reached her. "I have been daydreaming about seeing the Tacos all morning. Do you think your mom would drive us to the show?"

"I'll ask, but I don't see why not." Her eyes took on that thousand-yard stare they sometimes got before focusing back on him. "Are you going to invite *you know who* to ride with us?"

"I dunno. I kind of feel like I have to. He's the one who found out about the show. It only seems right for him to ride along with us. Don't you think?" He met her gaze, but she glanced away after a second.

"I mean, I could always lie and say my mom can't fit all three of us in her car."

"Yeah, that's true." Jonathan frowned, concerned. "But what if he asks us to ride with him?"

"Do you honestly think your mom would let you go to Peoria at night with a cute boy and no parental supervision?" She poked him gently in the ribs, tickling him.

Laughing loudly, he swatted her hand away. "Stop it!" He continued to laugh as they headed for the cafeteria, though he finally admitted, "Probably not."

Destiny nodded. "Besides, you know my mom is always up for a trip into Peoria. She can drop us off and go do her own thing while we watch the show. That way, we don't have to worry about parking or any of that."

"You're right. It would be easier just to have your mom take us, and my mom is more likely to say yes if your mom's driving."

When they reached the cafeteria, they dropped their backpacks off at their regular table, then got in the lunch line.

"All this talk about the Tacos makes me want Mexican food," Jonathan complained, eyeing the selection of pre-made sandwiches and mystery meat.

"Hey, have you two gotten food yet?"

Jonathan and Destiny turned around to find Chance standing there with a bag full of take-out boxes.

Jonathan rolled his eyes. "Not yet. Just mulling over the 'vast' selection." He gestured at the bag. "What's all that?"

"My dad dropped off food for me today. I guess the restaurant he went to for lunch messed something up, so they gave him more food to make up for it. Feel like helping me out?"

Jonathan traded a glance with Destiny. "Oh yeah," they said in unison and then burst out laughing. Getting out of line, they followed Chance back to their table, where he set out three containers of food.

"Let's see what we've got here." He opened the first box to reveal Spanish rice and refried beans. The second box had about a dozen rolled tacos, and the third held two quesadillas oozing cheese from the edges.

"Is this from Manny's?" Jonathan asked, amazed, as Chance pulled plates and utensils out of the bag and Destiny distributed them. "I was just telling Destiny I wanted Mexican food, and here you come with some of my favorites. I'd swear it was fate if I didn't know any better."

Chance and Destiny glanced at each other, Destiny looking smug.

"Believe me," Chance said, smirking, "if Fate were real, she wouldn't want you to have all the calories."

"Oh, I don't know, Chance," Destiny replied as Jonathan scooped rice and beans onto his plate. "You showing up with what Jonathan wanted means it was meant to be."

"Are you two going to eat?" Jonathan demanded as he put three rolled tacos on his plate and reached for the quesadillas. "I feel like I'm hogging everything over here." He watched the cheese stretch as he ripped off a piece of quesadilla. "I'm not going to stop, but I sorta feel bad for eating without you."

They all laughed, and Chance and Destiny started grabbing food.

"Hey." Chance caught Jonathan's eye once they all had food. "I'm sorry about yesterday. I shouldn't have done what I did, and you have every right to be mad at me. I dunno, I guess I couldn't stand by while they said those things to you. It never even crossed my mind that you might not be out yet."

Jonathan shook his head as he piled beans and rice on top of his quesadilla. "You're fine. I really wasn't in a great mood, and it had nothing to do with you or the situation. Luke and I have a weird history, which I couldn't have expected you to know about. And Mike is an asshat, plain and simple. I mostly ignore them when they say things about me, but yesterday I couldn't."

He took a bite of quesadilla, beans, and rice. Once he finished chewing and swallowing, he continued.

"And I *am* out. I just don't usually talk about it around school. If anyone asked, I'd be honest, and I have this little rainbow patch on my backpack." He lifted his backpack to show off his pins and patches. "But I don't go around announcing it to everyone. I'm the only out guy in school anyway, so it's not like I'm missing out on dating because I keep it quiet."

"For the record, I would date you." Looking suggestively at Jonathan, Chance shoved a large bite of rolled taco in his mouth. He seemed to think the slightly phallic shape of the rolled-up tortilla would be erotic in some way, but Jonathan could only laugh as he attempted to be sexy while shoveling food into his mouth.

"I appreciate the sentiment. If you weren't a black hole for food, I might date you too."

Destiny pressed a hand over her mouth to muffle her own laughter.

The remainder of the lunch period passed quickly, and together, the three ate every bit of food Chance's dad had dropped off. Jonathan was happy to have cleared the air with Chance, Destiny looked pleased once Jonathan said he wouldn't date Chance, and Chance appeared to be too busy checking out the other students to be bothered.

Saturday night couldn't come quickly enough.

Chance had done everything in his power—literally—to smooth things over with Jonathan, but telling him about the Telepathic Taco performance had been the only thing to produce any kind of results. Chance loved a challenge, though, and this was his best opportunity to show Destiny that his powers were just as important as hers. With that in mind, he'd opted to drive himself to the event to give himself time during the drive to devise a plan for the evening, which currently amounted to little more than separating Destiny from Jonathan and using every trick he could think of.

He arrived at the venue just as Jonathan and Destiny were getting out of a car out front. Wanting to meet them at the doors, he quickly pulled into a nearby lot and parked. Letting his influence spread out around him, he took in the patterns of downtown Peoria as people went about their business. When he looked across the street at

Jonathan and Destiny, though, the patterns disappeared. There was simply nothing there.

Here goes nothing. Taking a deep breath, he crossed the street.

"Wow, you're way earlier than I thought you'd be," Destiny said as Chance got in line with them.

He shrugged. "Normally, I wouldn't have been this early, but there was practically no traffic, and I found parking across the street. For free." Never mind that he'd used his powers to manipulate traffic lights, encourage everyone to drive in the right-most lane, and sweet-talk the parking attendant.

"That was lucky," Jonathan said, rubbing his hands together to keep them warm.

Chance snuck a glance at Destiny. "What are the chances, right?"

Before she could answer, the doors opened, and a tall, skinny man in a Telepathic Tacos shirt stepped out. He stopped short at the sight of them. "Are you here for the show?"

"Yes," the three said in unison.

"You know it won't start for another hour and a half, right?"

"Oh yeah, but we love the Tacos," Jonathan gushed, "and we wanted to be as close to the front of the line as possible!"

The man made a show of looking behind them at the complete lack of a line. "Well, mission accomplished, I guess. It's freezing out here; why don't you come inside? The band is doing a sound check. You can get a little preview of the show." Opening the door, he waved them in.

Jonathan and Destiny quickly ducked inside, Chance following close behind.

Any possibility of normal conversation was lost once they were inside. Music filled the space, making it hard to hear anything else as the band cycled through songs, playing small bits of each before moving on to the next.

Chance stopped by the bar as Jonathan and Destiny wandered toward the stage, Jonathan practically vibrating as they got close. Despite his obvious excitement, though, Jonathan glanced back at Chance to check on him. Chance smirked, pleased that Jonathan was still thinking of him despite not being affected by his abilities.

Since it was a small show, there was no designated seating. Choosing a small table to the right of the stage, closest to the lead guitarist, Destiny pulled out a chair and sat. Jonathan followed suit, moving his chair to give himself the best view of the band before settling in.

By the time Chance joined them, Jonathan and Destiny were in complete groupie mode, eyes glued to the stage. Chance sat on the opposite side of the table from Destiny, leaving Jonathan in the middle. Since Jonathan and Destiny were otherwise occupied, Chance watched the bass guitarist, who missed a few chords when he noticed Chance's attention and then struggled to catch up with the rest of the band.

The band wrapped up quickly after that. Without the music to overwhelm conversation, the three friends turned to face each other, and Jonathan and Destiny finally noticed that Chance had gotten them all drinks.

"Thank you, Chance." Jonathan picked up his Coke and took a large swig. He was mid-swallow when the band walked up to their table, and Chance watched as he struggled to swallow correctly.

"Hey, guys," the lead singer said. "Thanks for coming out to the show. And for being so early. My name's Cam.

This is James, Billy, and Alonzo." He pointed to the drummer, lead guitarist, and bass guitarist.

"We wouldn't have missed it!" Jonathan quickly assured, gaze glued to Billy's face. "My friend and I have loved you guys since we first heard you last year, but we live in Eureka, so this is the first time we've been able to make it to one of your local shows. I'm Jonathan." He touched his chest, before gesturing at the others. "And these are my friends Destiny and Chance." Taking a deep breath, he let it out slowly.

Chance chuckled, drawing the bass guitarist's gaze once more. He offered the bass player his hand and gently squeezed when he took it. "Nice to meet you, Alonzo. I'm Chance." He let a little bit of his power seep through their physical connection, pleased to realize his ability to influence through physical touch wasn't hindered even this close to Destiny.

Alonzo gulped. "H-h-hey there, nice to meet you," he said once Chance had released his hand.

Meanwhile, Billy was returning Jonathan's attention. "What do you think so far? Did everything sound okay to you?"

"It sounded amazing! You're amazing! I love you so much," Jonathan said automatically, before his eyes widened and he backpedaled. "I mean, you're all amazing. You're my favorite band!" He grimaced. "I already said that, didn't I?"

The band laughed and thanked him for the compliment. An awkward pause followed, and Jonathan seemed to flounder for what to do or say next.

"Hey," Destiny said, standing up with her phone out. "Would you mind if we got a picture with you?"

Cam spoke up. "Not at all! You still have another hour

to wait for the actual performance, so it's the least we can do." He moved toward their equipment. "Would you mind getting our logo in the photos and tagging the band if you post them online? We're working on getting our name out there."

She agreed. Once Jonathan was in place, she turned and held her phone out to Chance. "Here, Chance, would you mind?"

"Not at all." He smirked as he took the phone, knowing she'd asked him on purpose to keep him out of the photo. "Everyone get close together."

They all moved around until they got into a comfortable position.

"Jonathan, would you trade places with Destiny? She's blending into the background."

Once they'd switched places, Jonathan stood next to Billy, who wrapped an arm around his lower back, squeezing Jonathan's side slightly. Chance waited a few seconds, pretending to fix some settings on the phone so he could get the best shot, which gave Jonathan's cheeks a chance to go from deep red to a more normal shade.

"All right, here we go. Everybody say Tacos!"

He took a few photos, having them change poses a few times before he let them all relax. Before returning Destiny's phone, he grabbed Alonzo for a selfie, wrapping his arm around Alonzo's shoulders.

"Thanks," Chance said as he let Alonzo go.

Destiny held out her hand, lips quirked in amusement. "Can I have my phone back now?"

Chance flashed her a smile and handed the phone back with a slight bow. "My lady."

She rolled her eyes. "You're such a dork." Her tone was teasing, and Chance could see from her body language that she was relaxed and enjoying herself, something he rarely saw. But he knew better than to push his luck by trying anything with her.

Destiny opened her photo gallery and held it out so Jonathan and Chance could see the shots. There was one where Billy looked at Jonathan instead of the camera, which she saved as a favorite.

The band excused themselves to finish preparing for the show, and the three friends ordered some food to help pass the time. Chance ordered a cheeseburger and fries, while Jonathan and Destiny ordered some appetizers to snack on, since they had eaten beforehand.

"What's your favorite song of theirs?" Chance asked as he shoveled fries into his mouth.

Jonathan grinned. "My favorite is 'Guacamole Love.' It's sexy and funny and sweet. It fits a lot of situations and occasions."

"Oh yeah, I love 'Guacamole Love,'" Destiny agreed. "But I think my favorite is their newest one, 'Taco 'bout It'—about how relationships can be hard, but things get better when you 'Taco 'bout It.'" She said the song title slower the second time, as if to drive home the point.

Chance nodded. "That makes sense, I guess. But I tend to think that whether someone likes you or whether a relationship works out is all up in the air, random chance. You can talk about things or kiss and make up, but it doesn't mean it will last."

Destiny's patience was beginning to run out, but she kept making her case. "Sometimes it's not about the relationship lasting; sometimes it's about what you learn from the experience. Not every relationship is 'the One,' but that doesn't mean it isn't important."

As she spoke, energy built within her in a way she'd never experienced before, let alone around Chance. To her shock, it culminated in a flash of vision that showed Jonathan kissing someone. Steadying herself against the table, she tried to follow the path of the vision, but it quickly disappeared.

She whipped her head around to stare at Jonathan, even as she tried fruitlessly to pull the image back up in her mind's eye. Why would she have had her first vision of Jonathan now, after seventeen years? And how, when Chance sat right across the table from her?

"What? What is it?" Jonathan glanced over his shoulder frantically. When he turned back around, he held his chest. "Fuck, don't scare me like that!"

Destiny wanted to say something—apologize for scaring him or make a joke about him freaking out—but she was still struggling to deal with what she had seen and couldn't make her mouth form the appropriate words.

Narrowing his eyes, Jonathan glanced back and forth between her and Chance. As the silence they'd fallen into lengthened, he shifted awkwardly and eventually turned to Chance.

"Well, anyway, back to relationships. Chance, do you like anyone at school?"

"Me?" Chance raised his eyebrows. "No. I'm a love-'em-and-leave-'em type of guy, but ultimately, I prefer to keep things casual. I've never said no to a good time, and not many people have said no to the good time I can show them, if you know what I mean." He smirked. "But I'm not looking to get caught up in a relationship; I prefer to leave myself open to new opportunities. If your hands are always full, you can't grab on to new experiences."

"Sounds like you think you could hook up with just about anyone you want," Jonathan said, even as he glanced at Destiny worriedly. Having recovered from her shock, she squeezed his hand lightly to let him know she was fine.

"Oh, no question," Chance replied confidently. "It's almost too easy."

"And how about you, Destiny?" Jonathan added. "Do you like anyone from school?"

Destiny frowned, wondering what Jonathan was up to. He already knew she didn't do nonplatonic relationships. She'd told him she was asexual at the end of ninth grade—and when he told her he thought he'd never find a boyfriend, she'd told him she was also aromantic and had no desire to date. Early in their freshman year, she'd gone on dates with Jade Miller and Keenan Price just to be nice, but she told them after one date that she didn't feel a connection. After that, everyone pretty much left her alone.

Jonathan didn't relent, though, so she shrugged and answered anyway.

"Eh, you know how I feel about all that. By now, most people at school think I'm about as sexy as a potato." Despite her efforts to maintain a straight face, her lips twitched up at the corners.

Jonathan pointed at the fries Chance was still picking through. "I wanna be one of those french fries: hot and salty."

Destiny and Chance burst out laughing.

"I'm sorry, what?" Chance asked, even as he passed Jonathan the plate of french fries.

"I want to be like a hot and salty french fry," Jonathan repeated with a grin.

"Well, you're already hot, and you're definitely salty!" Laughing, Destiny dodged the playful swipe of Jonathan's hand.

"And you don't look like a potato!" Jonathan replied. "Even if you did, most of the girls in our class would kill for your looks, and most of the guys in our class want to mash you!"

Chance laughed as Destiny gaped at Jonathan. "I'm with Jonathan. I'd smash you if you'd let me."

Jonathan covered his mouth, but his eyes danced with amusement. "Well, if you two want to mash potatoes, please do it elsewhere. I'm already not hungry, and that might put me off food for a long time." He stuck his tongue out, and they all laughed loudly.

As the conversation continued more freely, Destiny leaned over, placed a hand on Jonathan's arm, and gave it a light squeeze. Still, she couldn't shake her vision of him—not just because it was the first she'd ever had of him but also because she hadn't been able to tell who he was kissing. She would enjoy the night's show and her time out with Jonathan, but she promised herself that she would get to the bottom of the mystery if it was the last thing she did.

Seven

By the time the band came out for the performance, all seats were filled and the standing-room-only audience crowded around the teens' table. Chance was glad they had gotten there as early as they had, even if it had meant sitting around for a while.

"Hey, everybody, we're the Telepathic Tacos!" Cam yelled over cheers and whoops from the audience. "Just want to give a quick shout-out to Destiny, Chance, and Jonathan, who have been here since our sound check over an hour ago. We wouldn't be anywhere without our fans, and we love you!

"With that in mind, Chance, Destiny, Jonathan . . . any song requests to get us started tonight?"

"'Guacamole Love'!" Chance called out, drawing all eyes to their table.

Cam pointed to their table. "'Guacamole Love' it is!"

As the band started playing, the audience screamed their approval. The music swelled and then quieted as Cam's voice filled the space.

Girl, you make me feel like I've got a crush,
Fighting every day against the risk of that rush.
Looking at my life, there's so much I wanna see,
But when I'm with you, I'm the man I wanna be.

'Cause our town's not big enough for you,
Not a girl like you, a girl like you.
And I don't know if I can give you what you need,
What you need, oh, what you need.

But your love is like guacamole, yeah,
Smooth and rich with a sweet swirl.
I want to taste your love tonight.
Don't worry, I brought my appetite.

When we're together, I know you want me too.
I see it in the way you look when I touch you.
And your body reacts the way I need.
I'm gonna go slow when I take the lead.

'Cause this night's too short for us to waste time,
We can't waste time, don't want to waste time.
By the time the night is over, I want you to know
That my love, yes, my love continues to grow

Cause your love is like guacamole,
Smooth and rich with a sweet swirl.
I want to taste your love tonight.
Don't worry, I brought my appetite.

Your love is like guacamole, yeah.
You got that guacamole love.
Your love is like guacamole, yeah.
You got that guacamole love.

You got that guacamole love.
That guacamole love.

As the song ended, they moved on to the rest of their set, and much of the audience, including Jonathan and Destiny, sang along the entire time.

When the show ended almost an hour later, Chance leaned over to Jonathan. "Thanks for coming out tonight. I know I made an ass of myself the other day, but I've had fun with you two. I hope you did too."

"Are you kidding? We've had a great time!" Jonathan gestured between himself and Destiny. "Thank *you* for the invite. And for being determined enough to keep trying with us."

Glancing at Destiny, Chance smirked. "My pleasure."

"You know," Jonathan added, "she might not want to admit it, but I think Destiny likes you. She's just protective of me, especially since my dad left. We've been through a lot together. When you're gay, not everyone is nice in a small town, especially when you don't fit the norm."

"Believe me, I know her type." Chance chuckled. "I knew a girl just like her a few years ago."

Remembering Fate at the height of her power, Chance could almost feel the pull of her power, drawing him toward some path he couldn't see. Shaking his head, he snapped out of the memory, and the pull faded. Only then did he realize Jonathan had been speaking.

". . . home tonight. Is that okay?"

"Um, yeah, that's fine. Whatever you want." Chance didn't know what he was agreeing to, but he didn't dare admit he hadn't been paying attention.

The band had already packed up their equipment and posed for photos and selfies with their fans, so the crowd was thinning. As the band made their way out, they waved goodbye to the three friends, though Chance noticed that Billy and Alonzo snuck a few extra glances.

Heading outside themselves, Chance, Jonathan, and Destiny waited for Destiny's mom to arrive, which didn't take long. When she did, Jonathan turned to Destiny and hugged her.

"I'm going to ride home with Chance, but I'll call you later, okay?"

Destiny opened her mouth but seemed to change her mind about saying something. Instead, she hugged Jonathan tightly and, after releasing him, turned to Chance. "If you hurt him," she said quietly, "I will hurt you. Make sure he gets home safely."

Chance laughed. "Yes, *Mom*." He casually threw an arm around Jonathan's shoulders and pulled him close. "Don't worry about us. We're going to be just fine."

Destiny didn't look convinced, but it wasn't like she could influence either of them or see how the night would turn out since they were both involved. Reluctantly, she headed for the car, but as she opened the front passenger door, she suddenly turned back around. "And don't do anything I wouldn't do, you two."

Chance grinned as she climbed into the car. "Where's the fun in that?"

Jonathan hit him lightly in the chest. "Don't be mean!" He waved at Destiny. "We'll be fine, don't worry. And I'll call you tonight when I get home so you know we made it safely."

Looking worried, she waved goodbye as the car pulled away from the curb and turned toward the freeway.

Chance leaned close to Jonathan's ear. "Now that she's gone, the fun can start!"

Jonathan squirmed and laughed, pushing Chance off him. "Oh, yeah? And what kind of fun do you think two teenagers could get up to at nearly midnight in Peoria?"

When several passing people looked at them askance, Jonathan took a few steps away from Chance. He seemed to do it unconsciously, but Chance hated that he felt it was necessary. Chance would have protected him if someone had tried to start something.

"Fair enough. Maybe the fun can start once we get back to your house." He gave Jonathan a flirtatious look and unleashed his influence; he knew it would have little to no effect, but he was curious to try it out again.

Jonathan's eyes went a little hazy, as if he were starting to fall for it, but then he shook his head and laughed. "We can always get on the road and see what pops up along the way." Blushing, he stepped into the street without looking—just as a car came down the road.

"Watch out!"

Chance forced as much power as he could into his voice and the space around Jonathan. The patterns of the world shifted around them, causing a nearby traffic light to change from green to red with only a flash of yellow. Confusion and honking followed immediately, and the driver slammed on their brakes. Jonathan turned toward the sound as Chance watched from the curb.

When the car stopped a few feet away from Jonathan, Chance breathed a sigh of relief. He may not be able to influence Jonathan directly, but at least he could change things around him. Now he just had to worry about what Destiny would say when she found out.

"You know, there are much better ways of making money than throwing yourself into traffic!"

Jonathan stared, mortified. The driver of the car only feet away from him was none other than the Tacos' guitarist, Billy. Fortunately, he was smiling as he stuck his head out the driver's side window.

"Oh my god, I am so sorry. I don't know what I was thinking. I'm such an idiot!" Jonathan laughed nervously as adrenaline coursed through his body. His arms started to shake, and his cheeks twitched.

Billy shook his head. "No big deal, Jonathan. Everyone makes mistakes." Jonathan gaped at him, shocked he had remembered his name. "And hey, since you're not thinking straight . . ." He rummaged around for a moment before scribbling on a piece of paper. "Call me when you get home so I know you made it, okay? Otherwise, I'll have to roam the streets of Peoria to make sure you haven't stepped in front of another car."

Jonathan stared at the paper Billy held out to him. "I, uh . . . I'm not going to do that again, I promise."

"Still, call me, just so I know for sure." Billy wiggled the paper insistently.

Jonathan stepped back into the street, checking both ways despite the empty road. As he grabbed the paper from Billy, their fingertips touched briefly. Gasping, Jonathan jerked his eyes up to find Billy staring at him, his pupils dilated. Blushing deeply, Jonathan dropped his gaze.

Billy chuckled softly. "Get home safely, you two." He pointed at the slip of paper Jonathan had clutched in his hands. "And I'm serious about calling me when you get there."

"I promise." Jonathan held the paper up to his head in an awkward salute but dropped his hand quickly when Billy raised his eyebrows. "But we don't live in Peoria, so it'll take a while before I get there."

"Don't worry, Eureka, I'm not going to sleep anytime soon."

Startled that Billy had also remembered where he lived, Jonathan stepped back, tripping slightly on the curb behind him.

Billy's expression slipped into concern. "Are you—"

"I'm fine!" Jonathan said, louder than he intended. "Fine, just a little clumsy." He cleared his throat, trying to look steady and unaffected. "Guess I'm still a little shaken up from earlier."

"If you're sure," Billy said, clearly uncertain he should drive away yet.

Jonathan nodded, insisting he was. "Thanks again," he added. "I'll talk to you later.

"All right, I'll talk to you later. Nice meeting you tonight." Rolling up his window, Billy slowly drove away.

When Jonathan turned around, Chance was grinning. "What?" Jonathan demanded.

Chance held up his open palms. "Hey, I didn't say anything. I'm just happy you didn't get hit, is all." He threw an arm around Jonathan's shoulders and guided him off the curb and toward his car. Though he doubted anything terrible would happen to them, Jonathan couldn't help keeping his head on a swivel as they crossed the street.

Once they were across the street, Jonathan relaxed and finally looked at the paper Billy had given him. "I can't believe that just happened."

Hey Jonathan,

It was great meeting you tonight. I'm not sure if you'd be interested in getting together sometime, but if you are, call me.

—B

At the bottom of the note, Billy had written his last

name and phone number, which Jonathan immediately put into his contacts. "Billy Moore," he said aloud as he saved the number. "I like it."

"All right, lover boy, let's get you home so you can drool over Billy without me having to watch." Jonathan scoffed, and Chance laughed. "Don't forget, you promised Destiny you'd give her a call. You've got a long night of Taco talk coming up."

Jonathan burst out laughing. "Taco talk! Oh my god!"

When they reached Chance's car, they climbed inside to get out of the cold, and Chance turned on the heater. As they waited for the car to warm up, Jonathan took the time to think through everything that had happened. There'd been a point where he thought Billy was flirting with him, but now that the shock and adrenaline had faded, he realized Billy was probably just being friendly. There was nothing to suggest Billy was even gay, other than Jonathan's imagination.

It was only when he noticed Chance watching him that Jonathan realized he was shaking his head. Jonathan grimaced. "There's no way someone like Billy would ever like me. Look at me." He gestured vaguely at his face and body. "He could have anyone he wants, which is probably girls his age, not some nobody gay guy from a tiny town."

Leaning over, Chance gently grabbed Jonathan's chin and pulled his face close enough that their lips nearly pressed together. Jonathan's breath caught in his throat, and he looked down at Chance's lips. Chance sat so perfectly still, Jonathan nearly closed the gap between them. Only the concentration in Chance's eyes held him back.

Jonathan shook his head to clear his mind, and the moment faded. Releasing Jonathan's chin, Chance sat back.

"What was that for?" Jonathan asked, breathing heavily.

Chance smirked. "You were being ridiculous, and I find the best solution when someone is speaking nonsense is to distract them with something else." As Jonathan continued to stare, Chance sat back. "I'm sorry. It seemed like a good idea at the time. I didn't mean to upset you."

"No . . ." Jonathan shook his head again. "No, you're fine. It's just that . . ."

"What?"

Jonathan reached for the seatbelt. "I've never kissed anyone before." He kept his eyes averted as he buckled himself in. "I thought that was going to be my first."

"What do you mean, you've never kissed anyone before?" Chance asked, voice pitching higher than normal.

"I mean, of course I've kissed people, but they were family members or childhood friends, so they don't count. I've never been kissed by a guy I might actually have a romantic opportunity with."

Chance cleared his throat. "Well, I'm sorry if I made you uncomfortable. But I hate hearing you talk that way about yourself."

"It's fine," Jonathan replied quietly. "Really!" he insisted when Chance raised an eyebrow in disbelief. "It . . . distracted me, so job well done, I guess." He turned his face away but laughed.

"Oh, is that so?" Chance placed the tip of a finger beneath Jonathan's chin and turned him back around until their eyes met. A wave of warmth spread over Jonathan's face, and he shivered. "If you want to fix that whole never-been-kissed issue right now, I'd be down to make out." He licked his lips.

Jonathan didn't turn away, but he didn't move in for a

kiss either. Despite the shiver of temptation, his mind was still firmly focused on Billy and what they would talk about later tonight. "You look like you're probably a good kisser, but I'm okay."

Chance shrugged. "The offer stands if you ever want to take me up on it." Straightening in his seat, he put the car in gear and carefully pulled onto the road.

By the time they got back to Jonathan's house, it was nearly 12:30 a.m. Destiny had started texting him fifteen minutes ago to make sure they were on their way home and that Chance was driving carefully on the slippery roads. Jonathan assured her everything was fine and that he would give her a call when he got home. But when they pulled up to his house, she stood outside waiting for them, wrapped up in an oversize sweater, pink fleece pajama pants, and tennis shoes.

"I told you I would call when I got inside," Jonathan said as he climbed out of Chance's car. "You didn't have to wait out here for me."

Destiny pulled her sweater sleeves down over her hands. "I tracked your location so I would know when you were pulling into the neighborhood. I just walked outside a second ago."

Chance leaned his arms on his side of the car, eyes locked on Destiny. "Well, *Mom*, we made it home in one piece, despite Jonathan's best efforts. But I assure you, I did everything in my power to make sure he was safe."

Jonathan watched their exchange silently. Destiny nodded to Chance so subtly that Jonathan would have missed it if he hadn't been looking right at her.

"He told me he went and stepped into traffic"—she hit Jonathan in the arm on each of the last three words—"but got Billy's number out of it, so I'd say it sounds like a win at the end of the day." Her enthusiasm felt forced to Jonathan, but he was too busy rubbing his arm to care. "Thank you for driving him home, Chance, and for inviting us to the performance. I think I speak for both of us when I say we had a great time."

"I'm glad it all worked out for the best. And with that, I'd better get my ass home before my dad wonders what happened to me. See you on Monday!" Jumping back in his car, Chance sped off down the street.

Destiny sighed as she watched him drive away. "Just when I start to change my mind about him, he does something like that." Wrapping her arms around herself, she turned to Jonathan. "Let's go inside. I'm cold."

Jonathan led the way inside, quietly shutting and locking the door behind them. Tiptoeing down the hall to his bedroom, he turned on the lamp in the corner of the room and flopped down on his bed. Destiny settled beside him.

Once they were comfortable, Jonathan jumped right in. "Chance was great toni—"

"Enough about him," Destiny cut in. "Tell me all about Billy!" Eyes bright, she turned her back to Jonathan and scooted into the circle of his arms.

"Oh! Billy!" Jonathan pushed himself up into a sitting position, grabbing his pillow and hugging it. "I have to call him to tell him I made it home. Do you think it's too late?" His voice wobbled.

Destiny smacked his knee playfully. "Absolutely not! He told you to call him, so you should call him."

"Maybe I'll text him instead. I don't wanna bother him if he's already asleep or busy." Jonathan pulled the note Billy had given him out of his pocket and reread it. He had already added the number to his contact list, but having the note made him feel more confident.

> ***Jonathan:*** *Hey, Billy. It's Jonathan from earlier. You gave me your number and told me to let you know when I got home, so I'm just checking in. I made it home safely. Thanks again for everything tonight! It was great meeting you!*

> ***Billy:*** *Eureka, you made it! I was beginning to worry you wouldn't reach out. But I believe I told you to call me. How do I know this isn't someone who stole the piece of paper I gave him? There are some crazy fans out there, you know . . .*

> ***Jonathan:*** *A good point, I suppose. I could send you a photo of myself to prove it's me.*

> ***Billy:*** *Maybe the crazy fan stole his phone in addition to the piece of paper and would just use a photo from the phone's camera roll.*

> ***Billy:*** *If only there were a way for me to know for sure that this is the real Jonathan. A phone call, perhaps?*

Heart pounding, Jonathan showed Destiny the text. Taking the phone on the pretense of needing a closer look, she hit the call button and put the call on speakerphone before Jonathan could take it back.

"I hate you," he said, laughing. Shrugging it off, she laughed along with him.

"I guess you do know how to call," Billy said when the call connected.

Clutching the phone in his hands, Jonathan stared at the screen intently. "Yeah, sorry about that. I didn't want to bother you in case you were busy."

"Nah. After a show, we usually go somewhere to kick back and relax, but I went home to wait for a phone call I was expecting. But then I just got a measly text instead," Billy teased.

"You know, some people prefer texting and never actually use their phones to talk," Jonathan teased back. "Maybe this person you asked to call you is one of those people." Jonathan's stomach felt like it was doing somersaults.

"That's true," Billy conceded. "I'm not usually a big talker myself when it comes to phone calls, but I also never give my number out to cute guys who come to my shows." Jonathan snapped his gaze to Destiny's and then silently rolled back and forth on his bed, freaking out at Billy calling him cute. "Especially when they step in front of my car later. Looks like I'm stretching outside my comfort zone all over the place tonight." He chuckled.

"I . . . um . . . I didn't mean to step in front of your car." Still freaking out, Jonathan's brain and mouth struggled to work in unison.

Billy guffawed. "I tell you I think you're cute, and you respond to the part about stepping in front of my car? Who are you, Jonathan No-Last-Name?"

"Daniels," Jonathan choked out.

Billy paused. "I'm sorry?"

"Daniels, my last name is Daniels. Jonathan Daniels."

He was finally getting past the initial shock of being called cute by one of the Telepathic Tacos.

"Here again, I call attention to the fact I called you cute, and you ignore it. Well, I can take a hint, Jonathan Daniels." Despite the words, Billy's voice still sounded light and amused. "If you don't think I'm cute, too, you can just say thank you. You don't have to keep avoiding it."

"No, I do! I do think you're cute. Are you kidding me? You're cute! I mean, look at you. Well, you do look at you, I'm sure, when you're getting ready or see your reflection or whatever . . ." Jonathan hit his forehead with the palm of his hand as he tried to stop the deluge of words streaming from his mouth. Destiny clutched her sides, laughing quietly.

"Thank you. See how easy that was?" Billy's voice was warm and confident but not cocky. Jonathan felt like he could listen to him forever.

"Yeah, sorry about that. I guess my nerves just got the best of me," Jonathan admitted. "But I do think you're cute. And once I get over the fact that you've called me cute a few times tonight, I'll be back to my normal, dorky self. I promise." Jonathan laughed uncomfortably.

"That's good. I happen to like dorks. I mean, I'm in a band called the Telepathic Tacos. If I didn't like dorks, I would never have made it work with these guys." He laughed again. "We're all a bunch of dorks."

Jonathan grinned. "I'll believe it when I see it. But I like you, so if you're a dork, I guess I like dorks too."

"Good to hear. Not only do you think I'm cute, but you like me as well? This night keeps getting better and better!" Muffled voices came over the line before Billy returned to the call. "Well, before anything else can happen, I'd better call it a night. I have to get up early to run some band-related errands. But I'll text you afterward, just in case you're busy."

Jonathan laughed. "Okay, I get it. I'm weird. But I'll let you go, and I look forward to that text when you're done with your errands. I hope you sleep well, and thanks again for everything. It was great getting to talk to you for a little bit."

"The pleasure was all mine, believe me."

Billy said goodbye and hung up, leaving Jonathan and Destiny stuck in silence for a few moments before Jonathan burst with excitement. He jumped up off the bed and danced around in a small circle.

"OH MY GOD! BILLY SAID I WAS CUTE!"

"I know! That's amazing!" Destiny joined in the excitement. "I never even knew he was into guys. Did you?"

"I had no idea." Jonathan shook his head. "I'm so excited! And just think, if Chance hadn't found that flyer, we wouldn't have even known about the show, and I wouldn't have gotten to talk to him. And if he hadn't distracted me, I wouldn't have stepped in front of Billy's car and gotten his number. Maybe Chance is having a good influence on my life."

The cold pit in Destiny's stomach returned, and she was suddenly uncertain about how to respond. She had seen a vision of Jonathan kissing someone, but she didn't know who. Hearing that Chance might have caused the events that unfolded tonight made her question whether Billy was the one in her vision. And exactly how much was Chance using his abilities around Jonathan when she wasn't there?

"Hello . . . ? Destiny?" She blinked and refocused on Jonathan. He looked concerned. "Where'd you go?"

"Sorry. I guess I'm more tired than I realized. I'd better get home and get some sleep." She felt uneasy lying to Jonathan, but there was nothing she could say that would detract from this moment of happiness. "I'll talk to you in the morning, okay?"

"Yeah, that's fine." Jonathan hugged her, then walked her to the front door. "Sleep well."

"You too," she replied stiffly and walked out the door.

As Destiny walked home, she thought through the evening's events again. They had been debating whether things were destined or based on random chance when she'd received a flash of Jonathan kissing someone. Not only was it the first time she had ever seen anything about Jonathan or his future, but it was also the first time her powers had ever worked around Chance. She hadn't had time to really think about everything at the time, and the vision had quickly faded, but she was sure it was an important event.

But is it Billy he'll be kissing? Or someone else?

Hoping for more information before Jonathan went to bed, she texted him.

Destiny: *I forgot to ask how the rest of the drive home and everything went with Chance?*

Jonathan: *It was mostly fine. Nothing happened on the drive home. We talked about other music we liked, sang along to the radio, and he told me about some of his favorite places he's been . . .*

Destiny: *Oh, okay, I guess I didn't miss out on anything important, then.*

Jonathan: *Yeah, nothing too crazy, unless you count me going down a self-induced hate spiral* *after getting Billy's number, where I refused to believe he could like me.*

Destiny sighed, feeling better now that she knew nothing had happened on their way home and that Chance had behaved himself. As for the self-induced hate spiral, she was quite familiar with Jonathan's moods. Whenever he felt self-conscious or uncomfortable, he would pull back into himself, delete his social media accounts, remove photos of himself, post angsty quotes, or stop talking to people altogether. His reaction to getting Billy's number didn't surprise her.

> **Jonathan:** *Fortunately, Chance snapped me out of it pretty quickly.*

> **Destiny:** *How'd he do that?*

> **Jonathan:** *He offered to make out, haha.*

> **Destiny:** *He WHAT?*

The next morning, Destiny got up at sunrise, determined to find Chance and talk to him without Jonathan around. As she dressed, she was startled to realize that the paths unfolding in her mind were sharper than they had ever been since her reincarnation.

Is that why I had a vision of Jonathan last night? Because I'm getting stronger?

That might explain, too, why she'd had a vision with Chance nearby, though that was something she'd never experienced even before they were reincarnated.

But Chance said his power is only a fraction of what it used to be. Maybe that was it? He's not getting his powers back as quickly as I am, so he can't block me anymore?

Knowing she wouldn't be able to reach any solid conclusions by herself, Destiny focused on finding Chance and left her house. She didn't make any conscious decisions, nor did she second-guess the path opening before her. She simply walked, changing direction as the need struck.

When her abilities began to fade, she stopped in front of a single-story home with a large shade tree out front and an old blue-and-white pickup truck in the driveway. The front door opened to reveal Chance, who stopped on the threshold, shocked. Despite the snow, he wore a bathing suit and a white tank top and carried a bucket full of soapy water.

"What are you doing here?" Looking around, probably for Jonathan, Chance headed toward the truck. "And how'd you find out where I live?"

She wandered up the driveway. "Oh, Chance, what a silly question. You know I can find you if I try. I've simply never had a reason to." She gestured at him and the bucket he carried. "What the hell are you doing with all that?"

Setting down the bucket, he took off his tank top and plunged his hands into the water. He pulled out a giant sponge and slapped it against the truck, wiping it back and forth. He tossed Destiny a grin. "I gotta give the neighbors a show."

"You're ridiculous. Isn't there some other way you can make a fool of yourself?" Picking up the discarded tank top, she threw it at his head.

Chance dropped the sponge to catch the shirt. Pulling it back over his head, he gave her his full attention. "Okay, what have I done now?"

Stepping closer, Destiny lowered her voice, not wanting the neighbors to overhear. "Do you really need to ask after what you did last night?"

Chance raised his hands, palms out. "I had nothing to do with what happened last night. I swear!" He sounded sincere. "Sure, I tried to use my influence, but around you, it barely worked, and on Jonathan, it was utterly useless."

"I'm talking about the kiss, Chance." She crossed her

arms and cocked her hip out. "You know, the thing you promised you wouldn't do. Ring any bells?"

"I promised a friendly interaction. Jonathan was being negative about himself, and a friend would try to cheer him up. Besides, I didn't actually kiss him. I just said I would if he wanted." He leaned against the truck, his eyes boring into hers. "And I never promised I wouldn't touch him. But I also didn't push the issue when he turned me down." He crossed his arms, mirroring Destiny's stance. "You should thank me for snapping him out of his bad mood."

Destiny's eyes were surely glowing as her power built. "You knew what you were doing when you offered to kiss him. You knew it would give you an excuse to try to influence him."

Chance sighed, and his head drooped, even as his shoulders rose. "Okay, fine, you're not wrong. I wanted to know if physical intimacy would give me an in. As you said, there's some block in place that prevents my influence from taking hold, and I thought a kiss might break through that wall somehow." He held his hand out toward her, palm up. "Plus, I'd exhausted myself forcing traffic lights to change to stop him from getting run over."

He fell silent for a moment, studying his hand. "Oddly, I felt some of my power return after that traffic light stunt, though. It was almost like . . . like . . ."

"Like helping Jonathan unlocked a piece of yourself you didn't know was missing?" Destiny asked quietly.

"Yes! That's exactly what it felt like." Chance frowned. "But that doesn't make sense. Does it?"

"I don't know, maybe? Once, when we were in elementary school, I helped calm him down after he scraped his knee, and I felt the same thing. I still couldn't see his path, so I didn't realize it until later, but I did feel different after that." Walking over, she leaned against the truck as well, careful to leave enough space between them that they wouldn't touch. "Then last night, I felt something I've never felt before. For a split second, I thought I saw . . ." She hesitated.

Chance leaned closer. "Thought you saw what?"

She waved the question away. "I'm not sure. Forget I said anything. We have bigger things to worry about." Straightening, she walked toward the tree, giving herself some space. She wasn't ready to share what she'd seen yet.

"Okay . . ." Chance eyed her but didn't press. "What do you think it means, then, that we've both felt our powers grow after helping Jonathan?"

"I have no idea." Destiny turned around to face him again. "What I do know is if you try to kiss Jonathan again, you'll regret it." Marching back over, she punched him in the arm and wagged her finger at him. "And I'll know if you pull that shit again, so don't even think about it!"

Wincing, Chance rubbed his arm. "Despite what you think of me, I'm not interested in forcing someone to do something they don't want to. I have no intention of kissing him unless he's the one who initiates things. And based on the looks he was giving Billy last night, I'm guessing you have nothing to worry about."

Destiny smiled. "That may be the best news I've heard all week. However, I'll always worry about him, so don't break your promise to me again. If you do, I'll break something of yours in return." She forced as much power as possible into her final words.

"Yeesh, someone woke up on the wrong side of the bed this morning." He poked her gently in the arm.

She glared at him. "Oh no, I always wake up like this when someone lies to me and tries to manipulate my best friend. My mood has nothing to do with how I slept." Almost silently, she added, "I'm not going to let this become another Daniel Cooper situation."

Destiny could still recall the mortal's face when he lost everything after Coincidence spent years manipulating the patterns around him. According to Coincidence, they'd met at a casino when Daniel asked Coincidence to help him pick a number. One legendary winning streak later, Daniel had been permanently banned from all the casino's properties and their friendship was sealed. Addicted to the good luck and fortunate circumstances Coincidence provided, Daniel left his entire life behind to follow Coincidence everywhere he went.

By the time she found out, Daniel had already begun to lose everything as the patterns Coincidence had changed slammed back into place to restore the balance. Only her direct intervention had kept Daniel from losing more. Unfortunately, he disappeared in the early 1970s, and no matter how she searched, she hadn't been able to find him—as if he were somehow outside the scope of her abilities.

As far as Destiny knew, neither of them had heard from him since.

All signs of amusement faded from Chance's face, and he nodded somberly. "I know I said it already, but I *am* sorry for breaking my promise to you, for what it's worth."

Destiny sighed. Chance at least sounded sincere, and they would have to continue playing nice if they were going to get through the rest of the year without a more significant incident. "I accept your apology, but next time you slip up, you may just find yourself waking up in a new body somewhere else."

Destiny doubted she had any control over that, but Chance didn't know that.

As his eyes widened and his mouth fell open, she chuckled and walked away, waving farewell over her shoulder. "Have a great Sunday. Don't do anything I wouldn't do."

"That doesn't give me many options!" he yelled after her.

Returning home, Destiny took a shower and made breakfast for her and her mom. They ate in silence until her mom asked if Jonathan had made it home safely.

"He did," Destiny confirmed. "But Chance almost took advantage of him in a moment of weakness, and I'm upset with him for it—and with myself for not making Jonathan come home with us when I knew better."

Her mother gave her a pointed look. "*Mija*, I know you care about Jonathan and want to protect his heart, but you have to let him make decisions for himself. How can he grow if you stop him from exploring the world, even the parts that might hurt him?"

Destiny grumbled but silently admitted that her mom was right. "You sound like Abuela," she teased. "I'm not trying to stop him from experiencing things. I just don't think Chance is a good influence on him."

"How could you know that, *mi amor*? You only just met him yourself, no?" Standing, her mother carried her plate to the sink, where she washed and dried it before putting it away. Her distraction gave Destiny time to think about her answer.

"Mama, you know I've always felt things about people. Who's good, who's bad, when something big is coming . . ." She was careful not to say too much, hoping her mother would fill in the rest.

"*Sí, claro. Pero* don't you think you may have a little blind spot regarding Jonathan?"

Destiny froze, and her face grew cold. She'd never said anything about her inability to see things related to Jonathan's future to her mom. "What do you mean?" she asked, heart hammering.

"I just mean he's your best friend. You two have been together since birth. Have you considered that what you *think* is best for him is, in reality, more for your own benefit? Like keeping him all to yourself?" Drying her hands on a paper towel, she turned to look at Destiny expectantly.

Destiny relaxed, able to breathe again. "You might be right, Mama. When it comes to Jonathan, I can be a little possessive. But not because I'm afraid of him letting someone else in. I just don't want to see him get hurt."

"*No hay peor consejo que el que no se pide*—no one likes advice when they didn't ask for it, *mi amor.*" Kissing Destiny on the forehead, she headed out of the kitchen. "Why don't you give yourself a break from worrying? Do something just for you today. Don't focus on the things you cannot change."

That, Destiny realized, was exactly what she needed to do. She'd woken up feeling stronger, and she needed to see what the full extent of her abilities was now.

She jumped up from her seat. "Thank you for the advice, Mama! I'm going to go for a walk. I'll be back later!" Gathering up her jacket and backpack, she left the house for the second time that morning. This time, she was determined to figure out how far she could push her abilities and get to the bottom of what was causing them to grow.

Destiny made her way to the college, which was the closest place guaranteed to have enough people for her to watch. It would also allow her to blend in and sit for a while without anyone wondering what she was doing.

It was quiet for a Sunday morning, but she grabbed a coffee, pulled out her English reading and a notebook, and settled in for a nice long morning of people-watching. She alternated between taking notes as she read and observing people and their paths. She took comfort in the familiar certainty she saw for them as they headed toward the library, the residence hall, or the dining room for breakfast. After a little while, she could even close her eyes and feel their futures opening up to her. Each was like the track of a rollercoaster: it might twist and turn, drop suddenly, or even send the rider for a loop, but staying on the track always meant ending up at one's destination.

She was focusing on a freshman who had moved from St. Louis and was still getting used to life on the small college campus when she felt the first tickle of something that wasn't quite right. She did her best to ignore it, but the longer she sat there, the more insistent and annoying it became. It changed from a tickle in her mind to an almost audible hum.

She was so busy trying to ignore it, it took her a while to realize the freshman was long gone, leaving her with no one else to drown out the annoyance. Finally, unable to take it any longer, she turned around to search for the source of the mental commotion.

On the other side of the courtyard, Luke Martin sat at a table, his head lowered over what appeared to be a tablet. He didn't seem to have noticed Destiny yet, but she could no longer ignore him. The buzzing grew even louder, as if he were surrounded by static electricity. She could even see tiny bolts of something she'd never seen before shooting off him in every direction.

"What the hell is that?"

In her frustration, she spoke louder than she meant to, and Luke looked up. He made eye contact with her but quickly returned to his tablet.

She turned back around. The buzzing had stopped, but she could still feel the energy shooting off him. She had never come across anything like this in the past, and no matter how hard she focused, she couldn't see a clear path for him. It wasn't a complete absence of information, as it was when she tried to read Jonathan. It was almost the opposite, where an infinite number of options fought for her attention. She couldn't remember what she had seen from him in the past, but she knew it hadn't looked like this.

Something had changed, and she needed to figure out what it was.

Ten

$\mathcal{J}$onathan's alarm came much earlier than he would have liked. He had spent much of Sunday and well into the early morning hours of Monday texting back and forth with Billy. In the few weeks since the concert, they had texted pretty regularly, though never at times convenient to Jonathan's schedule. Because the Tacos' performances were usually at night, Billy was up late and slept late. Jonathan didn't have the same freedom to sleep through his 5:45 a.m. alarm, but he hit the snooze button three times anyway before finally making it out of bed.

Jonathan: *Kill me now!*

Destiny: *What happened?*

Jonathan: *I was up late texting with Billy, and it feels like I got 30 minutes of sleep.*

Destiny: *Well, you know the solution to that problem . . .*

Jonathan: Skip school and hope I don't get caught?

Destiny: I'm going to pretend you didn't just say that, because the Jonathan I know would never let some boy get in the way of his near-perfect attendance record.

Destiny: What if I promise to get ready fast enough that we can get coffee on the way to school?

His eyes opened a little wider at the mention of caffeine, but the idea that Destiny would be ready early was almost as unlikely as him skipping school because of lack of sleep.

Jonathan: Don't play with my emotions. I'll be outside your door in 30 minutes. If you're not there, I'm leaving you and getting coffee without you!

It was an empty threat, and he knew she would see right through it, but it was worth it if it helped her speed up her morning routine.

Destiny: You would leave me for coffee?

Jonathan didn't immediately reply, instead hopping in the shower. As his phone notifications went off again and again, he decided not to bother shaving the stubble on his chin and rushed through the rest of his morning routine. Grabbing some jeans and a hoodie from the closet, he re-checked his texts.

Destiny: OMG, Jonathan!

Destiny: HELLO?

Destiny: *You wouldn't dare!*

Destiny: *Okay, fine. I'll be ready in 10.*

She'd obviously mistaken his silence for determination. Wondering if she would be ready as promised, he decided not to respond and just see what happened.

When he walked into the kitchen, his mom was eating a blueberry bagel with peanut butter and looking through something on her phone. She looked up when he came in. "Good morning." She paused. "You look . . . different this morning. Is everything okay?"

Jonathan suddenly felt self-conscious. "Yes, why? Do I not look okay?"

"No, it's not that. You just look more worn down than you usually do. Did you not shave this morning? And is that a hoodie?" She set her phone on the kitchen table and peered at him more closely. "Your eyes are all red. Are you coming down with something?"

Jonathan shook his head, relieved that that was all she meant. "I'm fine, Mom. I just didn't sleep well last night. I'm tired, but Destiny said she'd get coffee with me this morning, so I'm going for speed rather than style today."

"All right, babe, as long as you feel okay." She picked her phone up again and took a bite of her bagel, leaving a smear of peanut butter on her upper lip.

"I promise I'm fine, but thank you for worrying." He kissed her on the cheek to avoid the peanut butter. "I'm gonna head out now. I'll see you later. I love you."

"I love you too! Tell Destiny I said hi." By the time she finished her goodbye, she was fully focused on her phone.

"I will. See you tonight." Leaving the house, he was surprised to see Destiny doing the same next door. "Well,

well, it looks like you made it out of the house on time. I guess miracles can happen.”

“I’m gonna give you a pass on your sarcasm because you’re tired, but I have some stuff I need to do this morning anyway, so this worked out.” Destiny grabbed his hand and pulled him down the street. “Now, let’s go before the line gets too long.”

They went to Night Owls, the coffee shop across the street from the school. It was the only coffee shop in town open later than 9 p.m., but it was also open early and popular with students, teachers, and other people on their way to work. Fortunately, most opted for the drive-through, so the line inside wasn’t that long.

As Jonathan opened the door, he turned to say something to Destiny, only to have the reflection of the sun flash across his eyes. Turning away from the blinding light, he smacked into someone who was walking out, knocking their drink to the ground. As it landed, the lid popped off, skidding across the floor, and the hot liquid splashed across Jonathan’s shoes and the floor around him.

“Watch where you’re going!”

A sense of déjà vu overcame Jonathan, but he couldn’t see well enough to tell who he’d run into. “I’m so sorry. I couldn’t see where I was going for a moment there.”

Blinking as the bright spot in his vision faded, Jonathan looked up and finally saw who he’d run into: Luke Martin. Luke’s expression was impossible to read, but he eventually bent down to clean up the mess.

Jonathan looked at Destiny, who stood to one side, hoping for support or maybe interference between him and Luke. However, she was focused entirely on Luke. Still struggling to see clearly, Jonathan crouched down and reached out for anything that might still be on the floor.

When his hand wrapped around Luke's fingers, they both stood up immediately, and Jonathan quickly dropped Luke's hand.

"Sorry about that," he said, refusing to meet Luke's eyes. "I-I couldn't see." Even he wasn't sure if he was talking about the collision or the hand-holding. "Do you want me to buy you a new drink?"

"It's fine, whatever." Luke's eyes darted toward and away from Jonathan's face. He glanced at Destiny, who continued to stare at him with a pinched expression, as if trying to dissect him with her gaze.

"Don't worry about it," an employee said as she walked over with a mop. "We'll make you another one." She began to clean up what was left of the hot coffee.

"Thanks!" Realizing what he'd said, Jonathan added, "I mean, I'm sorry for the mess." He shook himself mentally. He just couldn't communicate properly with anyone today. This was definitely the last time he stayed up all night texting.

"It happens. No big deal." Setting up a caution sign, she took the mop back behind the counter to put it away and wash her hands. "Mark can help you at the register."

Luke turned quickly and walked toward the counter. Jonathan followed, dragging Destiny along with him, and stood back, waiting their turn. Luke gave the barista at the counter his order so he could remake it and then turned around to face Jonathan and Destiny. "You two are here early." His blue eyes squinted, as if it took effort for him to be anything other than hostile.

Jonathan stared at Luke, surprised. "What?"

Glancing away, Luke pushed a hand through his dark hair, ruffling it and pushing it out of his eyes. "Forget it."

Destiny watched the interaction between Jonathan and Luke. The strange lightning-like energy she'd seen around Luke at the college was in full effect today, but when he and Jonathan had touched earlier, everything had focused in on Jonathan. Now there was a steady connection between them that hadn't existed previously. It was small, almost like a string, and emitted a soft pulsing light, as if marking a heartbeat. It stretched and collapsed as they moved around each other but never broke.

"How was your weekend?" Jonathan attempted. Destiny belatedly realized she'd missed the look he'd cast her.

Luke turned his head and grunted when he realized Jonathan was speaking to him. "Fine. You?"

"It was pretty uneventful, like most weekends. The only exciting thing to happen to me recently was a few weeks back, when Chance invited us to a concert in Peoria, and we got to see the Telepathic Tacos play. Have you heard of them?"

Luke shook his head, but the connection between him and Jonathan had snapped, piquing Destiny's curiosity further.

Wanting to test a theory, she chimed in. "Yeah, but Chance is such a flirt, he tried to go home with a bunch of different people that night."

Luke glanced at her, and his eyes widened a little, but nothing happened on an energy level, much to her disappointment. "Huh. He does seem like the type to hit on anyone and see where it gets him." Luke seemed to be trying for nonchalance but didn't quite manage the easy, unbothered tone.

Jonathan laughed. "I'm so glad I'm not the only one

who's noticed that. He's tried to flirt with me, and it's flattering, but it never feels like he's being serious. I thought I was crazy."

Luke's nose scrunched up for a split second, but he turned away as the barista who had cleaned up the spill set his new drink on the counter. "Here you go. Try to make it out the door with this one," she joked.

"Thanks." Slipping the cup into a sleeve, Luke moved aside so Jonathan and Destiny could order their drinks. He carefully sipped his coffee and watched Jonathan as he decided what to get.

Jonathan debated aloud which pastry looked the best, but he couldn't make up his mind. By the time he decided, a line had begun to form behind them. "I'll have a large, iced caramel macchiato with whole milk, please. And can I have a cherry tart and slice of banana nut bread too?"

Destiny ordered her usual drink, a blended iced mocha, and got a muffin to go with it. Once they'd ordered, they moved to the other end of the counter to wait for their food and drinks.

"Did you forget to shave this morning?" Luke reached out to rub the stubble on Jonathan's chin. The casual touch surprised Destiny, though no more than it seemed to surprise Luke himself, who froze after dropping his hand.

Jonathan's eyes cut to Destiny, who covered her smile with her hand as she pretended to yawn. "I had a late night and just did the basics this morning."

"It looks good."

Luke apparently registered what he'd said at the same time Jonathan did, his eyes widening as Jonathan gasped. "I'm gonna go," Luke said brusquely, just as Jonathan thanked him. Their eyes locked, and the connection between them popped back into place.

Destiny looked back and forth between them, both surprised and excited. She watched as Luke backed up toward the door, almost running into another person as they walked in. Fortunately, he paused long enough for them to scoot out of the way this time. When he turned around and hurried out, she thought she saw the flash of a pathway opening in front of him, but he disappeared into the sun's glare off the door, making it impossible for her to confirm.

"Okay, what the hell just happened?" Jonathan whispered.

Tempering her smile, Destiny shook her head. "Your guess is as good as mine."

"But that was weird, right?" he asked, sounding genuinely confused. "It's not just me?"

"Oh no, it wasn't just you. He was almost nice. Well, I'm not sure I'd go that far, but he definitely wasn't the same guy he normally is when we're at school." She was equally confused, though not for the same reason.

"I swear, I thought he would push me or say something when I made him drop his coffee. I did *not* see a compliment on my appearance coming." Jonathan shook his head. "That's about the last thing I'd have thought would ever happen in my life."

Eleven

Jonathan made his way to his first class in a bit of a daze. He was barely aware of taking his regular seat, let alone the lecture Ms. Halpern jumped into on *Othello* and how its themes were still relevant to the modern world. Only when Chance leaned over and flicked his ear softly did Jonathan really become aware of his surroundings.

"Hey, what's wrong?" Chance whispered. "You look like I imagine Emilia feels at the end of all this."

Confused, since he hadn't read the whole play yet, Jonathan glanced at Ms. Halpern to make sure she was facing the whiteboard and then turned toward Chance. "What do you mean?"

"Well, I hate to spoil it for you, but she dies." Jonathan stared at him, horrified, but Chance waved his hand dismissively. "It is what it is, but what's wrong with you? You look terrible."

"Thanks," Jonathan replied, a little louder than he had intended.

Ms. Halpern turned around to face the class. "What was that?"

Jonathan faced forward again, cheeks burning, but before he could respond, Chance spoke up.

"I was just thanking Jonathan for letting me borrow a pencil. Sorry for disrupting."

For a long moment, Ms. Halpern stared at them. Curious, Jonathan glanced at Chance, but he was sitting in his seat doing nothing.

Finally, Ms. Halpern shook her head and averted her eyes. "No problem." She slowly turned back to the board, where she stood motionless for a few seconds, as if in a trance.

Jonathan waited until she'd begun to write again before turning back to Chance and whispering, "Thank you. I was up late talking to Billy last night and had a weird run-in with Luke this morning, so I'm running on autopilot."

"What happened with Luke? Do I need to teach him a lesson? I warned him not to mess with you." Chance's nostrils flared. "I could ruin Luke's social standing without lifting a finger. Say the word and I'll end him."

Jonathan shook his head. "No, don't. He was . . . nice to me?"

Chance blinked a few times, his mouth opening and closing. It took him a moment to respond. "That's not where I thought this conversation was going." His face relaxed, and to Jonathan's surprise, so did the rest of the class. Frowning, Jonathan looked around. Chance seemed oblivious to the change, but even Ms. Halpern shook off some tension at the front of the room.

"Believe me," Jonathan hissed as he turned back to Chance, "this isn't something I ever thought I'd say, but he actually complimented me. It was . . . unnerving."

Jonathan felt a little bad for speaking negatively about someone else, but it was so different than what he was used to from Luke. When he thought back on it, though, Jonathan realized that Luke had never really done anything terrible to him beyond some rude comments. He was usually in the background when someone else was teasing Jonathan. And he certainly hadn't touched Jonathan since elementary school.

Until today. This was the first time Jonathan had seen Luke outside class without his friends around.

"If Destiny hadn't been there with me," Jonathan added, "I probably would have assumed I was hallucinating from lack of sleep."

"I may need to pay Luke a little visit to see what that was about," Chance said under his breath.

"And say what?" Jonathan lowered his voice, pretending to be intimidating. "Hey, I heard you were nice to my friend. What the hell, man?"

Chance coughed, covering laughter. "Is that how you think straight guys talk?" He lowered his own voice. "Hey, bro, what the hell, man? Leave my buddy alone, pal!"

Jonathan laughed. Ms. Halpern didn't even seem to notice and just kept lecturing. "First of all, I don't believe for a second that you're straight. Secondly, yes, that is how I think straight guys talk. Though they'd probably throw in a ball scratch or something, just to drive it home."

"A ball scratch!" Chance wheezed, and they both dissolved into laughter.

When he could finally speak again, Chance shook his head. "You're honestly probably right on both counts. But if you don't want me to say anything, I'll leave Luke alone. Buddy." He grinned as Jonathan rolled his eyes.

"Whatever makes you happy, bro." Jonathan softly

cackled. "And yes, please don't say anything to Luke or his friends. I don't want them focusing on me more than they already do. Being friendly isn't a crime, even if it's entirely out of character, and I will not be the one to point it out. Especially since I'm the one who knocked the coffee out of his hands in the first place."

Chance perked up. "You didn't tell me that part. No wonder he was nice to you. He's probably afraid of you now that you stood up to him with violence!"

"Uh, yeah . . . about that. It wasn't so much violence as a complete lack of attention on my part."

Chance shrugged, undeterred. "Whatever it was, good for you!"

"I'm not sure there's anything to congratulate me on, but thanks." Chuckling, Jonathan replayed the whole situation from the coffee shop in his mind. He was still lost in the memory when the bell rang.

"Make sure you read the next fifty pages for homework tonight," Ms. Halpern said, raising her voice to be heard as students gathered up their belongings. "And review the themes for the quiz on Friday."

Jonathan was making his way through the crowd of students toward history when Chance called, "Wait up!"

"I can't wait," Jonathan called back without slowing down. "Mr. Wright doesn't wait for anyone! See you in math!" He turned down the social studies hallway, and Destiny fell in beside him along the way.

"Your cell phone just went off. You better put that on silent," she said. "You don't want Mr. W reading your juicy 'no, *you* go to bed first' texts with Billy." She laughed and jumped out of the way as he reached for her. "Am I wrong? Did you not write that?"

Not bothering to deny it, Jonathan pulled out his

phone. He did have a text from Billy, but it was a message from Chance that had caused his phone to go off. "That's weird. It was silenced. How did you hear it?"

"You know I have excellent hearing! So, what did he have to say?" She peeked around his arm as he read.

"The notification you heard was from Chance. He said, 'Mr. Right will wait for you, I promise, but Mr. Right Now will not!' with a bunch of eggplant emojis." He laughed. "And Billy just said, 'Good morning,' and that he was sorry for keeping me up so late talking last night."

Jonathan's pulse quickened, and he shook out his hands before responding to Chance's crude message. Response sent, he put his phone away.

"Are you all right?" Destiny asked as they walked into class.

"Yes, I'm just . . . I like Billy so much! He's so funny and nice and cute!" Jonathan's smile widened, and Destiny giggled at his excitement.

"I'm happy for you. I can see how happy he makes you." She turned mock serious. "Which he better keep doing, if he knows what's good for him."

"The more I get to know him, the more he seems like a genuinely good guy, not like I imagined he could be as a semi-celebrity." Just as he finished speaking, the final bell rang for class and Mr. Wright launched into the day's lesson.

Jonathan's mind wandered throughout class, but he made sure to refocus on Mr. Wright every few minutes to make sure he didn't miss anything too important. Once class ended and he could pull his phone out again, he sent a quick text to Billy: "Looking forward to tonight!" They had made plans to video chat that night.

When he walked into math, Chance was already

there, an evil grin on his face that only got bigger as Jonathan got closer. "What's happening tonight?"

Jonathan dropped his backpack beside his usual desk and sat down. "What do you mean?"

Chance leaned in to Jonathan, dropping his voice to a whisper. "You sent me a text that said you were looking forward to tonight. What're we doing?"

"Wait, what?" Taking out his phone, Jonathan realized he had sent his last text to Chance and sent "You're an ass!" to Billy instead. He frantically typed out an apology to Billy, but before he could finish, Mr. Davies shut the door and told everyone to put their phones away. Slipping his phone into his lap, he tried to finish the message, but he wasn't as sly as he thought.

"Mr. Daniels! Either you're on your phone when you know you're not allowed to be or you need a lesson in consent, since no one in this room agreed to you doing anything else under there. Stop what you're doing and keep your hands above your desk."

Face burning, Jonathan scrambled to put his phone away in his backpack and placed his hands on top of the desk.

"The next time you do that," Mr. Davies continued, "it's mine. And I'm talking about your phone, if anyone is recording this."

The class burst into laughter, and Jonathan ducked his head as embarrassment blazed through him.

"What a dick," Chance said under his breath.

"What did you say?" Mr. Davies demanded as the room grew silent again.

"I said you're being a dick," Chance said for the whole class to hear. "Yes, he was on his phone, so tell him to get off the phone. You don't need to suggest that he's doing anything else. You're the only one talking about things like that."

Mr. Davies's cheeks flushed slightly, but his expression remained unmoved. "Get out of my class right now!"

Standing up, Chance collected his belongings. "With pleasure. I don't want to sit here and listen to you say sexual things about your students to embarrass them." He walked out, but not before turning to Jonathan and giving him a small salute.

Jonathan wondered how long it would take for the story about this incident to get around school and hoped that his classmates would leave out the part about him being the reason everything started. He appreciated Chance sticking up for him with Mr. Davies and with Luke, but being friends with Chance made Jonathan a lot more gossip-worthy than he had ever been on his own.

Given the theatrical beginning of the class, the rest felt pretty standard. And while it felt like the class lasted longer than usual, the bell eventually rang, and Jonathan practically ran out the door. As soon as he was through it, he checked his phone, but Billy hadn't responded. Mentally berating himself, he sent his apology text about the mix-up as he hurried toward the cafeteria. When he reached their usual lunch table, he sat down, dropped his head on his folded arms, and waited miserably for his friends to join him.

Twelve

As Destiny and Chance sat down at the lunch table, Jonathan moaned into the circle of his arms. "I'm such an idiot."

"What? No, you aren't!" Destiny argued immediately, even though she had no idea what he was talking about.

At the same time, Chance said, "I'm not going to disagree with you, but who isn't?"

Whipping her head around, Destiny glared at Chance and mouthed, *Shut up.*

He shrugged and rolled his eyes, sighing. "Whatever," he said under his breath.

"No, Chance is right," Jonathan corrected without lifting his head. "I sent Billy the wrong message, and now he isn't responding to me. He said he was sorry for keeping me up late, and I told him he was an ass." Jonathan softly banged his head on his arms, which made enough noise to draw the attention of nearby students.

"Why did you call him an ass for that?" Destiny asked, doing her best to keep her voice neutral.

"I thought I was responding to Chance's text about Mr. Right Now not waiting for me. So instead of telling Billy I was excited about getting to talk to him tonight, I called him an ass!" Jonathan had begun to laugh-cry, which at least meant he had stopped feeling sorry for himself.

"Hey, Jonny Boy. I heard you got it up in Mr. Davies's class this morning," called out a football player as he and his friends walked by. "I knew you were gay, but I didn't know you were into old dudes."

His friends laughed, and Jonathan froze in his seat.

Before Destiny could speak up, she was distracted by a connection slamming into Jonathan from a few feet away. Turning quickly, she sought the source and found Luke sitting a couple of tables over, head down.

After a few seconds, he lifted his head, but when he saw her looking, he dropped it again. A few seconds later, the connection to Jonathan faded, and the mass of energy surrounded him as it had before, shooting off in all directions but never sticking to anyone else. She still didn't know what it meant, though with Chance sitting so close, she was surprised she could see anything at all.

"Don't worry about them," Chance told Jonathan, dragging Destiny's attention back to them. "They're not worth your time." He grabbed Jonathan's shoulder and squeezed.

"I agree. Chad is not worth worrying over." Destiny lowered her voice to a stage whisper. "After all, he carried a blanket to school until second grade."

Jonathan and Chance laughed.

Once they'd calmed down, Jonathan sighed heavily. "Thank you. I know I shouldn't worry about those guys. Honestly, I don't even care about what he said. It's just that I don't want to be the focus of gossip again, especially not that kind of gossip. You know it'll only get worse, until eventually the story changes to me having sex somewhere and Mr. Davies walking in on it or something equally random." He dropped his head back onto his hands and sighed. "I wish today were over already!"

"Well, I can't help with the gossip, but I can help with the school day being over." Chance kept his voice low so a passing teacher wouldn't overhear. "Let's go!"

He stood up, and Jonathan and Destiny followed suit. Destiny glanced back at Luke, whose eyes were fixed on Jonathan. When he saw her looking, he ducked his head again and refused to look up again, no matter how she tried to catch his gaze.

"Destiny, are you coming?"

Turning, she found that Jonathan had stopped a few feet away. He waited as she gathered the rest of her things and hurried to join them.

"Let's do it."

As they headed for the student parking lot, Jonathan whispered, "How are we going to get by the teachers and security? There's always someone watching the lot."

"I'm not sure, but I feel like it'll work out for the best." Chance locked eyes with Destiny, who nodded.

Jonathan sighed. "I wish I could be more like that."

"What do you mean?" Chance asked.

"You seem so carefree, as if nothing ever bothers you, and no offense, but it doesn't seem like you think things through. You just kind of do stuff, and whatever happens, happens."

Destiny smothered a snort. Jonathan had no idea just how close to the truth he was.

Chance shrugged. "None taken. Honestly, I don't like to make plans. I just sort of go with the flow. If something happens along the way, great. If not, that's okay too. Maybe it will lead to something better, right?"

He glanced at a teacher as they approached her. Following his gaze, Destiny watched the teacher's eyes glaze over as Chance pushed his power out around the three of them. The teacher let them walk right past as if she hadn't noticed them.

Too nervous to notice the strange behavior, Jonathan continued his stream of questions. "How does that work? Every other day, someone asks me what I want to be when I grow up or what I want to study when I go to college. I don't understand how you can get away with not planning for anything!"

His voice cut over the lunchtime chatter around them, and the teacher who had let them walk by turned around. "Where are you three going?"

This time, Destiny spoke up. "I forgot my textbook in my friend's car. They're just walking with me to keep me company while I grab it."

She didn't look convinced, but there were no rules that said students had to stay inside during lunch. Eventually, she nodded and made a sound that might have been approval, before turning and heading on her way.

"Sorry," Jonathan whispered as they continued toward the outer doors. "I didn't mean to be so loud. But I still don't understand how you can just not make plans."

"That all sounds like too much pressure. How are you supposed to know what's coming in the next hour, let alone the next year? And who can legitimately expect a seventeen-year-old to know what they want to do for the rest of their lives?" Chance pushed open the door, and just like that, they were halfway to freedom.

"I get where you're coming from," Destiny chimed in,

giving Chance a serious look, "but I think you could know what you want to do with your life even at seventeen. Some people know what path their life is supposed to take, and they follow that path and never have to worry about what'll happen next."

"Sure, but where's the fun in that?"

"Life isn't always about what's fun," Destiny said. "It's about doing what's right and what we're meant to do. And when you do the things you're meant to, you'll always find happiness."

In the next moment, she looked around. A security guard was about to intercept them. "We need to duck behind this bush." Grabbing Jonathan, she pulled him down next to her.

As soon as Chance crouched with them, the security guard rounded the corner and moved off to their right. "You're welcome," Destiny said unprompted once the security guard was far enough away.

"I guess knowing people's paths sometimes does come in handy," Chance admitted.

"I wish I knew mine," Jonathan piped up as they continued walking. Chance and Destiny exchanged a look. "Then I wouldn't make so many mistakes and wouldn't have to wonder if Billy will ever speak to me again."

Chance laughed. "Okay, I think you're being overdramatic now. Life isn't about *not* making mistakes, and even if there were only one path for you to take, you might stay on that path by making those mistakes."

Destiny stared at Chance, shocked, but added, "And like Chance said, maybe those mistakes would take you in a new direction that leads to better things."

"I'd rather just know what was coming so I could stop worrying about what would happen in the future."

Jonathan suddenly tripped, landing on his hands and knees. Destiny and Chance bent down to help him back up, just as another security guard drove past in a golf cart.

"That was a close one!" Jonathan brushed dirt off his hands and jeans as he watched the golf cart drive away.

"See?" Chance said. "If you had known you were going to trip, you would have stopped yourself, and we would have gotten caught."

"Or I could have avoided the fall and still told you both to get down because I would have known it was the only way to avoid being caught."

"But if you knew you'd trip and tried to stop yourself from tripping, then you never would have tripped and would have had no reason to change the way you were walking, which would still have caused you to trip and ultimately stop the security guard from seeing us."

Jonathan and Chance stared blankly at Destiny, who laughed. "Just trust me, if you tripped, it's because you had to."

"That hurts my head," Jonathan replied, laughing as they finally made it to Chance's car and got inside without being spotted.

"It's like going into a maze where there are lots of options for where you can go. You can make a right, a left, or keep going the way you were going every time you come to a new opening, but you'll have to eventually follow the right path to make it out of the maze. So whether you get there as quickly as possible or not, there's only one way to get to the end." Destiny glanced back and forth between the boys expectantly.

Jonathan looked like he was about to respond, but his phone went off. Chance laughed. "Saved by the text message. Thank god."

Destiny slapped Chance's shoulder. "Shut up! You know what I mean!"

Chance nodded but then shook his head and laughed.

Jonathan smiled widely. "I have no idea what you said, but you'll never guess who just texted me!"

"Billy," Destiny and Chance said together.

"Okay, fine, maybe you will guess. But you'll never guess what he said. He sent a laughing emoji and said that he was sleeping and just saw both messages a minute ago, so he was never mad at me." Jonathan slouched in the front passenger seat, finally relaxing.

"I'm glad to hear he doesn't hate you forever for a simple mistake. It's not like you sent him unsolicited photos of your"—Chance pointed at Jonathan's crotch and waggled his eyebrows—"eggplant emoji."

Jonathan laughed. "Oh my god, could you imagine? I would have died." Frowning, Destiny slapped his arm. When he turned around and saw her disapproval, he grimaced. "Not that I've ever sent anyone an unsolicited picture of my . . . eggplant emoji."

Putting the car in reverse, Chance backed out of the parking spot and drove slowly toward the exit, where a line of seniors with early release were waiting to leave. As they got closer to the front of the line, Destiny began to worry they would be stopped and turned around, but then she saw an opportunity and decided to take it.

"Pull over to the right up there." Leaning forward so Chance could see what she meant, she pointed to where the line split for right and left turns out of the parking lot.

"But I have to make a left to get to Jonathan's house," Chance argued.

"Just do it."

Chance maneuvered into the right lane. Since the only

guard stood on the left side, he waved them on without bothering to look at them.

"You got lucky," Chance said as he turned right and then moved to the left so he could turn around and head in the other direction.

Destiny glanced at Chance in the rearview mirror. "Luck had nothing to do with that." Chance just rolled his eyes.

"Hey! If anyone is getting lucky, it should be me and my eggplant emoji!" Jonathan grinned, and they all burst into laughter that didn't stop until they made it to his house a few minutes later.

Thirteen

*O*nce inside, Jonathan led the way to the kitchen to see what they could eat for lunch. "We've got Hot Pockets, I could make sandwiches, or there's a frozen pepperoni pizza," Jonathan said as he looked through the refrigerator and freezer.

"I vote pizza," Chance said. "Honestly, even if you two don't want it, I could probably eat the whole thing on my own."

"We're not going to eat Jonathan and his mom out of house and home just because you have a bottomless pit for a stomach," Destiny said with a mock glare. "And I'm fine with the frozen pizza if you are." She glanced at Jonathan.

"That works for me. It was meant for me anyway, so my mom won't miss it." Pulling it out of the freezer, Jonathan turned the oven on to preheat and pulled a baking sheet out of a bottom cabinet. He was removing the plastic from around the pizza when his cell phone lit up on the counter.

Chance picked up the phone and read the text. "Uh-oh, looks like your Telepathic Taco is jealous you opted for pizza."

"What did he say?" Jonathan asked nervously, voice a little high.

"Oh my god." Chance snickered. "You need to calm down. I was joking with you. He was just asking about your day. I'm telling him you ran away from school like the delinquent you are." Chance turned his back to Jonathan as his fingers flew across the screen, tapping quickly.

Rolling his eyes, Jonathan tried to look over Chance's shoulder as he finished his message. "That's fine, as long as you remind him that delinquents are hot."

"Obviously," Chance replied. "I also sent him a shirtless photo of you that I found in your photo roll. I hope that's okay."

Jonathan laughed but leaned forward to make sure Chance hadn't scrolled down too far in his photos. "Just make sure it's the most recent one."

"¡*Ay, Dios*! Boys are weird," Destiny said from her stool at the kitchen island. "Why do you keep shirtless photos readily available on your phone?"

"Quick access," Chance responded.

"He's not wrong, but it's mostly a self-esteem thing for me. I take a lot more photos than I keep, and the ones I keep are photos I feel good about. That way, I always have a good photo even if I'm having a bad day." As the oven beeped, Jonathan returned to the pizza and slid it into the heat. "It's also easier to have one ready than to take a new one every time I want to post one or share it with someone." He laughed.

"I guess not having to worry about having topless photos ready at the push of a button is a benefit of being completely uninterested in dating. That, and I never have to worry about sending the wrong text to someone I might like." Destiny leaned over and gave Jonathan a quick hug as he sat beside her.

Jonathan hugged her back before holding his hand out for his phone. "What did you actually say, Chance?"

"Nothing, really. Just that you left school because you were feeling tired, and now you're having a ditch day with some friends. The shirtless photo was just a benefit that he seemed to like because he sent you one in return, but it's only his chest and stomach, not his face." Chance handed the phone back, and all three of them looked at the photo Billy had sent.

"Aw, he has a cute little birthmark," Destiny pointed out.

"I honestly didn't even see that," Jonathan admitted, his eyes glued to the phone. "It is cute, though, I agree."

"You need some alone time before we eat?" Chance teased, giving Jonathan's upper thigh a playful squeeze.

Jonathan squealed and jumped in his chair, his leg flying out and kicking the cabinets under the island. "Do not squeeze my leg like that!"

Chance squeezed again. "Like what?" he asked, playing dumb.

Jonathan jumped again, though he managed not to kick the cabinets this time. Face flushed, he stood up to get away from Chance. "I'm very ticklish, thank you, so I'd appreciate you not doing that to me. Ever again!" He struggled to keep a straight face as his body was still dealing with the effects of being tickled.

"Chance, leave him alone." Destiny gave him a stern look, and he put up his hands in surrender.

"I didn't mean anything by it. Jonathan is too head over heels for Mr. Taco anyway." He laughed.

"Can we please not call him Mr. Taco?" Jonathan asked seriously.

Destiny laughed. "Oh, now I think we have to call him Mr. Taco." She grinned at Chance, who grinned back. "Billy Taco has a nice ring to it, don't you think?"

The three of them continued coming up with potential pet names for Billy until the oven's buzzer went off, alerting them that their lunch was ready. Dividing the pizza among them, they devoured it as quickly as the hot cheese allowed.

They were still sitting around the island eating when Jonathan's cell phone began to ring. Chance and Destiny joked that Mr. Taco was calling, but when Jonathan saw the screen, all amusement washed away. He waved his hand to quiet them.

"Hi, Mom, what's up?" He attempted to sound casual but wasn't sure he pulled it off.

"What happened? I got a call from the school that you weren't in class this afternoon. Is everything okay?"

Jonathan's chest began to ache, and his fingers tingled. He hadn't meant to worry her.

Rubbing his fingers together, he scrambled for an answer. "I . . . uh . . . I wasn't feeling very well and knew you couldn't get away from work, so I got a ride home from a friend." He felt terrible for lying to her, and his voice had begun to quiver, which didn't help. He tried to shake out the nerves, with little success.

"Oh no, are you still feeling sick? Do you want me to come home?"

"No!" he practically yelled into the phone. "I mean, no, you don't need to leave work. I'll be fine. I think it might have just been a panic attack."

That wasn't that far from the truth, and he took a

moment to take a full breath for the first time since answering the phone. It might have been less than a minute ago, but it felt like it had been much longer.

"Are you sure you don't want to have someone there with you?"

"I don't want you to worry. I'll be fine. I'm already feeling better, and Destiny said she would come by after school, so I won't be alone for much longer." His voice shook with the continuous lying, and his nose felt cold as the blood no doubt drained from his face.

"All right, honey, if you're sure you're fine, I'll stay at work. But please let me know if anything changes. I'll call you in a little while to check in and see how you're feeling." She didn't sound fully convinced, but Jonathan knew she wouldn't leave work if she didn't have to.

"That sounds good, Mom. I'll let you know if anything changes. I'll probably just lie down for a little while, see if that helps." His heart fluttered.

"Okay. I love you, honey."

"I love you too, Mom. Thanks for checking up on me. I'll see you when you get home." Jonathan waited for her to hang up and then set his phone down. He sat there quietly, not looking at his friends as he realized this was the biggest lie he'd ever told his mom.

Destiny put her hand on his shoulder. "You okay?"

"I will be. I just feel terrible for not being honest with her." Turning around on his stool, he stood up and began to pace around the kitchen, rubbing his hands to make the feeling return to his fingertips.

Taking a large bite of pizza, Chance turned to Destiny. "Why don't you date anyone?" he asked through the mouthful of food.

"What?" she asked.

Chance finished chewing and swallowed. "You said the benefit of not dating anyone was not needing topless photos, but why don't you date anyone?"

Jonathan tuned out the conversation as he paced back and forth in the family room. He felt guilty for lying to his mom and for sneaking out of school. He'd been neglecting his schoolwork and staying up way too late, to the point he sometimes fell asleep in class. It was a miracle he hadn't gotten in trouble in class for not paying attention when his mind was constantly wandering off. He needed to do better, which meant not texting with Billy so late at night—even if it did give Jonathan butterflies in the best way and gave him the most amazing dreams for the one to two hours of sleep he did end up getting those nights they talked. From now on, he would absolutely not stay up past midnight, no matter what happened.

Probably.

"Ah, I knew there was a reason you didn't want to date me. It wouldn't be fair to all the other kids in our school who also want to date me. You can't keep a good man down. I appreciate you looking out for me."

Startled out of his emotional spiral by Chance's reply, Jonathan glanced over and noticed his huge grin.

Destiny smirked. "Oh yes, you got me. I haven't dated anyone my whole life because I was waiting for you, and I won't date you because you're a manwhore who can't commit."

"Don't let her fool you," Jonathan interjected, reclaiming his seat at the island. "She's not interested in you, because she's aro/ace." He smiled at her. "She told me a long time ago."

When Jonathan's phone buzzed again, he picked it up, read the message that popped up, and winced. He had replied earlier to Billy's photo, saying he liked his cute birthmark. Billy's latest response was a request that Jonathan not show the photo to anyone else. Now Jonathan felt terrible because Chance and Destiny had seen it. However, he knew they wouldn't blab about it, and he certainly wasn't going to say anything about it to anyone else or show it around school. He answered Billy in the affirmative, though he immediately felt guilty for lying to someone for the second time that day.

After a few hours, Chance went home. Jonathan and Destiny worked on their homework until his mom came home. She fussed over him for a bit, ensuring he was feeling better. Once she was satisfied that he was not, in fact, sick, she left them to their work. Destiny left soon after, and Jonathan spent the rest of the night not checking his phone as penance.

Fourteen

The following day, Destiny and Jonathan made it to school earlier than usual and waited just inside the front doors for Chance to arrive. As they leaned against the wall, Destiny took advantage of Chance's absence and Jonathan's distraction with his phone to see if she could sense anything else about Jonathan.

Such as who he'd been kissing in her vision.

Taking a deep breath, she relaxed and opened her mind to the pathways around her. Immediately, she experienced an influx of visual noise: paths, potential futures, and connections between students. She scanned through them quickly, discarding anything that didn't seem connected to Jonathan.

As if on cue, the now-familiar buzz of confusion surrounding Luke caught her attention, as did his connection to Jonathan, though it was weak.

To Destiny's surprise, Luke was smiling as he watched Jonathan. Curious, she focused on Luke and was pleased when the flashes of potential futures faded away in favor of the connection she was interested in. She saw Luke's continued infatuation with Jonathan, but as always, her friend was annoyingly absent from the vision.

Just as Luke took a step toward them, one of the other baseball players walked through the front doors. When Luke turned toward his friend, his connection to Jonathan faded away.

"C'mon, give me something!"

"Sorry, what?" Jonathan asked, eyes never leaving his phone.

"Nothing, just talking to myself . . . mostly." It looked like she would have to have a talk with Luke if she wanted to find out what his deal was and get to the bottom of the strange energy he was giving off.

It took a few hours for Destiny to get Luke alone. Her opportunity came in the media center, where Luke sat by himself, none of his friends in sight. The energy bolts, as she had come to think of them, were flying off him in every direction, to the point Destiny found it difficult to look directly at him. Refusing to be deterred, though, she focused on her task and took a seat next to him.

Looking up when she sat down, Luke started to move his stuff out of her way. "There are other tables available, you know," he grumbled.

"I saw that, but I need to talk to you." She kept her voice low so as not to attract the attention of the other students scattered around the room.

"What do you want?" he asked, keeping his eyes averted.

Destiny decided to try a direct approach. "What's going on with you and Jonathan?"

The moment she said Jonathan's name, all the energy around Luke combined and shot out across the school, probably toward Jonathan.

Luke squirmed in his seat but feigned nonchalance. "I don't know what you're talking about; nothing's going on. Why?" he added, his voice pitching up in interest that belied the casual manner he'd adopted. "Did he say something about me?"

"No, I don't think Jonathan has mentioned you except in passing since middle school." As she spoke, the connection split back into smaller bolts.

"Then what do you mean? He doesn't talk about me, and I don't talk about him. And we definitely don't talk to each other." He finally glanced up at her, though not before his eyes darted around the room warily.

"Well, that's not true. You just talked to him the other day at the coffee shop." She reached for his hand, wondering if a physical connection would help her decipher the strange energy.

Pulling his hand back before she could touch it, he started to protest but then stopped, his mouth opening and closing silently.

"I was just being polite," he finally managed, sounding a touch panicked. "What, would you rather I yelled at him? Maybe push him into a table and threaten him?" His voice rose as he spoke, and he lowered his head and hunched his shoulders as other students glanced their way. Lowering his voice, he added, "Why do you care anyway?"

"Because he's my friend, and I want what's best for him. But I want what's best for you too." One of the splintered paths surrounding Luke extended toward her, as if testing her out, but in the end, it moved slowly away from her and disappeared.

"Why do you care what happens to me?" he asked incredulously. "We're not friends; we never have been."

She shrugged. "That's sort of who I am. I care about people. All people." When Luke looked at her with a furrowed brow, she quickly added, "Not in a romantic way, obviously, just in a platonic, 'I want to see the right things happen to people' kind of way. I want people to get what they deserve."

Luke stared at her as if seeing her for the first time. Before he could respond, the bell rang, signaling the end of the class period, and he gathered his stuff and stood up from the table. Instead of immediately heading off, he hesitated.

"You're not who I thought you were," he finally said.

"Neither are you." Climbing to her feet, she added, "I know we're not friends or anything, but I am someone you can talk to if you ever need to vent or whatever. It can be just between us if you prefer. I promise not to tell anyone."

"Probably not." He walked away but turned back just as he reached the door. "Thanks."

He disappeared through the door before Destiny could reply. Not exactly how she had seen the conversation going in her mind, but it was a start. She had begun to learn more about Luke, which could help her figure out his connection to Jonathan.

Destiny joined the flow of student traffic toward the cafeteria and found Jonathan and Chance waiting for her at their regular table.

"Where've you been?" Jonathan asked. "Your classroom isn't in that direction."

"I got release time to go to the media center to work on a project."

Jonathan's brow rose. "What project?"

"Just a research project for extra credit," she replied vaguely.

Chance seemed to understand her desire not to elaborate. "Can we please get in line? I'm starving, and I don't care about her research. Sorry, not sorry." He and Jonathan laughed and led the way to the shortest line.

As they waited in line, Destiny noticed a pathway connected to Jonathan. She turned and saw that Luke and his friends had passed by. Even though multiple bolt-like paths were coming off Luke, his connection to Jonathan remained.

Suddenly, she blinked and straightened. She could see Luke's pathways even though Chance stood right beside her! Glancing quickly around the cafeteria, she realized other paths were becoming easier to see—maybe not as strong as they had been in the morning, but clear enough that she could make out some of the things in her classmates' futures.

"There's a party this weekend," Destiny said absentmindedly. "We should go."

Chance grabbed a bag of chips and a bottle of water. "Who's having a party?"

"I'm not sure. Someone at that table over there." She jerked her chin toward the table in question.

Jonathan turned to look at the table of girls they only vaguely knew. "How do you know?"

Too late, Destiny realized her mistake, but she covered the slipup smoothly. "I could hear them talking about it: what they're going to wear, whom to invite and how—stuff like that."

As if on cue, one of the girls at the table turned and spotted them. Standing up, she walked over, eyes on Chance. "Hey, my friend's parents are out of town this weekend, and we're throwing a party. Would you maybe wanna come?"

Chance was all smiles, and Destiny could tell his power was engulfing the poor girl. "Can my friends come too?" He gestured toward Destiny and Jonathan.

She eyed Destiny and Jonathan dismissively. "Sure, bring any *friends* you want." Leaning closer to Chance, she added, "The more, the merrier, or whatever." Destiny suspected she was trying to sound sexy.

Chance grinned. "Looking forward to it. Text me the address."

As the girl returned to her table and sat back down, her friends all leaned in and began peppering her with questions. Destiny watched the group swoon as they slowly came down from Chance's influence.

"Well," Chance said cockily, "I guess we're going to the party."

Destiny watched as news of the party spread around the room, quickly followed by shifting paths. She couldn't yet see what would happen, but she could tell the three of them needed to be there.

Twenty minutes later, Chance elbowed Jonathan, distracting Destiny. "You should invite Billy Taco!"

"Oh my god, I thought we agreed *not* to call him that?" Jonathan laughed and shook his head. "But that's not a bad idea." Pulling out his cell phone, he began to text Billy.

"We never agreed to that," Destiny teased. "You just wanted us to."

Gathering their belongings, the three friends made their way to class.

Jonathan was on his way home when Billy responded to his invitation.

Billy: *Who all's gonna be there?*

Jonathan: *I'm not sure. Mostly other people from my school, and maybe some of their friends from outside Eureka. The girl throwing it is a senior, so maybe some people from the college too.* 🙌

Billy: *What time do you think you're gonna go?*

Jonathan: *I dunno. I still have to ask my mom if I can go out, but probably around 9.*

Billy: *I'll think about it, but I can probably go for a little while if we don't have rehearsal.*

Grinning, Jonathan snapped a quick selfie and sent it to Billy, wanting to share how giddy he was. Though they had been texting and occasionally talking since the show, this would be their first time seeing each other in person since Billy gave Jonathan his number.

Jonathan: *It would be nice to see you again. And I can make everyone jealous that I brought such a hot date!*

Billy: ☠️

Billy: *I don't know that anyone would see me when they have you to look at, especially if you're showing off that body like you do in these photos!*

Laughing, Jonathan scrolled back to look at the photos, trying to see himself through Billy's eyes.

Jonathan: *Trust me, no one at school looks at me like that, but I'm not going shirtless to this party. No one needs to see all this!*

Billy: *What if they—or more importantly, I—want to see it all?* 😶

Jonathan: *For you, I'd consider it, but only if you were shirtless too. Everyone else at the party would be looking at you, then, not me, so it would be less embarrassing.*

They continued texting until Jonathan had to get ready for dinner and Billy had band practice, but Billy promised to let Jonathan know whether he'd be able to make it to the party.

Jonathan couldn't wait for the weekend and the chance to see Billy again. He daydreamed about what he would wear, what they would talk about, and what the other kids from school would say when they saw them together. Sure, it wasn't a secret that Jonathan was gay, but he'd never actually dated anyone before, so as far as his class-mates were concerned, he might as well have been aro/ace, like Destiny.

The thought of showing up to a party with another guy felt like a statement he was ready to make in his high-school career. And if things went well, maybe they could go to prom together.

Jonathan's mind raced, imagining what their pictures would look like and wondering if he would be able to get the couples discount on tickets. That led him to imagine the two of them as a couple. Would Billy write songs about their relationship and play them with the band? Could Jon-athan talk his mom into letting him travel with the band during the summer?

He was getting way ahead of himself. He knew he needed to calm down, but he could so easily imagine the next few months and the more significant moments of the following years.

Before he could get too carried away, Jonathan went through his closet and picked out the best-looking outfit he had—a pair of jeans that were a little too tight for school but that showed off his assets nicely and a navy-blue Henley that, left unbuttoned, showed off the little bit of chest hair he had grown last summer.

Imagining Billy's reaction to seeing him, Jonathan smiled. "Maybe their eyes will be on me." He laughed at his sudden confidence. "I guess I'll find out on Friday."

By Friday, Jonathan had gotten permission from his mom to go to the party. In fact, she'd been happy to see he was getting out and living a little.

"Don't get me wrong. I love Destiny—she's a good influence on you—but your high-school years shouldn't be limited to a single friend and hanging out at home every weekend."

Billy had agreed to go to the party but wasn't sure what time he would show up, so Jonathan was going with Destiny and Chance. When Chance came to pick Jonathan up, his eyes practically bulged out of his head.

"My god, you look practically pornographic in that outfit!" Chance joked as his eyes roamed freely over Jonathan's body. "Who knew you could fill out your pants like that!" Reaching out, he pretended to grope Jonathan in several different places. Jonathan laughed along and spun to show off the full effect of the slightly too-tight pants. Gasping, Chance lightly smacked Jonathan's butt before he could finish the turn.

"Hey," Jonathan protested, pretending to be upset. "Don't get fresh with me, sir. Mr. Taco may not like to share." Saying goodbye to his mom, he closed the door as they left to get Destiny. Once the door was shut, his anxiety got the better of him. "Does it really look good, though, or were you just saying that?"

Chance leaned into Jonathan's side. "Honestly," he whispered, "if I thought I had a chance, I'd try to work my magic on you and take advantage of you right here on your front stoop."

Laughing, Jonathan hit his arm playfully. "If I thought you were legitimately interested in me, I might let you try."

As they walked up the path to Destiny's front door, Jonathan glanced at Chance out of the corner of his eye. He had to admit, Chance looked good. He wore a black button-up shirt with the sleeves rolled up and the top three buttons undone, exposing his bare chest. His dark jeans looked like they had been sculpted onto his body rather than purchased at a store, and his dark hair was styled so the curls resembled waves, like the ocean at night. His brown eyes shone in the amber glow of Destiny's porch light, making them look golden.

If Jonathan hadn't been hoping for a first kiss from Billy tonight, he might have responded differently to Chance's continued flirtation.

Catching Jonathan's look, Chance smirked. "Give me the opportunity, and I'll show you that sometimes the best things are the ones you know won't last forever."

Jonathan's heart skipped a beat. "Uh . . . I . . ." He cleared his throat as Chance's smile widened. "Spoken like a true player. Besides, you'll have lots to see and plenty to do once we get to the party." He rang the doorbell. "Don't make me reject you again."

"Who's getting rejected?" Destiny asked as the door opened, startling Jonathan. "If it's Chance, can you do it now so I can watch?"

Destiny's curls were carefully sculpted, framing her heart-shaped face beautifully. Her red spaghetti-strap top hung delicately from her shoulders, and her patterned stretch-cotton skirt clung to the swell of her hips before cascading over her thighs.

Jonathan held his hands out to his sides and offered her a bow. To his amusement, Chance only stared, his mouth hanging open and his quick wit apparently rendered useless.

Destiny smirked at Chance. "I guess it was you getting rejected. Maybe a theme for tonight, what do you think?"

Recovering from his shock, Chance gave a hearty laugh. "Baby, if you're doing the rejecting, I'll keep trying until I wear you down!" He undid another button to show off more of his tanned skin.

Jonathan watched quietly as Destiny and Chance seemed to share a moment but spoke up after a couple seconds of silence.

"How quickly I'm forgotten." Jonathan pressed the back of his hand to his forehead in mock dismay. Then he grinned. "But let's just keep this PG, okay? I don't want anyone to tell my mom about the three teens undressing on our front lawn."

Laughing, he grabbed Destiny's hand and hauled her toward Chance's car, where they waited for him to unlock the doors. Jonathan opened the back door for Destiny, waited for her to climb in and situate herself, and then closed it carefully. Quickly taking the seat in front of her, he buckled his seatbelt.

"Sounds like someone's a little excited to get this party

started!" Reaching forward, Destiny rubbed Jonathan's shoulders to help him relax. "Have you heard from Billy yet? Does he know what time he's going to be there?"

Jonathan put a hand on hers and squeezed gently. "I haven't heard from him, but he said he would text me once he was on his way. They booked a last-minute gig and needed to make sure they had everything in order before they leave town. It sucks because I was hoping we might be able to see them play again."

Shifting the car into drive, Chance pulled away from the curb. "We could always try to surprise them if it's close enough to drive. Did he say where it was gonna be?"

"Not yet, but I'll see if I can get more details tonight."

The drive to the party was relatively short since everything in town was less than thirty minutes away. As they drove, they made bets on what would happen during the party, to make things more fun.

When they pulled up to the house, the nearby parking was already taken, and they had to drive a couple of streets over to find any. As they walked back, they joined the flow of people, some familiar and some not, heading in the same direction.

Nudging Jonathan, Destiny pointed to a group about a hundred feet ahead of them: Luke Martin and some of his teammates.

"Oh great," Jonathan groaned, exasperated. "I should have realized they'd come to the party too." Firming his jaw, he shook his head and refused to stop walking. "As long as they leave us alone tonight, I'll be fine."

"They better leave you alone tonight," Chance added, voice deeper and oddly more substantial than usual. "Or they'll have to answer to me. And if it comes to that, they won't know what hit them!"

Jonathan just nodded.

"You never know," Destiny chimed in. "Luke was weirdly nice the last time you ran into him." She smirked.

Jonathan's brow furrowed. "Pun intended, I assume?"

"Oh, you know it was!" She laughed. "I'm just saying, sometimes people will surprise you if you let them."

A wave of heat burned through Jonathan, and he stopped in his tracks, forcing Destiny and Chance to stop with him. "Sometimes people will surprise you? What the hell is that even supposed to mean? We've known most of those guys for at least five years. Have you ever once been surprised by them in a good way?" Despite his anger and frustration, he tried to temper his tone. He might not understand where Destiny was coming from, but she was his best friend and she hadn't really done anything wrong. "Because I remember the time Mike put a brownie on my chair so I would have a brown stain on the seat of my jeans for the rest of the day. And the time they all got together during PE and decided to play 'smear the queer.'"

The humor drained from Destiny's face, and she and Chance stood there silently staring at Jonathan.

"I'm sure in ten or fifteen years, when they're older and more mature, they'll all be great guys in their own way or whatever it is you want to believe. But tonight, at this party, I just don't want them to start something in front of Billy." He folded his arms tightly across his body. "It would be nice if you'd take my side and not try to sugarcoat things."

Turning away, he continued toward the party, leaving Destiny and Chance behind.

Destiny didn't argue. Jonathan was right to think and feel the way he did about the guys who had bullied him for years. She just wished there was a way she could make him understand that Luke was struggling with his own issues and needed a friend, if nothing else, to help him figure things out.

As the group of baseball players turned a corner, the wind picked up, and one of them looked back toward the three of them. When he said something to the rest of the group, Luke glanced back as well. He must have locked eyes with Jonathan, because the path connecting them lit up.

To Destiny's surprise, she realized the connection was much more solid than it had been before. As she focused on Luke, she realized he was also easier for her to look at, as most of the energy that used to spark off him had disappeared or been redirected.

Luke had stopped walking when he'd caught sight of Jonathan, even as his friends continued on. After a moment, he dropped to one knee and reached for his shoe as if to tie it, but his eyes never once left Jonathan. When his friends finally noticed his absence, they stopped to wait for him, but Luke didn't seem to notice.

As Destiny watched, Jonathan uncrossed his arms and pulled the hem of his shirt down, dragging the fabric over his chest. The movement drew Luke's attention down, and the path flared brighter as if ignited.

"Yo, Martin, you comin' or what?" yelled one of his friends, annoyed.

The use of his last name seemed to finally snap Luke out of his daze. Glancing toward his friends, he mumbled something about tying his shoe before standing and hurrying over to rejoin them.

"Hey, Destiny," Mike Lawler called. "You're looking good tonight. You oughta ditch those two losers and hang with me. I guarantee I can show you a better time than they can." He grabbed his crotch, pretending to adjust himself.

She shot him a fierce grin. "I look good every night. And I'm more than satisfied spending the night with my friends." Tossing her curls over her shoulder, she grabbed Jonathan's hand as she caught up to him and pulled him past the group of baseball players, Chance following along. Once they were far enough ahead to be out of earshot, she whispered, "He's so gross, I wouldn't even touch him with Chance's body."

Jonathan nodded.

"Fucking stuck-up bitch," Mike yelled.

Chance stopped, and Destiny felt him throw his power back at the group. Mike tripped and landed hard on his hands and knees, and his friends burst out laughing.

Not bothering to acknowledge Mike's outburst, Destiny focused her own power on him until she found what she was looking for. As Mike yelled something else, she turned to Jonathan and whispered, "If I didn't know Kelly was going to break up with him this weekend, I would do something about his wandering eyes. But it seems like she already knows."

Destiny immediately realized the mistake she'd made in her anger, but Jonathan didn't question her intimate knowledge of their classmate.

"He's such an asshole. I wish he would . . ." Jonathan hesitated, apparently struggling to pin down an appropriate punishment. "I dunno what, but something bad."

Chance chuckled but remained silent.

After a few seconds of silence, Jonathan spoke again, finally asking the question that had no doubt been bothering him since they passed the jocks. "Why was Luke staring at me? Is there something wrong with my shirt? Did I spill something on it? Do I look too gay?"

"What does 'too gay' even look like?" Chance countered. "And who decides when you've reached that point? As for your other questions, there's nothing wrong with your clothes. You haven't spilled anything on yourself, especially," he added, gently teasing, "since there has been a complete lack of anything you could have spilled since we left your house."

"Maybe he was checking you out," Destiny offered.

"What?" Jonathan demanded, voice pitching up.

Destiny shrugged. "Maybe that's why he was looking. Because he was checking you out." Not bothering to wait for an answer, she headed up the driveway to the house where the party was taking place and walked right in.

When Jonathan finally caught up with her, he spoke directly into her ear to be heard over the loud music. "That would almost be hilarious if it weren't so impossible."

The press of the crowd pulled them deeper into the party and into the kitchen, where a keg sat on the ground. The kitchen island was covered in random bottles of alcohol, mixers, and soda, as well as bowls of chips and a tray of brownies—the latter of which smelled like a little something extra had been baked in.

Grabbing some cups, Chance handed one each to Destiny and Jonathan before filling his with beer from the keg. Destiny and Jonathan opted for soda, wanting to ensure they had a reliable ride home at the end of the night.

"This'll be my only drink tonight, I swear!" Chance yelled over the music. "You guys can drink whatever you want. I'll make sure we get home safely."

Jonathan shook his head. "My mom would kill me if

I came home smelling of alcohol, and I'm not risking jail time for some house party."

"Suit yourself." As Chance shrugged, the girl who had invited him to the party swooped in and pulled him toward the backyard. "I guess we're going outside," he shouted, allowing himself to be led away.

Following behind, Destiny and Jonathan exchanged looks. "Chance ditched us in less than five minutes," Jonathan said. "I guess I owe you a drink."

She laughed. "You should know better than to bet against Destiny. I'm always going to win, especially when it comes to him. He's too easily sidetracked by whatever new thing pops up. He's like a puppy with ADHD, impossible to keep focused."

Jonathan joined her in laughter.

Once they had made it to an area with a little more room, they began to mingle with some of the other people at the party. Every few minutes, Jonathan would check his phone, no doubt looking for a text or missed call from Billy. As time passed, his expression grew pinched, and he began to roll his eyes every time he looked.

After thirty minutes of standing around and listening to other people talk, he leaned over and whispered in Destiny's ear. "I'm about to lose my shit. Where the hell is he? And why are we hanging out with these people?"

She laughed at his last question but shook her head and shrugged, unable to tell him where Billy was or why they'd been sucked into the current group of people they were standing with. She was about to suggest going somewhere else when she noticed someone heading in their direction.

"Don't look now, but he's staring at you again."

Turning, Jonathan scanned the crowd. Destiny bit her

lip but didn't bother telling him that Luke was approaching from his other side.

"Hi, Luke," Destiny said, facing the new arrival to their small group. She narrowed her eyes, hoping he'd understand the warning against being rude. She didn't think she needed it, though, as the energy around him was reaching out for Jonathan.

"Hey, Destiny." He met her eyes for only a moment before glancing to her side. "Hey, Jonathan," he said with a little more volume.

Just as Jonathan opened his mouth to respond, his phone rang. "Sorry," he said, looking at the screen. "I have to take this."

ey, I just parked. Meet me out front."

Billy's voice had been hard to make out over the sounds of the party, but Jonathan had heard enough that he started to head back inside. On the way, he accidentally bumped into one of Luke's friends, who made a snide comment, but Jonathan refused to care or even acknowledge it. He was too excited to see Billy again.

The lights were turned down low inside, and someone had brought out strobe lights that flashed different colors all over the place. The living room had become a makeshift dance floor, where partygoers were crammed together in an almost-solid mass of gyrating bodies. It made it a little challenging to get through the crowd, but Jonathan pressed forward, until he finally reached the front door.

Walking outside, he checked both directions for any sign of Billy but came up short. He sent him a quick text to find out where he had parked, and a couple of seconds later, his phone rang again.

"Hey, where are you?" Jonathan asked excitedly.

"I'm still two streets away," Billy replied, sounding a little irritated. "I couldn't find anything closer. Gimme a minute."

"Where'd you park? I'll start walking that way."

"I'm on Hilldale heading toward Maple, I think."

"Okay, I'm on my way. I'll meet you in the middle!"

Jonathan jogged in the direction Billy had mentioned. Turning the corner, he spotted Billy on the opposite side of the street, a little way down. Picking up his pace, he waited for a few partygoers to drive past on their hunt for parking before running across the street, where Billy finally noticed him.

Jonathan couldn't help but stare. Billy wore an unbuttoned blue plaid shirt over a T-shirt for a band Jonathan had never heard of, as well as a pair of dark jeans with a hole in one of the knees. His medium-length reddish-brown hair was pushed back out of his eyes, which was how Jonathan liked it best.

"Hey," Jonathan said shyly as he stopped in front of Billy. He wasn't sure if he should try to hug Billy or not, but he itched to wrap his arms around Billy's slender body and breathe in his scent.

"Hi," Billy replied, voice void of his earlier irritation. He looked Jonathan up and down appreciatively. "You look amazing!" Gently taking Jonathan's hand, Billy encouraged him to spin in a circle, looking at him as if for the first time. "Like, really amazing. We could just go make out in my car for a while instead of going to this party, if you want."

The offer was tempting, but Jonathan couldn't tell if Billy was being serious or just teasing him. Laughing, he leaned in close, until their lips were only a few inches apart. "Can't we do both?"

Billy swallowed audibly as his eyes locked on Jonathan's lips. Glancing around carefully for anyone else walking or driving by, he leaned in to close the distance between them.

Jonathan closed his eyes, preparing for the kiss he had imagined ever since Billy gave him his phone number. He thought about how soft and full Billy's lips would be and what they would feel like pressing firmly against his own. He pictured their tongues tangling with one another as their kiss deepened.

The honk of a nearby horn snapped Jonathan back to reality, and he and Billy straightened, looking around for the car. It turned out to just be the sound of someone locking their car, but the mood was ruined.

They both laughed nervously, but their tension had eased when they realized no one had seen them, and the moment had passed.

"Well, we better head back to the party, or my friends will think you kidnapped me," Jonathan teased.

Billy groaned but fell in step with Jonathan as he began walking back toward the party. "Who's throwing this party anyway? One of your friends?"

"No, some girl from school invited Chance, and he got Destiny and me an invite. Well, technically, she said he could bring any friends he wanted; we just happened to be the friends in question. Her name is Amanda, but we're not close or anything."

"Ah, it's one of those parties."

Jonathan leaned closer so their arms would brush as they walked. "What do you mean?"

"A high-school house party with tons of random people you don't know that well."

"Well, not really. There are less than five hundred

kids at our school. I may not be close with them, but we all know each other and have been in the same school since kindergarten. My freshman year, Amanda was in my American history class, but we never spoke."

Shrugging, Jonathan grabbed Billy's hand. "Let's cross here." He pulled Billy into the road. Billy stumbled but easily caught up with Jonathan, squeezing his hand. When they got close enough to hear the music spilling out of the front door every time it opened, Billy slipped his hand out of Jonathan's and touched his back, encouraging him to lead the way. "I'll follow you," he said into Jonathan's ear.

Jonathan led him past the few people gathered out front and through the crowd dancing in the living room, which seemed to have grown in the few minutes he'd been gone. They stopped in the kitchen so they could each get a drink and Billy could grab a couple of snacks, before making their way into the backyard, where Destiny and Chance waited.

A crowd surrounded them, listening as they seemed to tell a story, though Jonathan wasn't close enough to hear what it was about. Taking turns speaking, they looked more comfortable with each other than they had at any other time in the past few weeks.

When Destiny spotted Jonathan and Billy, she waved to them, which seemed to break the magic of the story. The crowd slowly broke apart, and people went back to their smaller groupings around the yard.

"What was that all about?" Jonathan asked when he and Billy had closed the distance.

Destiny shrugged casually. "Nothing really, just waiting around for you to get back." Reaching past Jonathan, she grabbed Billy's hand. "I'm so happy you decided to come. How have you been?"

At the same time, Chance asked, "Billy Taco, how's it going?"

Billy laughed. "Billy Taco?" Turning to Destiny, he added, "I'm happy to be here, wherever we are."

"We're glad you came so our little Jonathan can finally stop talking about you and make his move." Chance waggled his eyebrows.

"He's joking. I don't talk about you," Jonathan said quickly. "Not that much anyway," he added quietly.

"Oh, that's okay. I think my bandmates are probably sick of me telling them about you and the things you've told me. But they do enjoy the additional inspiration I'm bringing to the songwriting, so that helps." Billy smiled at Destiny and Chance and then at Jonathan, who blushed, cheeks and ears flushing with heat.

"You guys are working on new songs?" Destiny asked excitedly. "Do you think you'll release any for download soon? I want to be able to get my Tacos fix, streaming, on demand!"

"We've been talking about maybe looking into releasing some stuff on a couple of music-streaming platforms to see if they'd pick up any traction. But before we do that, we want to make sure we cover our social media bases and post videos to go with them."

Billy continued telling Destiny about their plans—the videos, the website, the social media rollouts, and everything else he and his bandmates had talked about—almost as if she were the soundboard he needed to see how things would fit together in the future. At some point, Billy seemed to go on autopilot, his voice slowly losing inflection and emotion the longer he spoke.

Suddenly, someone burst out of the house and got sick all over the bushes. Everyone nearby quickly ducked out of the way. Billy snapped out of his stupor, and looking at his phone, Jonathan realized Billy had been talking non-stop about their plans for over five minutes.

"Sorry about that." Billy shook his head. "I guess I got a little carried away." He offered them a smile, but there was confusion in his eyes.

"Sounds like you guys have a lot coming up in the future. That's exciting to hear!" Jonathan said, doing his best to ease Billy's sudden awkwardness. "I hope I can come to some video shoots or help out somehow!"

Billy's face lit up with genuine enthusiasm. "Yes, that would be fantastic!"

"Don't get too bogged down with plans, man," Chance interjected. "You have to remember to have fun, too, and let things happen to you. You never know when you may coincidentally run into your next big break. Sometimes literally." Chance clinked his plastic cup against Billy's. "Right, Destiny?"

She grumbled but laughed. "Whatever you have to tell yourself to get out of bed in the morning."

Billy turned to Jonathan and stage-whispered, "Are they always like this?"

Jonathan laughed. "Usually worse. This is honestly them being nice to each other."

"Oh my god, Billy Moore?" A girl with short dark hair started walking toward them as she rummaged around in her purse. "You're Billy Moore, right? From the Telepathic Tacos? Can I get a selfie with you? My friends aren't going to believe you're here!"

She didn't wait for him to respond. She just walked up, threw her arm around his waist, and held her phone up to take a photo of them. He put his arm around her for the picture and left it there when she was done.

"I should *not* be telling you this because you're, like, here, but you're so hot, and I have the biggest crush on you!" Her words slurred together—due to an abundance of alcohol, excitement, or a combination of the two—but she clearly had no idea Billy was there with Jonathan.

Though she probably wouldn't have cared if she did.

Laughing, Billy kissed her cheek. "Thank you. You're pretty hot yourself." Reaching up, he slid a stray strand of hair behind her ear. "I hope you enjoy the rest of the party!"

"Oh my god, I will now that I have this." She held up her phone to show off the photo of the two of them. "What are you doing here? Do you know these kids?" She gestured to Jonathan, Destiny, and Chance.

Billy suddenly looked uncertain. "Oh, yeah, sort of. They came to an all-ages show we had a while back. I'm just hanging out," he added dismissively.

"You should come say hi to my friends; they love you too. They're inside dancing. They are not going to believe you're here!" Once again, she didn't wait for him to respond before walking back toward the house.

"I'm gonna go with her. Gotta seize those opportunities to meet the fans when I get the chance, right?" He raised his glass to Chance again, who nodded slightly.

Jonathan watched as Billy disappeared back into the house with the girl he didn't know and then turned to his friends. "Am I somehow drunk and imagining things, or did he just ditch us for some random girl?" He crossed his arms as his face burned, though this time less from embarrassment than anger. "He acted as if he barely knew us and wasn't inches away from kissing me thirty minutes ago."

"You guys kissed?" Chance and Destiny asked at the same time.

He hesitated. "Well . . . no. But we were about to before a car honked and ruined the moment." He sighed, dejected.

When he looked back at his friends, neither one was paying attention to him. Destiny's eyes had glazed over in her hundred-yard stare, while Chance seemed focused on something just beyond Jonathan. Before he could turn to see what had grabbed Chance's attention, someone behind Jonathan spoke up.

"Hey, I thought you might want a drink."

Screw this, Jonathan abruptly thought. *And screw Billy.*

"Do you dance?" Jonathan asked the person behind him, not bothering to turn around.

"What?" The person behind him sounded confused.

"Do you dance? Do you like to dance?" Jonathan continued to stare at the door Billy had disappeared through.

"Um, yeah, I dance—"

"Great, let's go." Jonathan stomped back toward the house.

Seventeen

$\mathcal{J}$onathan shoved his way to the center of the makeshift dance floor and began dancing, not caring who else was around him. All he wanted was to lose himself to the movement of his body and not think.

When someone pushed their way into his personal space and started dancing with him, Jonathan stopped, startled. After a second, he realized it was Luke and, in nearly the same thought, decided he didn't care what anyone else was doing; he was going to dance.

"I like this song," Luke said.

Jonathan eyed him, confused. "What?"

"I said I like this song." Luke pointed to his ears.

Jonathan hadn't noticed what music was playing when he started dancing, but now that he listened for it, he realized it was one of his favorite songs. "Oh yeah, it's good."

Looking around for Destiny and Chance, Jonathan spotted them making their way through the crowd and waved them over. Once Destiny was close enough, he leaned in and asked if she had seen Billy on her way inside. She shook her head.

"Whatever. I'm not going to let this ruin the rest of my night!"

Destiny smiled. "I'm glad to hear you say that. It looks like you've caught someone else's attention anyway." She glanced at Luke, who was still dancing, though he now looked like he felt awkward about it.

"Why is he here?" Jonathan asked her.

She frowned at him. "What do you mean? You asked him if he could dance and then just walked away. We all followed you inside."

He furrowed his brow, confused, but then realized he hadn't looked to see who had walked up to him earlier.

Now panicking, he stared at Destiny pleadingly. "What do I do now?"

She shrugged. "Dance." She turned him to face Luke and gave him a little push in the right direction. Tripping over his own feet, he fell into Luke, who caught him under the arms.

"Whoa, you okay?" Luke helped him to his feet. "How much have you had to drink tonight?" He looked concerned.

"I'm fine," Jonathan replied, cheeks warming again. "I don't drink. I'm just clumsy."

Luke kept one arm around him, as if worried he'd need to steady Jonathan again. "I'm not sure I believe that, but I'm happy to help either way."

Jonathan wondered if his cheeks would ever cool down. Deciding he'd rather not call attention to the intimacy of their position, he went back to dancing. He did cast Destiny one last pleading glance, but she only smiled and shrugged. Then, waving goodbye, she grabbed Chance and disappeared into the crowd.

As Destiny dragged Chance away from Jonathan, he protested. "What are you doing?"

"Giving the two of them space; they don't need us around to watch them. They're fine."

"Are you kidding?" Chance ripped his arm from her grip. "Luke Martin's a dick; he's probably just doing this to embarrass Jonathan later. With all your knowledge of the future, I'm surprised you can't see that!" Turning, he began to push his way back toward Jonathan.

Destiny grabbed his arm, stopping him in his tracks. "Do you really think Billy is any better for him? He *did* embarrass Jonathan by leaving him alone outside to go off with some random girl. And something's going on with Luke. I don't know what it is, but I know he's not doing this to hurt Jonathan intentionally. Besides, you know we can't control what Jonathan does, and even if I could, I would never intervene, knowing the potential damage it could cause." Forcing her way around Chance, she planted herself firmly between him and the other two, determined to hold him back, no matter their difference in height. "I'm not about to let you go mess this up either!"

Chance grumbled. "Billy was talking to a fan. There's nothing wrong with that. How was he supposed to know he'd be recognized? I mean, look around, Eureka isn't exactly a hotbed of indie band activity. Besides, he said he was writing a song about Jonathan. Doesn't that prove he has feelings for him?"

Destiny laughed. "No, he said he was using Jonathan as *inspiration* for new music. He never said he was writing a song about him, let alone that they were romantic. Plus,"—her voice rose—"Billy said he told his bandmates the things Jonathan had shared with him! If that's not a bad sign, I don't know what is."

"So what? Jonathan has told us almost everything Billy has said to him—and shown us some of his selfies." Chance smirked. "What's the difference?"

Destiny narrowed her eyes. "*We* aren't writing a song about it, and *you* scrolled through and looked at the photos. Jonathan didn't show you them willingly, so it doesn't count."

Abruptly, the music changed, quieting as a slow song came on. Destiny and Chance glared at each other, but without the loud music to cover their argument, they shook their heads and walked away from each other and the dance floor.

Destiny did turn for one last look at Jonathan and Luke before she extricated herself from the dancing mass. Stuck in the middle of the crowd, Jonathan and Luke had no choice but to continue dancing. While it looked like Luke had eventually let go of Jonathan, now that the music had slowed down, he seemed determined to hold on to him again.

"Why are you doing this?" Jonathan suddenly asked as he and Luke swayed back and forth with the crowd. "Why are you being nice to me? And more importantly, why are you slow dancing with me?" He gestured to his arm, which Luke had grabbed on to once the music slowed.

"I dunno. It just seemed like the right thing to do." He dropped his hand from Jonathan's arm but didn't move away. "You asked if I could dance, so I followed you in here. Then you practically fell on me, and we were getting pushed around a lot in the middle, so I wanted to make sure you were okay."

"Okay, sure, I guess, but why do you care if I'm okay? You and your friends used to be the ones pushing me around, and the last time I ran into you, you almost hit me." Jonathan wasn't about to forget the day they almost fought in the hallway, which only Chance's interference had prevented.

Luke's lips twitched up on one side in a half smile. "Technically, the last time you ran into me, I got coffee spilled all over me."

Jonathan watched a red flush creep up Luke's neck and suddenly realized that Luke's eyes looked unfocused. "Are you drunk?"

"No!" Luke protested, though he immediately added, "Yes." Frowning, he seemed to think for a moment. "I mean, maybe. I've had a few drinks, but that's not important." He lightly grabbed Jonathan's wrists and held him in place. "Look, I'm sorry for how my friends and I have treated you in the past. I never stopped it when I could have, which makes me just as guilty even though I never would have actually done anything."

Jonathan twisted his wrists out of Luke's loose grasp. "Why should I believe you? You were still a dick to me, even if you never actually did anything."

Luke leaned in close. "You make me feel things I don't know how to express. At first, I was angry at you because I couldn't stop thinking about you. Being angry was easier than being scared," he admitted quietly. "But that wasn't fair to you, so I tried to avoid you, but we always ended up in classes together, or I'd see you and get angry again. Whenever my friends did those things to you, I didn't stop them because I was afraid they would ask me why I cared, and I didn't know how to answer that."

By the time he finished and backed away a little, his eyes had focused on Jonathan's, and he almost looked like he might cry, until he hiccuped.

"What changed?" Jonathan asked, shocked by Luke's admission, even if he was a little intoxicated.

Luke hung his head. "Chance said he was your boyfriend, and I wanted to punch him. I didn't know why at the time, but I realized later I was jealous."

"Of me?" Jonathan asked, assuming Luke was as enthralled with Chance as everyone else.

Luke lifted his head and crowded forward again. "No, of him, for dating you."

He spoke a little too loudly, and some of the nearby dancers glanced over. Luke backed up again and lowered his voice.

"Chance stood up for you—protected you when I was being a dick—and I hated him because I hated that I wasn't the one doing it. It took me a few days to realize you two weren't dating, but I still couldn't make myself talk to you even then. When we ran into each other at the coffee shop, I thought that would be my shot, but I chickened out. Then Destiny talked to me and helped me realize I was being an idiot and that if I wanted something, I needed to get off my ass and do something about it." He reached out and pulled Jonathan closer as the next slow song came on.

"What're you doing?" Jonathan looked around at the surrounding people. "People can see us, you know."

His head was reeling, especially at the mention of Destiny talking to Luke about all this. She hadn't said anything to Jonathan about it, other than her line before the party about people being surprising.

This had certainly been a surprise, that was for sure.

Luke didn't seem to hear Jonathan's protests. "When I saw you walking toward the party earlier, I knew I could tell you everything tonight, but I couldn't get away from my friends, and by the time I did, you were with that other guy. I didn't want to get in the way, so I backed off, but then he walked away and left you. I grabbed you a drink as an excuse to talk to you, but you barely even acknowledged me before walking off yourself, so I followed you, and here we are." Shrugging slightly, he clasped his hands behind Jonathan's back and pulled him closer.

Jonathan opened and closed his mouth as he tried to figure out how to respond to everything Luke had just shared. Never in his wildest imagination had he considered that Luke Martin, baseball-playing jock and one-time bully, might end up liking him.

Despite his shock, though, Jonathan could smell the alcohol on Luke's breath, and he worried that this might all be a setup or a big joke at his expense.

"Say something, please," Luke urged, his eyes locked with Jonathan's. "You're starting to freak me out."

"I'm not sure what to say, Luke. I'm honestly speech-less. I . . . I mean, what does this even mean?" Lowering his voice so no one would overhear, he added, "Are you gay?" Jonathan might not trust Luke, but even he didn't deserve to be potentially outed by another person.

"No. Yes. I don't know." The words slurred together a little. "I haven't thought that far ahead. I just know how you make me feel, and it's not like anything I've ever felt before."

He glanced around before focusing back on Jonathan. Wiping his sweaty forehead with the back of his hand, he seemed to struggle with what to say next. His eyes were unusually wide as he stared at Jonathan, and he licked his lips.

"Can I kiss you?" he finally blurted out.

Jonathan's eyes went wide, and he pulled away. Before he could reply, a hand grabbed him by the shoulder, and he turned around.

"There you are," Billy said as he pushed past the final group of people between them. "I've been looking all over for you. I went back outside when I was done, but you were gone. Where're Chance and Destiny?"

As Billy looked around for Jonathan's friends, Jonathan glanced back at Luke—except he was gone. Chance and Destiny were also missing.

"Oh, I'm not sure. They must've gotten tired of dancing." Honestly, though, he had no idea. He hadn't even noticed their absence before now. "I'd better go look for them."

Billy caught his arm as he turned to walk away. "I'll come with you. I don't wanna lose you again."

"Yeah," Jonathan said with a humorless laugh. "I wouldn't want that either."

Billy pulled Jonathan up short before he could get far. "Are you okay? You seem upset for some reason."

For a moment, Jonathan just stared at him. "Am I okay?" he finally repeated. "Seriously?" He rolled his eyes. "Yes, I'm fine. I love inviting someone to a party to spend time with me, just for them to ditch me at the first opportunity for some rando they don't even know! It's my favorite thing ever!" Jonathan kept his voice low, but he refused to hold back his anger and frustration.

Billy shook his head, his expression turning condescendingly patient. "Look, I'm sorry if I can't afford to miss out on any potential fans. We're trying to make this music thing happen for real, which means we have to do whatever it takes—like talking to new people at every opportunity. That's how I met you, you know."

Jonathan's cheeks flushed. "Yet you don't think abandoning two of your biggest fans in this town—not to mention the one who invited you to this party—is a big deal?"

"You know what I mean," Billy replied.

"I get it. You have to do what you have to do. And that's fine. If you had said, 'Hey, I'll be right back,' or told her you were going to hang out with me for a bit but they could find you later, or even just waited for them to come to us—any of that would have been fine. But you acted like you didn't know me and then took off without a backward glance. I've been so excited to hang out with you, and you just walked away as if I were nothing."

Tears stung the corners of his eyes, but he refused to let them fall. Maybe he was being ridiculous, but he was upset, and no matter how he tried, he couldn't stop the tears. Turning away, he pretended to look for Chance and Destiny as he quickly wiped his eyes. If there was one thing he wouldn't let Billy see, it was him crying on their first outing together.

Spying Destiny and Chance sitting on a couch together in the front room of the house, Jonathan started walking toward them.

"Hey." Billy caught Jonathan's hand in a soft grip but dropped it once he'd stopped. "I'm sorry if I hurt your feelings. That wasn't my intention. I assumed you knew I'd come back, but you're right. I should have said something, and I didn't. That's definitely my bad. Can you forgive me?" Looking into Jonathan's eyes, he offered a cute, lopsided grin that made Jonathan's heart race a little.

Jonathan sighed quietly. "It's fine."

Billy poked him gently in the side. "Are you still mad at me?"

Chuckling softly, Jonathan shook his head. "No. I'm not sure why I even got so worked up over it. It's not like we're dating. I just sort of thought you were coming to see me."

"I did come to see you. If I knew I would run into fans, I would have brought merch for them to buy." He gave it a few seconds and then laughed. "I'm joking."

Jonathan joined in. "You're so dumb. They probably already have it anyway; she seemed like the type."

Billy laughed and pulled Jonathan in for a side hug as they joined Chance and Destiny. "You have no idea!"

Jonathan tried to enjoy the rest of the night, but he couldn't shake the memory of Luke asking if he could kiss him. Here he was, with one of his favorite indie musicians, and he could do little more than pretend to listen to Billy talk about their new single while his mind wandered to a boy Jonathan had considered a bully only hours before.

When he finally realized his eyes were wandering as well, Jonathan tried to suppress the disappointment he felt that he hadn't found him again.

Eighteen

$\mathcal{J}$onathan grunted when his alarm went off Monday morning. He was not ready for another week of school, but it was the last one before spring break. Hitting snooze, he pulled the blue quilt over his head to get another few minutes of precious sleep, but his mind was already buzzing with thoughts of the past two days and what would happen when he saw Luke at school.

Hoping to distract himself, he grabbed his phone from the bedside table and pulled it under the quilt with him. There was a text message from Billy, telling him about the latest band rehearsal, and one from Destiny, letting him know she wasn't going to school today, so he'd be alone this morning. Groaning, he threw the covers back, just as his alarm went off again.

If he was going to walk to school alone, he was going to stop for caffeine at Night Owls before facing the mess that was sure to be waiting for him at school. He took a quick shower, brushed his teeth, and messed with his hair until it looked mildly acceptable. Grabbing his backpack, a heather-gray hoodie, and a granola bar, he headed toward the coffee shop for his morning iced coffee.

Stereotypical? Yes, but he didn't care.

When Jonathan turned the final corner, Luke was standing in front of the coffee shop. He attempted to duck back before Luke could spot him, but someone opened the coffee shop door before he could, drawing Luke's attention. When Luke turned, their eyes locked. Resigned, Jonathan straightened up, pulled the bottom of his hoodie down to smooth out imaginary wrinkles, and walked the rest of the way with what he hoped looked like confidence.

"All alone this morning?" Luke sniped. "Where're your bodyguards?" His tone was cold and angry, which Jonathan didn't understand but was unsurprised by. This was the norm for their interactions, with one glaring exception. Despite being outside in the frigid morning air, Luke wore athletic shorts and a T-shirt with cutoff sleeves. Jonathan couldn't help but notice that Luke's toned arms and shoulders were prominently displayed by the outfit he had chosen.

"Destiny said she wasn't coming to school today, and Chance never walks with us since he has a car," he replied, refusing to meet Luke's eyes. "I'm just getting coffee before school. Do we have to do this right now?" He reached for the door handle.

"What did they say when you told them what I said to you on Saturday?" Luke demanded, voice low. "You all probably had a good laugh at my expense, didn't you?"

Jonathan snapped his gaze up to Luke's. "I didn't say anything to them. I wouldn't do that." It hadn't been something they needed to know. "Now if that's it," he said, almost daring Luke to say something else, "I'm gonna go inside now." Holding Luke's gaze, he waited.

Luke looked surprised, but he took a step closer to Jonathan, blocking his path. Jonathan took a step back. "Why . . . why didn't you say anything? You could have outed me. I deserved it for how I've treated you." His voice was quiet, and he ran his hands through his hair, smoothing down strands that were already in place.

"Outing someone is fucked up, no matter what they've done." Sighing, Jonathan suddenly felt nothing but exhaustion, which pressed in on him like a physical presence.

He'd spent most of Sunday running through his conversation with Luke, trying to understand why he had said what he said and whether it was real or some mean trick he was playing.

"I already told you I wouldn't talk about someone behind their back like that, and outing someone—even you—is not only mean but potentially dangerous. You don't deserve that. No one does."

Offering Luke a closed-lip grin, he stepped around him and walked inside. The door caught before closing, so he assumed Luke followed him inside.

"I'm sorry," Luke whispered.

Jonathan turned back to him. "For what?"

"Everything. Being a dick, unloading all that stuff on you without warning on Saturday, asking to kiss you, and then disappearing." He looked around the coffee shop as he said the last part, no doubt making sure no one was listening.

"I saw that other guy come back, and I didn't want to get in the way of whatever else you had going on with him. And then I felt stupid for opening up to you without you reciprocating, but I never took the time to ask you how you felt, if you were single, or if you could ever even like a guy like me. Like, am I even your type? Do you have a type that you typically go for? Who was that other guy, by the way? Is he your boyfriend?"

Jonathan laughed and held up his hands to stem the flow of Luke's questions. "I'm sorry. That was just . . . a lot."

Luke exhaled loudly and then laughed in turn. "Yeah, sorry about that. What are you getting to drink? I'll get it for you."

"No, that's okay. You don't have to do that."

"C'mon, I want to. It's literally the least I can do for all the torment my friends and I have put you through. Plus, it gives me something to hold over your head to make sure you'll talk to me again."

Jonathan eyed him and smirked. "Oh, is that what you think? Well, in that case . . ." He stepped up to the counter. "May I please have a large blended caramel latte with no whipped cream? I'd also like a slice of banana nut bread. Actually, may I have two slices, please?"

Thanking the barista, he stepped out of the way so Luke could order and pay. When he was done, they moved to the side to wait for their drinks and pastries.

"Hungry, little guy?" Luke teased.

"I mean, I'm not paying. There's no reason to go small. Right?" He raised his eyebrows, waiting for a response from Luke. When Luke just shook his head and smiled, Jonathan laughed.

"Honestly, I'm getting off easy if all you wanted was this as payment for your time and answers to my questions. You owe me now, don't forget." He nudged Jonathan's shoulder with his own.

Once they both had everything they'd ordered, they decided to sit down for a few minutes. They had enough time before the first bell rang.

"So," Luke began, "how did you know you were . . . you know?"

"Gay?"

"Yeah." Luke glanced around again for eavesdroppers.

"Because my favorite flower is the hyacinth," Jonathan said with a completely straight face.

Luke struggled not to spit out his coffee. When he finally had his laughter under control, he asked, "What the hell does that have to do with being gay?"

Jonathan just smiled. When Luke finally seemed to realize Jonathan was teasing him, Jonathan considered the question seriously.

"I don't know. It wasn't any one thing." Jonathan had never been asked the question before, so he hadn't really thought about defining it. "I guess, when I would watch TV shows or movies growing up, if there was a shirtless guy on screen, I wanted to watch it, but if it was a woman, I just didn't care. That was a big sign. But I think the biggest thing was that Destiny and I have been friends forever and never dated. In sixth grade, when everyone else started saying they were boyfriend and girlfriend, I went around and asked five different girls to be my girlfriend, but I never thought about asking her. Then in seventh grade, when dating became even more common, I considered asking her out, but mostly because it would have been easy, not because I was attracted to her. Which was exactly how I felt about every other girl in our class."

Taking a sip of his coffee, Jonathan realized Luke was staring at his mouth.

"Don't get me wrong; Destiny is gorgeous and so nice and smart. She's everything I would want in a potential girlfriend, but I still never developed any feelings for her. Yet when we came back from summer break or something, I would see how some of the guys at school had changed, and I'd think about them a lot. I knew I found other guys in our grade cute, but I didn't know what that meant," Jonathan admitted. "Being gay was always this terrible thing you didn't want to be because it meant you would get teased. But if someone had sat me down and told me what being gay *actually* was, I would have realized it sooner. It took me seeing two guys our age kiss on TV to realize being gay wasn't something bad."

Jonathan watched Luke as he silently nodded along. He was paying closer attention to Jonathan than he ever seemed to for the teachers in their shared classes. "Does that make sense? Is that how it feels for you?"

"I don't know if I am gay. I mean, I think girls are hot, and I've had girlfriends, obviously. I've also seen more of some of the guys on the team than I ever wanted to and never felt anything. I kissed a guy once as a dare, but I didn't feel anything, so I never thought about it. But freshman year, when you cut off all your hair, I suddenly saw you differently than I ever had before." Luke fell quiet, looking a little uncomfortable.

"Why did my haircut matter?" Jonathan asked, his curiosity getting the better of him.

"Honestly, I don't think it did. I think that was just why it started." Luke shrugged. "At first, I thought it was just because you looked different, so I noticed you more. But then I found that I was looking for you, and I didn't know why. That's when the bullying got worse from the other guys; they noticed you because I did, which made you more of a target." Luke shuddered and leaned away from the table. "I still can't believe I just stood by and let them do those things to you."

"It's okay," Jonathan said quietly, his eyes focused on his drink. He was doing everything in his power not to relive those moments in his mind, but it was a losing battle.

"No, it isn't. It's shitty!" Luke's outburst drew attention from others around the coffee shop, but they went back to whatever they were doing when he smiled and held up a hand in apology. He continued more quietly. "They are shitty. *I* was shitty, and I'm going to stop it! Not only for your sake but for everyone else's as well. There's no reason they should be picking on anyone, anyway. It's not like we're some amazing team. We lose half the games we play." He laughed, and Jonathan joined in.

Jonathan liked the way Luke laughed; his eyes crinkled up, and his top teeth became visible when he thought something was especially funny. The joy and humor were so evident on his face. He was unguarded.

Jonathan felt envious of his ability to be so carefree.

"We better get going, or we might be late. I don't want to be responsible for tarnishing your attendance record, which I'm sure is stellar," Luke joked.

Grabbing his backpack, Jonathan put the second slice of banana nut bread away for later. "I actually ditched some classes just last week."

Luke leaned back in his seat. "I can't picture that, but it does make me feel better about myself, knowing you're not as perfect as you seem."

Jonathan blew out a breath. "I'm far from perfect, that I can promise you. But that was the first time I've ever missed school, so other than that, my attendance record is perfect." He laughed and was glad when Luke chuckled as well. The intensity that had been building during their conversation had dissipated.

Jonathan's cell phone vibrated on the table, and when

he picked it up, there was a message from Chance asking where he was and whether he, like Destiny, was skipping school. When Luke asked if everything was okay, he nodded.

"Yeah, everything is fine, but Chance is probably minutes away from ditching, assuming Destiny and I aren't coming to school today. I can't be responsible for that again."

"Again?"

"It's a long story, but they helped get me out of school the day I ditched, so we all did it together," Jonathan admitted.

"What's the deal with him? He came in one day and was instantly popular with everyone—which I guess makes sense since he's new and interesting—but it seemed like he gravitated toward you two right away. Not to sound rude, but if he wanted to be popular, he had better choices for friend groups."

Jonathan laughed. "Wow, tell me how you really feel!" Luke started to protest, but Jonathan cut him off before he could say anything. "I'm just kidding. You're right. He definitely seemed to pick me specifically, and he and Destiny got stuck together because she was already my friend. I honestly have no clue why he chose me. I think it's because I don't let him get away with whatever he wants." Jonathan sent Chance a quick reply to keep him from leaving school. "For some reason, everyone else just seems to give him what he wants. Destiny and I don't do that, so maybe he knows we're willing to call him on his crap?" He shrugged and ducked under Luke's arm as he held the door open for him.

"Do you think he's hot?" Luke asked as they crossed the street.

"Yes and no, I guess. He's handsome, of course. Just ask him." They laughed together. "Uh, but he's definitely just a friend. I understand he's hot, but it takes more than that to interest me. I also don't think he's interested in dating just one person. He's told me he would hook up with me, but I'm pretty sure he'd say that to anyone if he thought it would work."

"So he isn't gay?" Luke pressed as they approached the front doors.

"Who isn't gay?" Chance asked, walking up behind them. They eased apart to make room for him as they walked to class.

"You," Jonathan said simply.

"Oh, well yeah, that's true. I'm an equal-opportunity lover. Why limit yourself, boys? The world is my oyster, and I want to sample everyone's pearl."

They all laughed, but Jonathan noticed that Luke appeared to be deep in thought. Once they took their seats, Jonathan got a text from an unknown number.

You still owe me more answers. That second piece of cake was expensive.

Glancing over, he saw Luke holding his phone. Luke pointed to it when he noticed Jonathan looking at him.

Jonathan quickly added Luke's number to his contact list and then replied.

Jonathan: *Technically, it was bread.*

Nineteen

Once school had ended, Destiny waited for Jonathan to stop by to check on her before going home to work on his homework. When he knocked, she sent him a text telling him to let himself in. He had a key to her house on his keyring in case of friendship emergencies.

She had spent the day working on her visions and had reached the point where she could open herself to the paths of anyone she knew—outside Jonathan and Chance, of course—even without having them nearby. Now she was relaxing in bed, watching a telenovela about two babies switched at birth—one raised by an incredibly wealthy family and the other raised by a poor family—and how their lives were still intertwined. She suspected one of her sisters or the Muses must have helped with its creation, as it had so many references to fate.

Jonathan sent her a quick *I'm inside your house* text and waited until she sent back laughing emojis and yelled for him to come into her room. They were close, but he never let himself into her room without permission.

As he slipped in, Destiny looked around to see what he would be taking in. She lay in bed with a bowl of chips and her laptop open. Her beaded curtains clicked softly as they swayed in the slight breeze coming through the open window. The citrus candle burning on her desk gave the room a warm and welcoming feel that screamed summer and brightness, even with the chill in the air and the dimness of the late-afternoon light.

"How are you feeling?" he asked as he cleared a stack of magazines off her desk chair to make room for himself to sit down.

"I'm feeling better; thanks for asking. How was your day without me?" She tried to relax her body so the question would seem casual, but her voice held a slight edge that surely betrayed how interested she was in his answer.

"Honestly?" He dropped his backpack onto the floor beside him and kicked off his shoes so he could put his feet up on her bed. "I've had better."

Destiny frowned at him, confused. She knew Luke had wanted to talk to Jonathan after the party. Even though she couldn't see the outcome because it involved Jonathan, she knew Luke would never try if she were around. Her staying home had been a way of allowing Luke to find Jonathan alone, which was rare.

"Really? Nothing interesting or unusual happened? As you got coffee, perhaps . . . ?" She floated the idea out to him and waited.

"How do you always do that?" He laughed loudly with surprise and frustration. "It's like you know what's coming before anyone else! If I didn't know any better, I would assume you were psychic and ask for the lotto numbers or something."

"Oh yeah, you know me, Madam Martinez the Magnificent, psychic to the stars of Eureka!" She laughed, and Jonathan joined in. "But seriously, spill the tea since you admitted to having some! I wanna know what happened!" She hit her bed to get him focused on his story, rather than the fact that she already knew something had happened.

"Well, as you somehow already know, I got coffee this morning and ran into Luke. It was like he was waiting for me, which was strange."

Closing her laptop, Destiny pulled her pillow into her lap.

"He wanted to talk about what happened at the party with Billy and me and you guys." Destiny could tell he was choosing his words carefully, but she didn't press the issue. "Then he asked me all kinds of questions about how I knew I was gay, who Billy was, how we met, what my type was . . . stuff like that."

"Interesting." Destiny knew he was keeping something from her, since he hadn't mentioned the tension between them or the connection she had seen forming that led to this encounter, but she decided to leave it alone for now, rather than pry. She was sure he would have a good reason for keeping it from her. "Maybe he was doing a research project and needed to talk to an actual gay person," she joked.

Jonathan laughed and stole the bowl of chips, popping a couple in his mouth. "You're probably right. A high-school exposé on the secret life of small-town gays and the boys they love." His smile dropped almost instantly, and he rushed to cover up his mistake. "Not that I love Billy or . . . or anyone really."

"You don't love me?" she teased.

"I do, but you weren't a boy last time I checked," he quipped.

They continued to joke and catch up on the rest of the things that had happened throughout the day, including Chance hiding from the girls and handful of guys who kept approaching their table at lunch to try to sit with them. Destiny just shook her head, realizing Chance was probably trying to win Jonathan over while she was gone, but the fact that Jonathan was sharing the story proved it hadn't work.

"What is wrong with him?" she asked, shaking her head to indicate she didn't expect Jonathan to have an answer.

"Your guess is as good as mine." He laughed and ate a couple more chips. "But whatever it is, I wish I had a little bit of it. I'd be thrilled to be in a position where I had too many people wanting my attention, instead of pining over a guy who ditches me at the drop of a hat."

Destiny hadn't had a moment to talk to Jonathan about what had happened with Billy at the party or how he felt about it. When she looked at Billy's path, it was almost singularly focused on his music. When she'd pushed him further about it at the party and he'd talked about the band's plans for the future, she had noticed that he never mentioned Jonathan in any of those plans. It didn't necessarily mean he didn't *want* Jonathan to be with him for those things, but it suggested he might not be willing to let anything get in the way of his potential fame.

Jonathan shared that they had texted a little more throughout the day on Sunday, but there had been nothing since then. He'd decided to wait for Billy to reach out first, rather than doing what he always did and try to smooth things over.

"Did he ever explain himself?" Destiny grabbed a chip from the bowl and took a bite.

"Only what he said at the party: she was a fan, and he couldn't risk alienating his fans, so he had to play nice. I get that; honestly, I do. But ditching the guy you've driven to the outer suburbs to see for a group of people you don't know? Why? Who does that?"

He started shoveling chips into his mouth without chewing. Destiny knew it was to keep his hands busy so he wouldn't grab his phone. She knew from experience that he was dying to send a text demanding the attention he really wanted.

"What does that even mean?" Destiny wondered aloud. "He can't alienate anyone? Ever? Does that mean he will always choose other people if they demand his time? What if you demanded it back?" She was doing her best to remain neutral, but her instincts as Jonathan's friend were making her question Billy's intentions.

"Right? Why don't I matter more than some random fan?" he mumbled around the mouthful of chips. He fell quiet for a minute as he chewed.

"Oh god," he said once he'd swallowed, staring at her miserably. "Do you think he thinks I'm just some random fan he talked to because it was good for the band?"

"What? No! Of course not!"

Even as she hurried to assure him, Destiny couldn't help but wonder about it herself. She hadn't considered the possibility before, but she had been too excited about meeting the band and Jonathan making a connection to worry about Billy's motives at the time. He was definitely career focused, so it wouldn't surprise her if that had been his initial reason for approaching Jonathan, but she didn't dare say that out loud.

"Don't think like that." Reaching out, she took the bowl of chips out of his hands so she could hold them. "You're not just a fan; you're an extraordinary guy, and you deserve to be treated the way you want to be treated." She squeezed his hands until he looked her in the eyes.

"Thank you." He relaxed enough for her to let go of his hands. "I know I'm being crazy, but I just like him so much, and he's so hot and cold. At the party, he wouldn't touch me when other people were around, which I sort of understand, but not even a hand on my shoulder or anything. I grabbed onto his forearm at one point when he told a joke, and he shook it off as if I was hurting him."

She shrugged. "Maybe you were."

They both looked down at his arms, which were slender and lacked the muscle strength needed to hurt someone just by touching them. "Oh yes, watch out, everyone. I'll crush you with my massive twig arms." He started laughing again and couldn't stop. "Could you imagine?" Jonathan held his arms up, hands shaped like claws. "Rawr," he said quietly, and soon the two of them were wiping away tears of laughter.

"Stop! Stop! I can't breathe!" Destiny begged as she gasped for air, only to laugh each time she had enough air to do so.

"Rawr," he repeated. He fell off her desk chair when he leaned over too far with the newest laughing fit.

Destiny sat up to make sure he was okay, but when his laughter got even louder, she burst out laughing again and attempted to crawl to the edge of the bed to look down at him as he lay on the floor. "You're a mess. We both are." She wiped away the tears that stained her face. "My stomach hurts so much," she complained as he continued to roll around with laughter.

"Mine too!" he said, his smile still wide. "Totally worth it, though."

"Definitely!"

When he finally sat up, he checked his phone. "I'd better get going. I have a paper due in English that I haven't started yet. Why do I do these things to myself?" Getting up, he grabbed his backpack, walked over to Destiny's bookshelf, and began to search for whatever book it was he needed for his essay.

"What if you were meant to go through everything you've been through? What if fate brought you to those points in your life and made sure you went through the things you did?" Reaching out, Destiny plucked a book from the shelf without looking, opened it to a random page, and began to read aloud. "You taught me a lesson, hard indeed at first, but most advantageous." Closing the book, she looked up and suppressed the smile that wanted to break across her lips at the look on Jonathan's face.

"Is that *Pride and Prejudice*?" He took the book from her hand. "How did you know I was looking for it?"

She smiled and shrugged. "I guess it's like you said earlier: I'm psychic."

He rolled his eyes and laughed. "That's sure what it feels like. Well, then, Madam Martinez the Magnificent, tell me what you see in my future?"

Despite the joke, his expression was serious. He was hoping for a serious answer, which Destiny sorely wished she could provide. Knowing it wouldn't do any good, she checked for any signs of paths or where they might lead and saw nothing. She smiled sadly, upset she couldn't help but also knowing she wouldn't have been able to directly interfere even if she had.

"I see . . ." She closed her eyes and held a hand up to

her face, concentrating. "I see you at your kitchen table with your laptop. There's a book with you, and it looks like . . ." She paused for dramatic effect. "I see you working on a paper that's due tomorrow. You finish it in time and though rushed, you still get a good grade."

She dropped her hand as though the vision had faded away and smiled at Jonathan, who didn't look very impressed with her psychic skills.

"Wow, it's uncanny," he said sarcastically. "Almost as if you were able to tell me that I will do what I already said I was about to do."

"To be fair, I did say you would get a good grade, and that hasn't happened yet."

He smiled evilly. "Yeah, but now I can just slack off and purposefully do terribly and prove you wrong."

"The Jonathan I know would never do anything terribly on purpose, even to prove a point. He has principles and high standards for himself, not to mention an insane need to be the best at everything he does," she teased. "But, yes, by all means, prove me wrong."

"You suck!" He laughed as he put the book in his backpack, which he slung over his shoulder.

She stuck her tongue out at him. "You and I both know that isn't true." Crossing her arms, she added haughtily, "And feel free to borrow that book you just stole. No big deal."

"It's mine now. Consider it the price of our friendship despite all your emotional manipulation." He walked out of her room laughing, which was the only reason she didn't worry that he was actually accusing her of anything.

She followed closely behind him. "I'll see you tomorrow," she said, giving him a hug before he left.

Now that she knew she was right about Luke and what he was going to do, she decided it was time she and Chance talked about his meddling in Jonathan's life. She had to get him to see that he needed to give it up and move on. She just hoped he would see it the same way she did.

Twenty

$\mathcal{P}$icking up her cell phone, Destiny dialed Chance's number. She had already changed and was ready to walk out the door.

He picked up after the first ring. "Please tell me why I kept running into red lights until I started driving toward your house." He sounded intrigued rather than upset.

"We need to talk, and it's always better when we do that in person, don't you think?" She left a quick note for her mom, letting her know she would be home before dinner, and then walked outside, just as Chance pulled up. "You're just in time for us to go on a little drive."

"Where are we going?" He lowered the air so she would be comfortable and adjusted the volume of his music so she wouldn't have to raise her voice to be heard.

"It's your car. Why don't we drive until we end up somewhere? That should work for you, right?" She smiled, knowing he wouldn't be able to resist the taunt.

"Baby, everything works for me. You know that." He laughed and put the car in gear. They sat in silence for a few minutes while he drove. It was nice not to feel like they had to create conversation or be careful to make sure they didn't say the wrong thing or give away too much information. The silence was pleasant. Friendly even, though Destiny knew it wouldn't last. She could feel Chance watching the random patterns of the world, waiting for the next one he liked so he could follow it.

Taking a deep breath, Destiny began what she knew could become a heated conversation. "I know you've been trying to use your influence on Jonathan even after we discussed it. You told me you wouldn't do it, but you haven't stopped." She kept her tone firm but not harsh.

He smiled a little. "Jonathan told you about the people flocking to our lunch table today, didn't he?"

"Yes, and I know that was because you were trying to get him to do something while I was gone. We both agreed to leave him alone, but you're not holding up your side of the agreement."

Chance lifted one hand in recognition of being caught. "You're right, but I had to try. It was the only time we've been alone over the last few weeks. You and I have both admitted that something is changing. I'm getting stronger again, even around you, but especially when you're not around. I had to see if it extended to him. As I'm sure you know, it didn't. He's still completely unaffected by my influence. I can change things around him, but he's immune somehow."

The light ahead of them turned yellow, and he sped up slightly, making a right turn that would take them away from the high school.

"But I don't think I'm the only one." He gave her a knowing look. "I see the way you watch him. Your eyes always focus past him, as if you're trying to see something that isn't there. What would happen if you saw his future? Could you leave him alone to wander into it without steering him in some way toward the shortest path to happiness? You talk about how I need to stop, but ever since I've been here, you've been doing everything you can to control what happens to him. So what is this really about?"

Destiny sat quietly, thinking it over. He was right. She had never been this close to someone whose life she might be able to improve, and the fact she couldn't see the direction of his life frustrated her to no end. If she could somehow see what would happen to Jonathan, she would have done anything to save him from heartache and hardships.

"That's why we need to talk," she said, eyes fixed straight ahead. "I admit, I have tried to see what was coming in his life. I've tried to do that for years without success, until recently."

Chance shot her a startled look. "What're you talking about?"

"The night of the concert, when you offered to kiss him . . . I saw a flash of him kissing someone."

"You never told me that!" Chance's anger seemed to fill the small car, but Destiny refused to feel guilty for keeping this one thing to herself.

"There are plenty of things you've never told me, so don't get all high and mighty on me over this. Should I have told you? Maybe," she admitted. "But it was only for a second, and it hasn't happened since. I still try sometimes, but I never meddle in the ways you have lately." She looked at him. His attention wasn't on the road, yet he still navigated it perfectly. "He's my best friend. I don't want to control him; I just want what's best for him."

Chance looked offended. "I'm not trying to control him!"

"You want him to fall for you so you can make him do whatever pleases you. What would you call that?" She spoke of it not as an accusation but as an undeniable fact.

Chance rolled his eyes. "I was just curious if I could. I wasn't going to do anything to him."

"And that's what I'm talking about. It's like you can't help yourself. You blew into town, and I told you to leave him alone. Instead, you used your power to win him over with the tickets to the Telepathic Tacos show. I asked you not to do anything to him emotionally or physically, and you almost kissed him. I said we needed to leave him alone to sort things out with Luke, and you tried to cause a scene, which you might have succeeded in doing if I hadn't been there to stop you. Then, on the one day I took off from school, you practically started an orgy during lunch because you tried to influence him!"

She had turned in her seat so she could look at him directly and was pleased that he looked a little remorseful for that last part.

"What do you propose we do, then? Neither of us can be trusted to leave him alone, but for some reason, our abilities don't have any power over him. We're already too connected to him to just leave him alone, and we don't know if leaving him alone would create some future issue he would have to face as a result."

Destiny raised an eyebrow. It almost sounded like he agreed with her. "Exactly. *We* can't just leave Jonathan alone, but *you* can."

He narrowed his eyes. "You want me to just ignore him from now on? Are you sure that wouldn't cause him emotional damage?"

"No, but I'll be there to smooth things over as I always do."

"And if I don't agree to leave him alone?" he asked, voice rising.

"I'll make you," she said coolly as the amber light of her eyes softly lit the car's interior. "We can't keep fighting to try to control him, so we need a truce."

She grabbed onto the handle above her window as he made a sharp turn, pulling into a strip mall, and parked the car.

With the car off, he turned to face her. "And what exactly is the agreement?"

"We agree not to attempt to use our abilities to influence Jonathan. I agree that whatever happens to our abilities due to our friendship with him happens. I won't intervene to get him to do what I think he should. You agree to stop trying to assert your influence on him, and you agree not to use any physical attraction Jonathan may feel to your advantage. And once he's ready, you'll disappear." Her tone turned saccharine. "Maybe you and your dad can throw another dart."

"Why would I agree to that?" Chance demanded. "There's nothing you can do to me without messing up the 'grand plan,' right? And you have nothing I want."

Destiny sat back and turned her attention outside the car. She watched people coming and going from the shops and restaurants around them as she tried to come up with some reason for Chance to agree. She hated it, but he was right that she wouldn't risk messing with things she couldn't see, and they were each a blind spot for the other.

Looking for some new option, she changed the subject. "What were you doing anyway?"

"What do you mean?"

"During lunch today. What were you trying to do that brought everyone and their brother to the table?"

"Oh, that." He laughed. "I was just asking about prom and if Jonathan thought he would invite Billy to go with him. I guess I was trying a little too hard with those vibes, because everyone seemed to notice. I was asked to prom by five different individuals and two couples."

"Only two?" Destiny laughed. "How disappointing that must have been for you."

"You have no idea!"

"What did Jonathan say about prom?" Destiny kept her attention focused mainly on what was happening outside the car.

"He said he wasn't sure he wanted to go."

"What?" She sat up straighter and looked at Chance again. "But that's such an important moment—or it could be," she added quickly. "Why doesn't he want to go?"

"I don't know. He didn't say. Then I got distracted, and I think he was upset I started getting all those invites." He had the decency to look embarrassed.

"We have to help him!" she said, determined to make sure he had a good time.

Chance laughed. "So much for leaving him alone, eh? After all, how do you propose we help him without being able to influence him?"

Destiny opened her mouth and then closed it, and she pursed her lips as tried to decide how to respond. Finally, she smiled at Chance. "Maybe he would go if he were invited."

"Why would I worry about whether he gets invited or not?" Even as he asked, it was clear he was already working through ideas.

"Because if you get him the invitation and he accepts it, I'll admit you're right," she offered.

He perked up. "And . . . ?"

"And I'll quit trying to control you and what you do in people's lives," she added, hoping that would be enough for him.

"And you'll let me take you out."

She lifted one hand and studied her cuticles. "I've never turned down free food."

Chance grinned, obviously confident he'd be able to get Jonathan a date. "I accept your terms."

"But when I win, you'll leave Jonathan and everyone else in Eureka alone. You let them follow their paths free of your influence." Holding her breath, Destiny waited.

"And just to sweeten the deal, if you win, I'll let you take me out," Chance said with a flirtatious smile.

"Permanently?" she asked, her smile wide.

Extending her hand, Destiny grasped Chance's. To her surprise, cold flooded through her stomach and chest, shooting down her arm into their clasped hands. When Chance also shuddered, she wondered what the outcome of their bet would be.

With the terms set to both their satisfaction, Chance started the engine and began the thirty-minute drive back to Destiny's home. It was a quiet drive, and Destiny spent it thinking about how she would approach the task of getting Jonathan to the dance. Her mind wandered through the many relationships she had seen over the last few millennia. She had watched people as they prepared to get engaged or married, people who had recently married and were very much in love, and those who had fallen out of love and were just going through the motions on their path toward heartbreak. She didn't want to throw Jonathan into a situation that would ultimately cause him emotional pain. But she didn't want to sit back and watch him miss out on things because he was afraid to put himself out there either.

"Why do you think we can't influence him?" Chance asked, pulling Destiny from her thoughts.

"What? Who? Jonathan?"

He nodded. "Yeah. You said you've tried to see his future, and I've basically tried everything on him. Why don't our powers work on him?"

She shrugged slightly but then realized he wasn't looking at her. "I've always assumed he was some sort of test or punishment for something I'd done in the past. A lesson I needed to learn by not being able to help the person I was closest to, perhaps. But when you showed up and weren't able to influence him either, that theory didn't make as much sense."

"What d'you mean?"

"Who would have the power to send us into these bodies *and* know we'd both be put in the path of the same person? Without us, the higher gods don't have control over the futures and fates of mortals, let alone other gods. I didn't see you coming; how could they?"

When Chance had been quiet for a few moments, Destiny looked at him. He looked surprisingly somber.

"What if he's another god?"

As they pulled up to Destiny's house, Chance noticed that the pattern he had been following before she called was back, leading in the direction opposite the one they'd taken for their conversation. The idea he'd shared with Destiny about Jonathan being a god had killed their conversation, and she didn't say anything as she climbed out of the car, almost as if she were in a trance.

Once he was sure she was safely inside, he followed the pattern as it shifted, folded, and unfolded in front of him. It took almost an hour of driving back and forth down the highway before he finally got to the end of the pattern and realized he recognized the building before him. It was where they had seen the Telepathic Tacos play. Music drifted from inside; if he wasn't mistaken, it was the chords for 'Guacamole Love.'

"This is going to be easier than I thought."

Stepping out of his car, he walked inside to have a quick conversation with Billy and the rest of the band about the possibility of a new gig they might want to explore. As expected, they jumped at the opportunity, and he was one step closer to winning the bet.

When he finally returned home, he slipped inside quietly, careful not to wake his dad.

Twenty-One

The rest of the week before spring break flew by in a series of midterm exams, projects, and fortunately, a few movie days. Jonathan couldn't wait for a week away from classes and homework, and with Destiny and Chance being unusually distant recently, having a little time to himself sounded like a nice change of pace. If they were going to be weird, he would let them be weird together.

Billy had been texting and calling Jonathan more lately and had been trying to make plans to visit since Jonathan would be available. However, the band had some new gig coming up that they had to prepare for, so they were still waiting for a chance to get together.

When Monday morning rolled around, Jonathan discovered he had forgotten to turn off his automatic alarm when music began blaring at 6:15 a.m. After turning it off and making sure it wouldn't go off again for the rest of the week, he pulled the quilt up over his head to block out the early-morning sun streaming through the windows.

Unfortunately, his plan to sleep until noon had been

completely ruined. Even as he closed his eyes and focused on relaxing, he couldn't help but focus on every part of his body that felt uncomfortable. His bladder, especially, did not seem to have gotten the memo about sleeping in, and it was quickly reaching the point where he would have to get out of bed or suffer the consequences.

Frustrated and exhausted, Jonathan threw the covers back, snapping his eyes closed as the light blinded him temporarily. Keeping his eyes closed so he could hold on to as much sleep as possible, he slowly made his way down the hall toward the bathroom. By the time he crawled back into bed, the idea of returning to sleep was little more than wishful thinking.

He might not have been able to fall asleep, but that didn't mean he had to get out of bed. Reaching over, he grabbed his phone and pulled the quilt back up over his head to keep it dark for a little longer.

He had two unread text messages. One was from Destiny, asking if he had any plans this week, but since she had sent it late last night, he knew better than to respond now and risk waking her up. The other was from Chance, who had texted a few hours earlier asking if Jonathan was going to see Billy this week.

Deciding to leave them both on read and deal with them later, he watched random videos for a while, until another text popped up. The notification banner caught his attention.

Luke: *Hey, have you eaten yet?*

Jonathan: *Hey. No, I haven't. Why?*

Luke: *I thought I might get some coffee and banana cake at Night Owls. You interested?*

Jonathan: *It was BREAD! I just woke up, tho. It'll take me 20 mins to get ready.*

Luke: *I'll see you in 30—you can answer the rest of my questions, lol.*

Checking the time, Jonathan realized he'd spent over three hours watching videos. Rolling onto his back, he took a deep breath in and let it all out through his nose in a long sigh. Then he threw his covers back and grabbed some boxer briefs, a pair of jeans, and a T-shirt that made his arms look a little less skinny than normal.

He showered quickly, brushed his teeth, and got dressed, before looking at himself in the mirror and trying to decide what to do with his hair. He typically let it fall into whatever style came naturally, but if he was meeting Luke for breakfast, he felt like he needed to put in a little more effort.

Why? It's not like you like him. Billy is the guy for you; he's the one you're dating. Or, well, sort of dating, anyway. Luke's whatever, and you don't have to make yourself look good just to hang out. He's seen what you look like every day for years. Why is this suddenly a big deal?

Despite his inner monologue, Jonathan brushed his hair in different directions and even added some pomade, trying to get it to stick to a style that looked intentional. After ten minutes of trying, he finally gave up, ran his head under the shower again, and started over.

The final result looked like a more polished version of what he usually did, which he figured was as good as possible.

His mom had already left for work and wouldn't be back until later that evening, so he didn't have to worry about her asking where he was going. He wasn't sure if it would be cold, so he grabbed a jacket that he could put on if needed, as well as his wallet, keys, and phone, and left the house.

When he got to the coffee shop a few minutes later, Luke wasn't there yet, so he ordered his usual drink, two slices of banana nut bread, and the drink he'd heard Luke order the last time they were there. He chose a table in the corner away from the door so any of their classmates who might come in wouldn't see them.

Sitting down, he waited.

When Luke still hadn't arrived by the agreed-upon time, Jonathan wondered if he was being stood up. He checked his phone, but he didn't have any unread messages, so he decided to give Luke a few more minutes before he headed home.

A couple of minutes later, the bells above the door jingled, and Luke stepped inside. As he did, the sun reflected off the door behind him, bathing him in glowing golden light for a split second before it closed again.

Jonathan admired Luke's broad shoulders and muscular arms, which didn't need the help of a specific type of T-shirt to look good. He had opted for shorts that showed off his large calves, which almost made Jonathan tuck his jean-covered legs under him to avoid any comparison.

Before he could, Luke stopped next to his chair and waited. When Jonathan finally stood up, Luke gave him what Jonathan would typically describe as a "bro hug"—one arm in front and one arm wrapped around his back. It was awkward for Jonathan, who generally opted for any other type of hug, but it was more physically intimate than they had ever been, so Jonathan kept his mouth shut.

Luke pulled back. "Hey! Sorry I'm late. Before I left,

my mom asked me to help my little brother get ready for a trip to Peoria that his friend's mom is taking them on." Looking down at the table, he smiled as he realized Jonathan had already ordered for them both. "Did you get me an iced Americano and banana cake?"

"Banana nut bread," Jonathan corrected, exasperated. "Yes, I did."

Luke laughed and took the other seat. "You hate when I call it cake, don't you?"

"No, I just . . . it's not cake. I don't like cake. It's sweet bread. It's different. That's all." Jonathan was aiming for casual but fell short. He didn't know why he was letting Luke get under his skin like this, but he realized he was being too critical and needed to relax. Taking a deep breath, he tried again. "So, you said you had questions for me?"

Now it was Luke's turn to be uncomfortable. Picking up his drink, he took a sip, and his entire face pinched together. "Oh god, that's—yuck—wow!" Standing, he grabbed a couple of sugar packets and a stirrer, before retaking his seat.

"Oh no, I'm sorry. I forgot to mention that I didn't add anything to it." When Jonathan had gotten Luke's drink, he had realized he hadn't paid any attention to how Luke would doctor it, so he'd left it alone, not wanting to mess it up.

"No worries. Thank you for ordering for me; that was very nice of you. I normally don't drink it straight up like that." He gave Jonathan a little wink and laughed.

"Yeah, me either. I like to gay it up first," Jonathan said seriously. Luke's mouth dropped open in shock, and Jonathan laughed. "Oh my god, your face! You look so scandalized!"

Luke joined in on the laughter, which helped them both relax. Something they desperately needed.

"I guess I don't 'gay' mine up. I just add sugar. Which maybe is '*gaying* it up'; I don't know." Luke's eyes remained locked on his coffee as he sipped it again and set it back down. "I'm still pretty new to this whole gay thing."

"This whole gay thing?"

"Yeah, I'm still figuring out how to act or talk. Like, if I'm gay, do I have to talk the way they do on *Drag Race*?" Luke asked earnestly.

"What? No! I mean, you can, but it's not like there are rules about how to act. You just act like yourself, whoever that is. If you're gay, you're gay, and how you act is how a gay person acts. How you talk is how a gay person talks. That's my experience with things anyway." He took a bite of his banana nut bread.

"Is that guy your boyfriend?" Luke asked suddenly.

"Who? The guy from the party? I honestly don't know . . . I don't think so, though. We've never talked about that before. I hoped he would be, but he doesn't always seem interested in a relationship." Jonathan was surprised he was sharing so much with Luke without hesitation. "Do you have a boyfriend?"

"No." Luke shook his head, smiling sadly. "Also, I kinda lied to you before." He kept his eyes glued on his hands, which were wrapped tightly around his coffee cup. "I told you I'd only ever kissed a guy once on a dare. That's not true." He peeked up at Jonathan through his lashes as if to gauge his response. "The truth is, I messed around with a guy at an athletic camp last summer. He's the one I told you about; we did kiss on a dare, but we didn't only kiss." He squeezed his eyes shut and started speaking rapidly, hurrying to finish the story. "He goes to a different school, and it only lasted for a couple of weeks. I haven't talked to him since." His voice was quiet, even in the nearly empty coffee shop. "I sorta thought it was a joke until I realized a few weeks later that I missed it and then had a dream about him."

Jonathan remembered Luke mentioning that he had kissed another guy once. To his surprise, hearing that it had been more made him a little upset, but he made sure to keep his expression neutral. Carefully, he nodded. "Are any of the other guys on the team . . . you know?"

"Gay? Not that I know of, though a couple of them have never had girlfriends. They don't give off any vibes that suggest they're not straight, but then, I guess maybe I don't either, so who knows?"

Shrugging, he picked up his coffee and swirled it absentmindedly. When he realized he wasn't talking, he set the cup down and looked back up at Jonathan, who sat patiently waiting for him to speak.

"Is he your type? The guy from the party? Is that the type of guy you normally go for?"

Jonathan thought about it. "Honestly, no," he admitted. "Don't get me wrong, I think he's attractive. But he's not the type of guy I typically find attractive. I prefer a guy with darker hair, someone tall and usually bigger than me, and a guy who can make me laugh. The rest is just icing on the—"

"Bread?"

Jonathan laughed. "Exactly."

"Have you ever had a boyfriend?" Luke asked, his foot sliding across the floor to sit next to Jonathan's.

"No. I've had crushes, but Billy—the guy from the party—is the closest I've gotten to dating anyone."

"What do you like about him?" Luke pressed gently.

"Well, at first, it was sort of a silly crush I had on him. He's in a band I like, which is how we met. He and the other band members came up and talked to us before they performed at a show not that long ago, and afterward, I almost walked in front of his car."

Jonathan laughed at the memory, but when he realized Luke looked horrified, he sat up a little straighter.

"Oh, uh, it wasn't as serious as that sounds. After I stepped into the street in front of his car, he stopped and gave me his number, and we started texting. He's cute and funny and talented. He writes some of the songs they sing and plays the guitar."

Nodding, Luke pulled his feet back under his chair. "He sounds like a great guy. You must be happy with him."

"Oh, yeah, totally." The answer sounded forced even to Jonathan's ears.

Luke eyed him. "Why am I finding that hard to believe?"

"It's stupid. I'm stupid. It's just that it doesn't always feel like he's into me the same way I'm into him. It's almost as if I'm a distant second choice, or maybe even third, behind everything that's happening with the band. And saying this aloud makes me sound like a crazy person who refuses to allow the guy they like to have interests, but it's not that. It feels like the band is his number-one priority, and I'm so far behind it that I'm barely an afterthought."

Reaching across the table, Luke lightly grabbed Jonathan's elbow. "You're not stupid. If that's how you feel, then it's something you have to deal with. It's okay for him to prioritize the band, but he should also prioritize time with you if he wants to be with you. If he can't do that, he should tell you so you don't hang on to something that won't happen." Luke's feet slid across the floor again and lightly brushed against Jonathan's.

Jonathan looked down at Luke's hand, then smiled up at him, surprised Luke had given him such good advice. "Thank you. I appreciate it. It feels good to talk to someone about this and get their honest opinion. Don't get me wrong, I love my friends, but sometimes it feels like they're fighting to get me to see things their way. And they almost never agree on what that should be!"

Returning Jonathan's smile, Luke let go of Jonathan's arm. "I know how that feels. My friends are the same way. But I'm always happy to listen if you need to vent or get something off your chest. Or if you want to work out and get those biceps even bigger," he teased.

Jonathan's mouth opened in fake indignation. "I think my arms look really good, thank you very much!"

Luke's eyes roamed over the arms in question before he nodded in agreement. "No complaints here!"

Twenty-Two

The next day, Jonathan slept until 10:30 a.m., and when he woke up, he had four unread texts, a missed call from Destiny, and a voicemail from Billy asking if he wanted to get together that afternoon. He stretched and yawned to wake himself up before responding to Billy. Then he fired off a response asking for more details.

Not expecting to get an answer from Billy anytime soon, Jonathan replied to Destiny, who had asked about binging the newest Netflix series that had just come out, as well as possibly grabbing lunch.

> **Jonathan:** *You know I'm down for a good binge-fest. What sounds good for lunch?*

> **Destiny:** *I'm easy. Pizza, tacos, that Chinese place over by the college?*

> **Jonathan:** *Ooooo, tacos! Let's go to Manny's, get the sampler and a few extra tacos, and make it a party for two!*

Destiny: *It's like you read my mind. 11?*

Jonathan: *I'll be ready.*

After the text exchange, Jonathan hopped out of bed and grabbed a change of clothes before heading to the bathroom to shower and get ready for lunch. He was just putting his shoes on when there was a knock on the front door, and Destiny called out after letting herself in.

"I'm back here," he called from his bedroom.

A few seconds later, she poked her head into his room. "Everyone decent?"

He laughed. "It's just me, and yes, I'm good."

"Just making sure. I would hate to walk in on something untoward," she teased, then plopped down on the edge of his bed.

"You're so weird sometimes, especially when you say things like 'untoward.'" Despite the joke, he eyed her seriously, as if examining her for some detail he had missed.

Standing up, she shrugged off the scrutiny. "I'm always weird when I'm hungry. That's part of my charm. And I haven't eaten since last night, so please hurry."

Laughing, Jonathan followed her out of his room and out the front door. Manny's Taco Shop was a few blocks away but worth the walk, especially for the mini chimis with their mix of spicy shredded beef and beans. Jonathan couldn't control what happened in his dreams, but if he could, they would feature those every time.

"So," Destiny began, "I saw Luke with his family last week."

"Yeah?" Jonathan asked, trying to keep his tone casual. Not being able to tell her about his conversations with Luke was killing him, but he had promised not to out Luke and he wouldn't, not even to her. "That's cool, I guess."

She laughed, and he could tell she'd seen through his attempt at disinterest. "Yeah, Chance and I went for a drive and ended up in Bellevue, and they were there."

"Why did you two go for a drive?" he asked, suspicious of the closeness he'd noticed between them in the past few days.

"Oh, I was helping him through some stuff he was dealing with. We didn't want to bother you."

"Are you two dating?" Jonathan asked plainly.

"What? No! Are you serious? One, you know I'm aro/ace—I don't have any interest in dating. And two, even if I did, it wouldn't be him." Her lip curled. "We're barely friends."

"That's what I thought until you kept disappearing together, and now you go for long drives, just the two of you." He stopped in the shade of a large tree branch that stretched over the sidewalk.

Destiny stopped, too, and turned around to look him in the eye. "We are not dating, I promise. You know I would tell you if something like that happened, just like you would tell me." She narrowed her eyes. "Right?"

Jonathan nodded once and attempted to cover up his guilt by deflecting back to her. "If I didn't know you better, I might not believe you, but you and I are the only ones immune to his unique charms."

Destiny laughed. "You can say that again! And thank goodness for that; he would be insufferable if he were your boyfriend!"

Jonathan laughed in agreement, finding it impossible to imagine a relationship with Chance. "You're so right!"

"Speaking of boyfriends who aren't boyfriends." She bumped his arm with her shoulder. "What's happening with you and Billy?"

"Nothing!" Jonathan said too quickly, thinking she was asking about Luke. He really needed to get his guilt under control before he said something he'd regret.

Her gaze intensified. "Ooookay, calm down, crazy."

He attempted to backpedal. "Not sure why I said it like that. I guess I'm just getting frustrated that nothing new is happening. But he did ask me to hang out this afternoon, so maybe that will change soon." He pulled out his phone to see if Billy had replied yet, but the message status still showed as delivered and not read.

"Well, you know I just want you to be happy," she said earnestly. "If he makes you happy, that makes me happy, but don't feel like you owe him anything if he doesn't."

"I know. Sometimes I think I'm over it and ready to let him go, but then he'll send me a text or a photo of a cute puppy and tell me he's thinking about me, and I'm right back in it again." He sighed. "When he's hot, he's boiling. But when he's cold, it's like he forgets I even exist."

"I can't imagine what that feels like. I wish I could help you," Destiny said, her mouth pinched into a tight line.

"It's fine, really. I just need to figure out what I want to do and stick to it. I mean, having a sexy rocker boyfriend would be pretty hot." He laughed.

Destiny laughed along with him, but they were quickly distracted by a loud rumble from Jonathan's stomach. "All right, I get it. You're hungry. I'm starving too, so let's run!"

She took off running, and Jonathan started after her. It only took him a couple of seconds to catch up, and by the time they made it to the door of the small restaurant, they were laughing and breathing heavily from the impromptu race. Getting there just before Destiny, Jonathan opened the door and waved her in ahead of him. "Losers first."

Destiny sniffed and lifted her head high. "I let you win," she proclaimed as she walked through the door.

Ever since Chance had filled her head with the idea that Jonathan might be another god, she'd felt a little uncomfortable around him. However, watching his awkward run and listening to him pant as he tried to speak helped her shake off that unease. Even as a mortal, she was in much better physical condition than almost anyone else her age, and she doubted another god would be able to hide their physical prowess well enough to perform like Jonathan when it came to physical exertion. It still didn't answer the question of how she and Chance had ended up in the same town, helping a random teen, but the fact that helping him was helping them regain their powers was proof enough to her that they were doing the right thing.

"Whatever you need to tell yourself to sleep better at—"

As Jonathan's response cut off, Destiny glanced around to find him staring at a particular table, where Luke was sitting with the other baseball players. Luke looked up, and a smile spread across his face when his eyes landed on Jonathan. Destiny looked back to see Jonathan pull at his left sleeve and tug at the bottom of his shirt to straighten it.

Pretending not to notice the sudden shift of Jonathan's attention and energy, she didn't tease him for not completing his thought. "Are you ready to order? Just the usual, right?"

Jonathan walked with her toward the counter, but as that only brought them closer to Luke, Destiny couldn't miss that his attention was still focused on the jock sitting to his left and smiling at him.

"Um, yeah. What?" Jonathan finally turned away from Luke to look at Destiny. "The regular, yes."

Destiny grinned up at him. "Why don't you go say hello?"

"Are you kidding me? He's with all his friends. They're not exactly the most welcoming guys at school. Plus, why would I even say anything to him? We barely ever speak." His tone was strained by the end.

"Okay, then let's order and go sit down." Grabbing his arm, she led him to the counter, where they ordered their food and got their drinks. Then they claimed a table on the other side of the restaurant that still allowed Jonathan to stare at Luke if he wanted to.

"I don't know why he's looking at me," Jonathan said finally, before taking a drink and popping a tortilla chip in his mouth.

She shrugged. "He clearly has a crush on you." She watched the connection from Luke wander all over Jonathan's body and laughed to herself as she realized it spent a lot of time on his face and arms. "I think he likes your biceps," she added softly.

Jonathan's attention snapped to her, his eyes panicked. "What? Why would you say that?"

Keeping her face blank, Destiny shrugged. "Just calling it as I see it." When the connection suddenly got even stronger, she looked behind her and saw Luke stand up. "Don't look now, but I'm pretty sure he's heading over here."

Jonathan immediately looked, and his face paled slightly. Pulling at both of his sleeves, he looked up at Luke, who now stood by their table.

"Hey, Destiny," he said, looking at her briefly. "Hey, Jonathan." Luke's voice dropped a little when he greeted

Jonathan, and his excitement was palpable. "How are you guys doing?" He didn't bother looking back at Destiny, so she kept quiet and watched the tension build.

"Good," Jonathan replied. "We were just out, um . . . we're good. How are you?"

"Yeah, we're good too." Luke looked over his shoulder at his friends, who were staring back, confused. "We had practice this morning, and now we're taking a break for lunch."

"Practice during spring break? Why?" Destiny asked when it was clear that Jonathan was still unsure what to do.

"We have a game against Heyworth next week, so we don't get a break." He kept his attention on Jonathan as if he were the one asking the questions. "What are you two up to today?" Luke leaned down a little, getting closer to Jonathan, and his front foot slid forward until it touched Jonathan's.

Jonathan sat up a little taller, bringing their faces closer together. "We're, uh, just grabbing some lunch before we go back to my place and binge that new Netflix series."

"Number twenty-one," called the woman at the register, interrupting the moment Jonathan and Luke were having, much to Destiny's annoyance. She glared up toward the register, but the woman had already walked away. Luke straightened and stepped back, making room for Jonathan to stand up so he could grab their food.

"I guess I'll just see you around, then, Jonathan," Luke said with a smile before turning and finally acknowledging Destiny again. "Destiny, always good to see you."

She nodded knowingly. "Luke, a pleasure. Don't be a stranger. We're always happy to grow our little group."

He nodded back and went to fill his cup before retaking his seat. Jonathan returned with their food and unloaded the tray, then walked it to the trash can by the doors. As he did, Destiny noticed that Luke's connection was firmly planted on Jonathan's ass. Shaking her head, she smothered her laugh as Jonathan returned to the table.

He eyed her questioningly but didn't say anything. When Luke and his teammates finally got up, they filed out of the taco shop without a word to Jonathan or Destiny, something that would not have happened in the past and didn't go unnoticed by either of them.

"What was all that about?" Jonathan asked.

"You tell me," Destiny said. "You're the one Luke Martin couldn't keep his eyes off."

Jonathan averted his gaze. "He was just being nice."

"When has he ever just been nice? I'm telling you, he has a crush on you. It's totally obvious." When Jonathan didn't respond, she continued. "He came up to you and brought you a drink at the party. Then he danced with you until Billy came back, and when you and Billy met Chance and me outside, Luke kept coming by every few minutes to check on you." She took a bite of her soft taco.

Jonathan's eyes widened. "What? You never told me that."

"You didn't tell me about your two coffee dates with him, so we're even." She smiled as Jonathan squirmed. "Don't look so uncomfortable. Luke told me."

Jonathan stared at her over his untouched food. "What do you mean, Luke told you?"

"I gave him my number a couple of weeks ago. Told him to text me if he ever needed to talk. People like to open up to me; what can I say?" Shrugging, she took another bite of her taco.

"What exactly did he tell you?"

"He said he confronted you the day I didn't go to school and found out you hadn't told us what he said at the party. I think he was checking to see if you were telling the truth about not telling me anything. Then he told me he liked you and wasn't sure what to do about it. He asked me about Billy and if you two were dating—"

"What did you say about Billy and me?" Jonathan's stomach clenched the more Destiny shared about her conversations with Luke. Why had she been talking about him behind his back?

She rolled her eyes. "I told him if he wanted to find out about you and Billy, or anything else, he should talk to you directly. Then he told me he invited you to get breakfast yesterday and would talk to you about it."

"Oh. So that's how you knew he had teased me about my arms?"

Destiny furrowed her brow and shook her head. "What are you talking about?"

"Never mind. I guess I was wrong." His phone vibrated in his pocket, and when he pulled it out, he had a message from Luke.

Luke: *You looked hot today. Breakfast tomorrow? My treat this time.*

Jonathan smiled, and Destiny didn't even bother to ask who it was. He typed a quick reply and returned his phone to his pocket.

Jonathan: *See you at 10.*

Twenty-Three

After they finished their lunch, Destiny and Jonathan went back to his house and watched a few episodes of the newest season of their show. Jonathan was distracted through most of it, thinking about Luke and Billy and what he would do. Still, he didn't want to make things about him, so he kept his internal struggles to himself, until Destiny finally said she had to go home and help her mother make dinner.

Jonathan walked her to the door. Realizing he still hadn't heard from Billy about hanging out later, he pulled his phone out of his pocket and sent him another message, which was read almost instantly. Three dots popped up, indicating that Billy was replying.

> **Billy:** *Sorry, been busy with rehearsals all day. It should be done by 8. I can come by and pick you up. Let's grab some ice cream.*

> **Jonathan:** *Yeah, that should work. I'll be around.*

Just let me know when you're on your way so I can make sure I'm ready.

Billy: *Will do. See ya ltr*

Jonathan waited for his mom to get home and then hung out in the kitchen with her until dinner arrived. They ate on the couch and watched an old episode of *House Hunters* until it was time for him to get ready. He took a quick shower and, after some contemplation, decided on an outfit for the date.

Billy pulled up to the house a few minutes later and sent a quick message to let Jonathan know he was outside. Grabbing his jacket on his way out, Jonathan told his mom when he thought he'd be back.

"Be careful and have fun. I love you," she said as he headed for the door.

"I will. I love you too!" He grabbed his wallet and keys and walked out.

Billy was waving at him from the passenger side of his car, where he stood waiting for him. When Jonathan got closer, Billy opened the door and waited for him to get comfortable in his seat before walking around to the other side and getting in.

"So, where do you wanna go?" Billy asked as they headed toward the end of Jonathan's street.

"If we're staying in town, we can go to Claudia's or Uncle Joe's."

"Your uncle owns an ice cream place?"

Jonathan laughed. "No, it's called Uncle Joe's. He isn't my uncle."

"Which one is better?" Billy asked as they idled at the stop sign.

"Honestly, they're both good. It just depends on

whether you want food or just ice cream, and then soft serve or hand dipped."

Billy smiled. "I'll go wherever you want to go. Just give me directions."

Jonathan smiled back. "You're lucky I have a craving, or we might have been stuck here for a while. Make a left and then a right at the next stop sign. It will be on the left down the road a little bit. I'll tell you where to turn."

Nodding, Billy made a left as instructed. "So, how have you been, cutie?"

"Good, I'm doing my best to ignore my homework until the last possible moment." Jonathan laughed.

"God, I don't miss that. I've only been out of school for a year, but it feels like a lifetime." Reaching for the stereo, Billy turned up the volume enough that Jonathan could tell he'd been listening to the Taco's first album.

"I love this song!"

"Me too, but I wrote some of it, so I'm biased." Billy laughed loudly. "I can't believe we're finally getting together, just the two of us!" He sounded excited, and he kept stealing glances at Jonathan, who was buzzing with the anxiety and excitement of finally having time alone.

"I know. On one hand, it's good that you're so busy lately, but I do miss our nightly talks, and not being able to hang out hasn't been great." Jonathan was determined to keep the mood light and happy since they were together now. "But tell me all about the new gig you got!"

"No, no, no . . . tonight is about you and me, not the band. I spend enough time with those guys, thinking and worrying about band stuff. Tonight, I want to focus on you and me. Other than avoiding homework, how has your break been so far?"

Surprised to hear Billy decline to talk about the band,

Jonathan considered what to talk about. "It's been good so far. I'm not excited that it's almost halfway over now, but I've enjoyed sleeping in." He laughed. "Destiny and I hung out today and watched some TV. Admittedly, I did try to get ahead on some projects and stuff for next week so I don't have a mountain of stuff to do right after the break, but I've mostly been relaxing."

Jonathan felt terrible about not mentioning his breakfast with Luke or the one he was going to tomorrow, but if he wanted to just focus on the two of them like Billy said, then leaving out the thing—or guy, in this case—who was pulling some of his attention away was also fair. He supposed it was also not worth mentioning since nothing had happened between them.

Unfortunately, by thinking about Luke, Jonathan's confusion reared its messy head, and he found himself comparing the two.

Billy was tall, taller than either him or Luke, which Jonathan genuinely liked, even if there was only about an inch difference between them. He was creative and emotionally expressive, and he said adorable and flirty things to Jonathan, which made him feel attractive. His reddish-brown hair and brown eyes were cute, but they weren't as dark as Jonathan usually preferred. His sort of indie rocker vibe was cool, but it sometimes made Jonathan feel like he wasn't cool enough to mix with the same crowds as Billy.

Jonathan's attention snapped back to the moment at hand as the car slowed, and he realized Billy had asked him a question. "Sorry about that. I was apparently in my own world. What did you say?"

Billy just laughed. "I was just asking if this was it coming up,"—he pointed to the sign for Uncle Joe's—"but I figured it out. Do you know what you want?"

"Yes, I'd like a small vanilla cone, in a cup, with chocolate and peanut butter on top, please." Jonathan spoke without hesitation, as he'd gotten the same thing every time he'd been there.

Billy smiled. "A man who knows what he likes. I like that. Can I have a bite if I promise to give you a bite of mine?"

"I guess that depends on what you get," Jonathan teased.

"Oh, is that so? The stakes are high, I guess. Do you have any recommendations for what else you like that I might want to try?"

"No way! I'm not giving you a hint about what to order just so you can have some of mine," Jonathan joked. "A person's ice cream order is personal and important. It says a lot about you. Maybe we don't have compatible palates, and we'd never be able to share a pizza or enjoy a home-cooked meal together." Jonathan's voice rang with a clear note of sarcasm.

"I see, so this is potentially a breakup-worthy decision." Billy's smile spread even wider. "Fair enough. I guess I'll take my chances and see how I do." Pulling up to the menu, he took a quick glance and then ordered Jonathan's vanilla cone with chocolate and peanut butter, as well as a chocolate cone in a cup with peanut butter and granola.

"I like what you did there, adding in a little texture but sticking with safe flavors," Jonathan said as Billy pulled forward. "It feels a little like you may have cheated, having already known my order, but I'm willing to share some of mine with you to try yours."

"I'm not sure." Billy looked serious now, and Jonathan's smile faltered slightly. "Maybe I want to keep all of mine to myself." Jonathan sat quietly for a few seconds before Billy burst out laughing again. "You should see your face. You look so sad! Of course I'll share it with you! I would have given you some of mine even if you had picked a gross flavor. You're cute, and you deserve all the ice cream you want."

Jonathan buried his face in his hands, embarrassed that he had fallen for Billy's teasing again. He was glad it was all a joke, though, and he was finally able to push Luke out of his mind and be completely present with Billy.

When he finally uncovered his face, Billy was still looking at him. Suddenly, Billy leaned toward Jonathan, reaching out as if to grab his leg. Jonathan's pulse began to race as he imagined what their first kiss would be like, soft and sweet, short but powerful . . .

Closing his eyes, Jonathan leaned forward a little.

"Sorry, I don't want to hit your leg, but I have to get in the glove box. My wallet's in there." Reaching past his leg, Billy pulled on the small handle of the glove box.

"Oh, sorry. I could have gotten that for you," Jonathan said, embarrassed that he had misinterpreted the moment.

"No worries, I got it." Billy seemed completely unaware of the misunderstanding that had just taken place.

After paying for their order, Billy made a right out of the parking lot and drove a few minutes up the road until he found a fairly empty parking lot. Pulling in toward the back, he rolled down the windows to let the breeze in and turned off the car. Once settled, they each had a few bites of their own dessert before switching and trying the other's.

"Well?" Billy asked once they'd switched back. "How do you rate my selection?"

"I like it! The crunch of the granola and the added sweetness are nice. I might add it to my order in the future." Jonathan smiled at Billy appreciatively. "What did you think of mine?"

"I think I like the chocolate ice cream better than the vanilla personally, but chocolate and peanut butter are a winning combo for me. Can't go wrong with that."

They took a few more bites in silence before they both attempted to speak again.

"What else are you—"

"How long did it—"

They both stopped, and Jonathan apologized for interrupting.

"No, it was me. What were you saying?" Billy happily took a large bite of ice cream so Jonathan couldn't get out of asking his question.

"I was just going to ask how long it took for you to write new songs. You said you were working on some new stuff, and I was curious when you might start performing them."

Billy smiled. "I wasn't going to talk about band stuff, remember?"

Jonathan blushed. "Sorry, I guess I did . . ." He wasn't sure what else to say, but Billy spoke up again.

"That's okay, I'll let it slide." He chuckled and looked out into the parking lot beyond the windshield. "I guess it depends on the song. Sometimes, I can sit down and write one in a couple of hours, maybe a day. Sometimes, it takes a couple of days or even a week if I just can't quite get it right. The longest it's ever taken me was about a month, but I wasn't trying every day. When it takes that long, I have to give it a break and do something else. That usually helps, but it can take a little while to happen." He watched the headlights of a car enter the parking lot to turn around and leave again.

"That's so impressive. I could never do something like that," Jonathan admitted. "I have no musical ability whatsoever, and even though I can write a research paper, a poem or song is way outside my comfort zone."

"It's not that hard," Billy said with a small laugh, "but it's a skill that takes practice, and if it's not something you do all the time, it can be a challenge."

Jonathan nodded. "I can see how it would get easier if you were used to doing it all the time, especially if you had other people there to help out with the process. It still sounds cool to me, and I'm impressed."

"I'll take that compliment, thank you." Billy reached over and squeezed Jonathan's leg before pulling his hand back.

Jonathan had another moment of panic, but he managed to keep his wits about him this time. He even reached out and did the same to Billy to show him that he liked the physical affection.

They finished their ice cream and continued talking about what the rest of the week held for them. Jonathan still didn't mention his upcoming breakfast with Luke, and Billy admitted that he was busy with more rehearsals for their new gig.

By 10:30 p.m., the breeze outside was beginning to get too cold, so Billy rolled up the windows and turned on the heat. Then he wrapped an arm around Jonathan and pulled him close, using his other hand to rub Jonathan's shoulder and arm to warm him up.

Elated, Jonathan relaxed into Billy's embrace while he could.

Twenty-Four

Eventually, Billy stirred, claiming he needed to get on the road soon, so he would have to take Jonathan home. Though disappointed, Jonathan understood, and he scooted back into his seat and buckled his seat belt.

When they pulled up in front of Jonathan's house, Billy turned off the car and shifted around to face Jonathan.

"I have sort of a surprise for you," he said.

"A surprise?" Jonathan looked around for a box or bag that he had missed. "What is it?"

"Well, the gig I told you about—the one we've been getting ready for—is going to be close by, and I wanted to see if you would come?"

Jonathan's eyes went wide with surprise, and he immediately forgot about any gift he might have received. This was the best news he'd heard in a while. "Yes! Whenever and wherever it is, I'm there! Are you playing at the college? I'm so freaking excited!" Jonathan's mood, which had soured slightly as their date ended, was back up to his pre-date excitement levels.

Billy beamed. "We're not playing at the college, no. We're performing for the high school."

"The high school? Why?" Jonathan asked, confused.

"Your friend Chance helped us get hired to play at your prom. We're going to be performing a week from this Saturday!"

Jonathan was too shocked and confused to respond at first, but if Billy and the Telepathic Tacos were performing, maybe he could show off how hot he was and that he and Billy were sort of casually dating. The more Jonathan thought about it, the more excited he became, until he reached over and hugged Billy without questioning it.

"That's amazing. I'm so happy for you and excited to see you perform!" Jonathan held on tight and was ecstatic when Billy wrapped his arms around Jonathan, returning the hug. It lasted for almost a full minute before Billy pulled away with a sad expression, saying he needed to go. Mood only slightly dampened by the farewell after the great news, Jonathan said good night and got out of the car.

Once in the house, he sent a quick text to Destiny to tell her the news about the Tacos performing at prom. Her reply came back almost instantly.

> **Destiny:** *WHAT? How did that even happen? We've never had a live band perform.*

> **Jonathan:** *I know! He said that Chance helped them out somehow. I didn't even know he was on the Prom Committee, but knowing him, he probably joined because some hot girl asked him to.*

> **Destiny:** *I can almost guarantee you he's not on*

the committee. Why bother doing the work when he can just smile at them and make them do it for him?

Jonathan: LOL. True story. Anyway, now I'm re-thinking my "no prom" stance, but it's probably too late to rent a tux and have it arrive on time. Plus, I'm not sure I have the money for one anyway.

Destiny: You don't think your mom would give you the money?

Jonathan: She would, but that, plus the ticket, plus the shoes, blah blah blah—it just adds up. I don't want to ask her for that kind of money if I don't have to.

Destiny: We'll figure out a way. It's the Tele-pathic Tacos! At our prom? We can't miss that, even if we have to volunteer to clean up at the end of the night!

Jonathan: I didn't even think that was an option. I'd do almost anything to make sure I get a chance to dance with Billy so the whole school can see us and how good we look together.

Destiny: The whole school? What about Luke?

Jonathan: I don't know what to do about him. He sort of told me that he might like me, but he hasn't said anything since then. It's probably because I'm literally the only openly gay guy at school. It's not like he has a whole line of guys to choose from.

Destiny: *I dunno. I don't think a lack of options has got you on his radar, but I'm not telling you what you should do.*

Jonathan: *We're meeting for breakfast again tomorrow—me and Luke.*

Destiny: *As I said, I don't think he likes you because there aren't any other options. I think he likes you for you.*

Jonathan: *What am I doing? I like Billy! What would he say if he found out I was going to breakfast with someone else? If he did that to me, I'd be so upset!*

Destiny: *I wouldn't worry about it. Nothing is happening between you and Billy at the moment, right? But enough about him, how do you feel about Luke?*

Jonathan: *I dunno. He's cute, I can't deny that. And lately, he has been nicer to me, which is a welcome change. But it just feels like it's some joke I don't get, or like at any moment, I'm going to find out he's been recording me somehow and showing his friends.*

Destiny: *LMAO. Okay, crazy, I don't think you need to worry about that. I've seen him around you, and I've seen him look at you when you aren't looking. There's something there, but if you're not interested, it doesn't matter.*

Jonathan: *I'm not not interested, but I'm with Billy, sort of. I dunno.*

Jonathan: *Why is this so hard?*

Destiny: *It's all part of the experience of growing up, I guess.*

Jonathan: *You're lucky you don't have to deal with dating drama, and I'm fortunate I have you to help me deal with mine!*

Destiny: *Hahahaha! I couldn't agree more. And I'm glad to see you recognize my value.*

They kept texting, eventually moving on to other subjects before calling it a night.

A few hours later, Jonathan's alarm went off, giving him enough time to make himself look presentable. Checking his phone, he found a message from Luke confirming they were still on for breakfast. He sent a quick reply and hopped in the shower.

As he got ready, his heart began to race for no reason, and no amount of deep breathing would help him calm down. Once he decided he looked as good as he was going to, he turned the lights off.

That's when the butterflies started.

"C'mon, why am I even nervous?" he asked himself out loud, not understanding why his body was betraying him now. "It's not like we haven't done this before! Besides, he probably doesn't even like me. For that matter, I may not even like him."

He squeezed his face into a look of superiority. "He's not even that . . . cute."

Jonathan snorted. Even to himself, he couldn't get that lie out without a pause. "This is stupid!" Opening the front door, he shut it behind him and stomped his way toward breakfast.

About halfway there, a strong breeze kicked up, and he could feel it undoing the work he had put into his hair. Nevertheless, he kept trudging on toward the coffee shop.

When Jonathan turned the corner, he noticed Luke standing outside waiting for him. Luke seemed to notice Jonathan as well and began walking toward him. With his nerves in full effect, Jonathan had to remind himself to play it cool and not make a fool of himself. He also reminded himself to walk slowly so he didn't appear too eager.

As they got closer to each other, Luke's eyes widened, and he laughed, though he tried to pass it off as a cough. Suddenly uncomfortable, Jonathan turned to see if Luke's friends were hidden somewhere or had followed behind him. When he didn't see anyone there, he turned back around and continued toward Luke.

"Hi," Luke said once they were close enough to hear each other without having to raise their voices.

"Hey," Jonathan responded without much enthusiasm, still feeling uncomfortable.

"I'm sorry. I just have to—" Luke reached up and ran his fingers through Jonathan's hair, smoothing it out. "There you go. You were rocking a look I don't think you'd intended for a little bit."

Blushing furiously, Jonathan laughed loudly with relief. "Thank you."

"Don't mention it," Luke replied with a smile. "You ready?" he asked and turned back to Night Owls.

"Yes." Jonathan fell in beside Luke as they walked back toward their breakfast spot.

They ordered their usual drinks, and each got a breakfast sandwich. Instead of two slices of banana nut bread, they decided to share a single piece, which made Jonathan smile. Once they had their items, they sat at their usual table in the back, far from the door. This time, Luke didn't even bother looking whenever people walked in the door.

"How was practice?" Jonathan asked.

"It was good, thanks for asking. It would have been better if you had come to watch."

"I'm not a big fan of sportsball, but maybe I'll come to a home game sometime."

Luke laughed and leaned in closer. "I'll hold you to that."

"What role do you play?

"Is that a sex question?" Luke joked.

"What? No!" Jonathan's cheeks and neck flushed.

"Are you trying to see *my* sportsballs, Daniels?"

Jonathan's eyes felt like they might pop out of his head if they opened any wider, and he struggled to come up with some appropriate response. Luke Martin had *definitely* just flirted with him.

"I'm just messing with you. Calm down." Luke patted Jonathan's shoulder, then squeezed it. "I play third base."

Jonathan took a sip of his drink. "That's the little pillow on the left, right?"

Luke tilted his head to the side, and he stared at Jonathan as if trying to figure out how to answer the question without teasing him.

"I'm just joking!" Jonathan finally said. "I played tee ball when I was younger," he added, trying to continue talking about something Luke enjoyed. "My dad wanted me to get into sports like him, but I was a right fielder. I don't remember much about it, other than doing cartwheels out there." He smiled at the memory. "And one time, I found a frog on the field and watched it so closely, I missed that the inning had changed over, and one of the parents had to come get me." Jonathan laughed to himself.

"That sounds exactly like I would expect," Luke said, tapping Jonathan's foot with his own. "Admittedly, I once spent half an inning trying to fix a wedgie I had, so you shouldn't feel too bad. Tee ball is like that for everyone. No one is good yet. No one hits the ball or knows what they're doing. I think it's more for parents than anything. It gives them a break from their kids during the practices." Luke's smile was genuine, making Jonathan feel less silly for sharing his story.

"When is the next home game?" To Jonathan's surprise, he legitimately wanted to watch Luke play.

"It's the one against Heyworth I mentioned yesterday. The Friday before prom." He hesitated before asking, "Do you think you're gonna go?"

"Yeah. I'll see if Destiny and Chance wanna come with me." Jonathan tried to imagine how his friends would react when he asked them to come watch the game.

"Oh, no," Luke clarified. "I meant to prom."

Jonathan's nerves returned with a vengeance. "I'm not sure yet, but I'm hoping to. How about you?" He tried to keep his tone casual.

"I'm planning to, yes. Got my tux and everything."

Before either of them could think of something more to say, the silence between them was broken by a different voice coming from right behind Jonathan.

"Hey, Luke, what are you doing here?"

Twenty-Five

Jonathan didn't recognize the voice immediately, but when Luke looked up, surprised, the recognition in his eyes made Jonathan realize it was someone from school. Turning around, he saw that it was Kelly Noe, the on-again, off-again girlfriend of Mike Lawler.

"Uh, hey, Kel, how—how's it going?" Luke asked, stumbling over his words.

He'd lowered his head as if trying to hide, and he kept his eyes averted from them both. It was suddenly excessively clear that no matter what Jonathan thought might be happening between them, there was no way Luke Martin would ever give up his social standing for someone like Jonathan.

"It's going okay. What're you two up to?" Her voice was higher than normal, and Jonathan could feel her stare drilling into his back.

"Oh, nothing, we were just, uh . . ." Luke paused, trying to find something to say.

"We were working on our presentation for a chem

project that's due next week," Jonathan said quickly. "This was the only time we were both available." He refused to look at Luke. "But I think we're done here."

Jonathan stood up and grabbed his jacket and coffee. "I'll send you the draft when I have it finished, and you can let me know what edits to make for your portion." Looking at Kelly, he nodded once, before turning back to Luke. "You two have a good one." With that, he walked out the door and quickly toward home, determined not to give the tears welling in his eyes the freedom to spill over.

The cold wind stung his eyes, and he had to keep wiping away tears to avoid looking like he was having an emotional breakdown on the sidewalk. The farther he walked, the stronger the wind became, until he finally had to duck behind a building for a break.

"Jonathan!"

He turned around to see Luke running after him, his cheeks flushed.

"Jonathan, wait up!" Luke called out, struggling to put his jacket on as he ran.

"What are you doing?" Jonathan demanded. "She's going to say something to Mike about us being together." He wiped his eyes again quickly, rubbing his hand on the back of his pants.

"I don't care what she says to him," Luke replied, his eyes fierce.

"But . . . you're not—you don't know if—you said you . . ."

Jonathan's mind raced to make sense of what was happening. Luke still hadn't confirmed if he was even gay, and despite the clear flirtation, he hadn't publicly claimed to be interested in Jonathan, so why was he acting like this?

"Do you want to go to prom with me?" Luke asked,

his eyes locked on Jonathan's. "Well, technically us—I'm going with a few friends—but I want you to come with us."

Jonathan didn't know what to say. He wasn't expecting an invitation to the dance from anyone, especially Luke, and since Billy would be there and Jonathan wanted to dance with him, he wasn't sure he could even say yes.

"Just think about it, okay? Promise?"

"Okay," Jonathan replied. "I'll think about it."

Turning, he continued walking home and immediately texted Destiny and Chance, asking them to meet him there in twenty minutes. They both replied they would be there, and he put his phone away. He needed to think about what he was going to do now.

Once home, he fixed his hair again and began to pace back and forth in the kitchen and family room, before finally taking a seat and waiting for the other two to arrive.

When Destiny and Chance arrived, Jonathan told them what had happened with Luke, what he'd done when Kelly arrived, and what he'd said about going to prom. Destiny couldn't help but smile at Chance, who was visibly disappointed.

"What are you going to do?" she asked.

"I don't know what I can do," Jonathan replied. "I like Billy, and he's going to be there. I want to dance with him, but now Luke has invited me to go with him, and it would be weird to go with Luke but dance with someone else."

"Why would it be weird?" Chance asked. "It's not like Luke asked you to be his date. He asked you to go with him and his friends. Maybe he was just being nice." He crossed his arms.

"Or maybe, Luke wanted to ask him to be his date,

but he already had plans to go with his friends and included Jonathan in those!" Destiny replied, her eyes locked on Chance. "Meanwhile, Billy only mentioned playing and never actually said he would be Jonathan's date."

The words slipped out before she'd thought them through. She turned to Jonathan, whose face had gone pale.

"Oh my god." Jonathan's expression had fallen, and a look of panic began to spread as his eyes widened and his mouth dropped open. "Do you think Billy won't want to dance with me?" Jonathan buried his face in a cushion on the couch they were all sitting on.

"I never said that," Destiny said, trying to backpedal.

"Why don't you ask Billy to be your date?" Chance suggested. "Give him a chance to say yes before you worry that he might not agree."

Jonathan lifted his face from the cushion. "He's going to be there whether I invite him or not. I just assumed he would want to dance with me since we're seeing each other—or whatever this thing is between us! God, I'm an idiot." He face-planted into the cushion again.

"You're not an idiot," Destiny said quickly. "You're just in a unique situation where neither guy has stepped up to clarify how they feel about you."

"What am I supposed to do about that?" he asked, sitting back up. "What if neither of them likes me like that? What if they both do? What if I'm alone forever because no one will ever like me?"

"Okay, now you're just spiraling and being way too hard on yourself," Destiny said, tone firm but full of affection. "I already told you, Luke definitely likes you. Is he the right guy for you? I don't know, but it's worth giving him a shot, right?"

"I agree with Destiny," Chance said, "don't think like that. Everything is going to work out for the best. You just have to give it a chance." He chuckled and winked at Destiny. "Billy was excited to tell you he would be at the dance, right? Maybe that was because he was excited to get to celebrate the night with you." He side-eyed Destiny.

"Exactly," Destiny bit out with more force than necessary. "Everything will work out exactly how it should. You just have to leave it up to fate." She glared at Chance with narrowed eyes.

Lifting his head, Jonathan looked at the two of them glaring at each other. "Are you two going to be okay? Did I miss something?"

"We're fine," they said simultaneously.

"Just a friendly disagreement on what you should do," Chance added.

"And what's that?" Jonathan asked, turning to face them both expectantly.

Destiny spoke up before Chance could. "It doesn't matter what we think is best, right, Chance?" She narrowed her eyes.

"Right," he agreed flatly.

"What matters is what you feel is right and what you want to do. We're not the ones who have to live with the decisions you make. We just get to sit back and support you as you make those moves." Reaching out, Destiny took Jonathan's hand and gave it a comforting squeeze. "And we will both be here for you, no matter what you do. Right, Chance?"

"Right," he repeated, but he also reached out and took Jonathan's other hand. "And if it doesn't work out, you can always come to me for some distraction." He slid Jonathan's hand up his thigh, dangerously close to his crotch.

Pulling his hand away, Jonathan laughed. "Hold that thought for now, but depending on how the next week and a half goes, I might need that kind of 'support,'" he joked.

Chance scooted closer and tried to retake Jonathan's hand, but Jonathan wouldn't let him; laughing the whole time, he kept pulling it away. "I'm here for you, whatever you need," Chance added with a waggle of his eyebrows that had Jonathan laughing even louder. "Let me help you unload your burden. We can unload together."

"You're just gross. You know that?" Destiny leaned away from the two of them, her nose flared and tongue stuck out a little in disgust.

"What did I do?" Jonathan asked incredulously.

"You're encouraging him! He's bad enough on his own. He doesn't need any help from anyone!" While her admonishment was honest, her tone was teasing.

"What am I going to do now?" Jonathan asked rhetorically once they'd all calmed down. They sat on the couch together, Destiny still holding his hand and Chance sitting close by. The silence seemed to stretch beyond the room, as if the house itself held its breath waiting for an answer.

Destiny turned her head to Jonathan. "Why don't you sleep on it and see how you're feeling tomorrow? Maybe you'll have a clearer head, and the right decision will be more obvious. Prom is still over a week away, and no one's demanding a decision from you today."

"I agree with Destiny." Spinning in his seat, Chance laid his head on Jonathan's leg. "Whenever I'm trying to figure out what to do next, I sit back and wait for the next move to pop up when and where I least expect it." He squeezed Jonathan's knee for emphasis.

Squealing, Jonathan kicked out his leg and laughed.

Destiny sighed loudly. When Jonathan looked at her

curiously, she shook her head and rolled her eyes before pointing her finger at the side of her head and spinning it in a *crazy* motion. Then she pointed at Chance.

"You should do whatever you want, even if it's something as useless as waiting around for something to pop up. Whatever you decide, I have faith that it will be what you're meant to do, and you just have to make that decision and move forward into your future." She gently squeezed his shoulder.

"We live in a universe of random chaos that is expanding every second of every day. Even if you believed in some higher power, what're the chances he's out there planning everything that happens to us?" Chance grinned slightly at Destiny, though he wiped the expression away when Jonathan glanced at him.

"Oh, I dunno, Chance," Destiny countered. "It seems entirely possible that there could be a higher power out there in the universe and that *she* could absolutely be aware of all the important parts of our lives and how they are going to play out." She gave him a serious look, daring him to say something else.

"Well, whoever or whatever is out there," Jonathan said, clueless about the meaningful glances passing between Destiny and Chance, "they don't seem to know or care about what's happening to me right now."

"Don't say that," Chance said, voice soft. He caught Destiny so off guard that she didn't try to comfort Jonathan as she usually would. "Sometimes, even when things seem like they're not going well, those struggles are just part of the journey. It doesn't mean we aren't being looked after or that no one cares. It just means that hurt, loss, confusion, and most importantly, how we deal with those things and move forward is part of the process of getting older."

Turning onto his stomach, Chance propped his head up so he could make eye contact with Jonathan, who listened closely. "Life and love can be hard, but you have us, and if nothing else, you can rest assured that both Destiny and I have a vested interest in making sure you always have someone here to support you, even when those tough things happen along your way." Giving Jonathan a small grin, he flipped back onto his back while Destiny and Jonathan sat silently.

"That was . . . surprisingly sweet, Chance. And it's true, we've got your back, no matter what." Destiny squeezed Jonathan's hand again.

"Just don't tell anyone about this," Chance said quickly. "I don't want anyone getting any ideas about me being soft or sentimental."

"Your secret is safe with us," Jonathan said with a small laugh. "Thank you both so much for listening to me and giving me advice, even if you didn't exactly give me the kind of advice I was looking for." He paused to see if they would crack. When they didn't, he continued. "I'll talk to Billy the next time I see him and ask him if he'll dance with me." Chance looked meaningfully at Destiny, but she just waited for Jonathan to continue. "And I'm going to ask Luke how he feels about me the next time I see him, because no matter what happens, I want to make sure I don't hurt either of them."

The smug look on Chance's face faded away, but Destiny could tell he wasn't upset.

"I think that's a great way to move forward," Destiny said finally. "Knowing where you stand with both of them and making your decision based on as much information as possible."

The three of them hung out for the rest of the day.

Destiny and Chance were still there when Jonathan's mom returned home from work in the evening. She offered to order them a pizza, which they accepted, and after making phone calls to their respective parents, the two of them ended up spending the night with Jonathan to help keep his mind occupied and off the future, at least for now.

When they woke the following day, Chance snuck into the kitchen to raid the refrigerator and see what he could make for breakfast. Destiny stayed with Jonathan, who finally looked at his phone to find two unread messages. One was from Billy, letting him know he couldn't wait to see him at their performance, and the other was from Luke, who asked if he had decided on the dance.

Destiny pretended not to notice the messages, but she could feel warring emotions coming from Jonathan, which was a first for her. It caught her off guard so badly that she missed what he said before leaving the room.

Once he'd left the room, she felt like she was able to breathe again, but she still felt as though she'd lost her balance. Her powers were increasing so dramatically now that she was almost back to full power. Yet still Jonathan's future somehow eluded her. She didn't know what it meant or who was behind it, but she was determined to find out.

Twenty-Six

$\mathcal{J}$onathan eventually responded to both Luke and Billy later that morning. He let Luke know he still wasn't sure what his plans were but that he would give him a heads-up as soon as he did. He told Billy he was excited to see them perform and potentially listen to any new music they might decide was ready by that point.

Luke responded a few minutes later to say that he was happy to wait, but he hoped Jonathan would decide to join them, and Billy sent a thumbs-up emoji a few hours later to acknowledge Jonathan's reply.

"I don't know what you see in him," Destiny said, looking over Jonathan's shoulder as Billy's response came through. They were sitting on his bed watching YouTube videos, killing time until lunch. Chance had gone home shortly after they'd finished breakfast, but Destiny had decided to stay and keep Jonathan company for a little while to prevent him from spiraling.

Jonathan pulled his phone away from her. "Uh, hello? I don't look at your incoming messages." Actually, he did, and she knew it, but she just laughed it off and doubled down on her stance.

"I mean it. I know he's cute and talented and taller than you, which is super dreamy." She fluttered her eyelashes. "But he also doesn't seem emotionally vulnerable or even interested in what you want to do. And he hasn't really made himself physically available to you either."

"To be fair, I haven't been up-front about what I want yet, so he hasn't had a chance to respond to the idea of us dancing. And he is cute, tall, and dreamy . . . he's also sweet, and he makes me laugh, and he didn't run me over that first night we met, so that has to count for something!" Jonathan paused the video they were watching and turned to face her. "Right?"

She hesitated, and Jonathan realized she was choosing her words carefully. "I love that he stopped his car before he could run you over. You're my best friend, and I'm not sure what would happen to me if you weren't here anymore."

Her expression and tone darkened, and she seemed to get lost in her own thoughts. Jonathan wondered if she was thinking more deeply and seriously about what could have happened in that moment than he had. Regardless of the reason for her look, he knew she'd always want whatever was best for him, and he loved her for it.

"But I also don't want you to settle for someone who doesn't always make you feel your best. I'm not saying he doesn't. I'm just saying that *if* he doesn't, you shouldn't feel like you have to stick it out on the off chance he one day will. A relationship will work out if a relationship is meant to work out between you two."

"Ugh!" Jonathan covered his face with his pillow and moaned into it loudly before uncovering his face again. "I just wish I could see what the right decision was, so I could stop worrying so much."

"Believe me," Destiny chimed in, "I know exactly what you mean. But like I said last night, whatever you decide to do will ultimately be the right choice. You just have to get over this hurdle and keep going."

"A sports analogy? Really?" Jonathan scowled before they both burst into laughter.

Even though Jonathan still wasn't sure what he should do, he felt better about whatever would happen. Then again, there was always the option to skip the dance entirely and just watch a video of the performance later or hide somewhere within earshot so he didn't have to face either of them. He kept that idea to himself; neither Chance nor Destiny would approve of him hiding from his problems. Then again, they didn't risk embarrassing themselves or being rejected by one or both of the guys they liked.

Jonathan's heart skipped a beat. Had he just thought about Luke as someone he liked as more than a potential friend? Was he actually attracted to the baseball jock who made him smile and teased him about his love of banana bread?

"Oh my god," he said quietly, plopping his face into his palms.

"What happened?" Destiny asked. "What are you thinking about? Your face is all pinched, and it looks like you're going to cry or you have to poop. Do you need some privacy? I can go home if you need me to." She stood up with a wide smile.

He laughed. "No, shut up, I'm fine. Just . . . thinking." He gave a heavy sigh and shook his head, laughing quietly to himself. "I'll be fine, I promise. I'm just trying to decide what to do."

Destiny sat back down and placed a hand on his knee. "I'm here for you if you need me, but I can let you have some alone time if you need to figure things out."

"Yeah, maybe it would help if I just thought things over. It may not help, but I also may not be that fun to be around while I try to figure this out." Sitting up, he gave her a small smile, attempting to look determined but falling short of that goal. His cell phone chimed, but he purposely ignored it, unwilling to take on anything else right now.

"Okay, I understand. I'm right next door if you need me. Just let me know if you want me to come back over or if you want to go for a walk or something." She looked at his phone for a moment and smiled. "I have a feeling you're not going to feel this way for long, but I'm around all day." Destiny hugged him and then stood up and let herself out of the house.

Jonathan lay in bed for another minute or two, contemplating his feelings for Billy and Luke and what it meant that he liked them both. *What if they both like me back? What if they find out I like someone else and stop liking me? What if they fall for each other and forget about me entirely?* Thoughts spiraled around in his head faster than he could process them, and he was beginning to get a headache.

When his phone notification sounded again, he decided to check it so the noise would stop going off. There was a text from Destiny.

Destiny: *Made you look*

There was another from Luke, which made his pulse race.

Luke: *Hey, wyd? Are you busy right now?*

Jonathan: _No, I'm just hanging out at home._
Why?

Luke: _Can I stop by for a min?_

Jonathan's panic level shot up as he looked around his messy room and imagined Luke in there with him. He started frantically picking up shoes and random piles of clothing strewn about the room and shoving them into the closet. It took another chime from his phone for him to realize he'd never actually responded.

Luke: _Hello?_

Jonathan: _Yeah, sorry, I was watching something._

Luke: _So . . . can I come by?_

Jonathan: _Yeah, when do you think you'll be here?_

Luke: _knock, knock_

A knock sounded from the front door a second after the text came through, and Jonathan's panic shifted into overdrive. Destiny hadn't been wrong; he was too stressed about Luke being there in person to worry about how he felt about anything else. He scanned his room one more time to make sure it was semi-decent and then checked his reflection in the mirror before finally answering the door.

When he opened it, Luke stood there with a slight sheen of sweat on his face despite the cool breeze. He was dressed in dingy-looking baseball pants that looked a little small—though Jonathan certainly wasn't complaining—and a T-shirt over a long-sleeved shirt. He also wore a hat that was pushed up off his forehead just enough for Jonathan to see his whole face.

"Hi," Jonathan said, a little out of breath from his frenetic cleaning.

"Hey," Luke replied. "Sorry for the short notice. I was sort of in the area and thought I'd see if you were around."

"How . . . how did you know where I live?" Jonathan asked, confused. Even though they'd been friends in elementary school, they'd never visited each other's houses. And while Eureka wasn't that big, Luke knowing where he lived still struck Jonathan as unusual.

Luke smiled. "I might have gotten your address from someone at school so we could work on that chemistry project we have."

"You know that was just a cover, right? We don't actually have a project due next week." Jonathan said it almost automatically, still shocked to find Luke Martin in his baseball gear standing on his front porch.

"Yes," Luke teased. "I'm an athlete, not an idiot."

"Right." Jonathan laughed, relieved. "Sorry."

"It's okay; I'm just messing with you," Luke replied. "Do, uh . . . do you think I might be able to come inside at some point, though?"

Jonathan's face flushed, and he stepped back. "My bad, absolutely, please."

Luke squeezed past Jonathan, giving his arm a gentle nudge as he did so. Once the door was closed, they stood in the entry, just looking at each other. Suddenly realizing Luke was inside his home, Jonathan started walking toward the kitchen.

"Would you like anything to drink? We have water, OJ, milk, Coke . . ." Jonathan trailed off as he opened the refrigerator, looking to see if they had anything else he could offer.

Following Jonathan into the kitchen, Luke sat at the table. "I'd take a water bottle if you have one. Otherwise, just tap water is fine, with a little ice, please."

"Sure!" Jonathan pulled out a pitcher of water. Grabbing two cups, he filled them with ice and water. Putting away the water pitcher, he carried the cups to the table and offered one to Luke. "Here you go."

As Luke accepted the cup, their fingers brushed together, and Jonathan nearly dropped the cup in his haste to snatch back his hand. "Sorry," he said, embarrassed.

"For what?" Luke asked, looking confused.

"We just, uh . . . you know what, never mind." Jonathan took the chair next to Luke and took a sip of water. "So, what were you doing in my neighborhood?"

"Oh, I was . . . well, honestly, I wasn't just in the neighborhood. I came by to see you, and when I was halfway here, I realized I probably should have asked before showing up out of the blue, but I also didn't want to chicken out, so I texted you when I was a few minutes away, and by the time I was walking up to your house, you finally replied."

"Did you see Destiny when you got here?"

"No." Luke shook his head. "Should I have?"

"No, not necessarily. She was just here a little bit before you; I thought you might have seen her leave." *Or she might have seen you.*

"Nope, I didn't see anyone." Taking a drink, Luke looked around the kitchen. "You have a really nice house, Daniels. I like it."

Jonathan blushed and his stomach fluttered at Luke's use of his last name. For some reason, it made him feel like they were equals in that moment.

"Thanks, Martin," he responded, then wrinkled his

nose. "Nope, don't like that at all." It didn't sound right when he tried it.

Laughing, Luke took Jonathan's hand and pulled him out of his seat. "C'mon, give me the grand tour." He tugged Jonathan back toward the front of the house.

"Well, that was the kitchen, obviously, and this"—he gestured to their left—"is the family room."

"Very nice."

"Over there"—Jonathan pointed behind them as they paused near the foyer—"through that door is the mud-room, where the washer and dryer are. My mom's room is down that hallway, and back to the left is the office slash workout room." Leading Luke toward his bedroom, Jonathan continued pointing out what was through each door. "This is the guest bathroom, which is also my bathroom, and then my bedroom."

"Can I see your bedroom?" Luke asked, eyes bright with curiosity.

"Um, yeah, sure." Jonathan laughed nervously. "It's not very exciting, but why not?" He peeked inside quickly just to make sure he hadn't left any underwear or the like lying around by mistake. Once he was satisfied that it was as clean and embarrassment-free as it would get, he stepped inside and waved Luke in.

Luke walked around the room and took in the small collection of video games stacked on the small shelf under the TV and then the books on the desk, including *Pride and Prejudice*, which Jonathan realized he needed to give back to Destiny. Next, Luke looked at his poster collection, which covered the walls above his bed, and finally examined the collage Jonathan had created on his closet door from images he'd torn out of magazines.

"What's all this?" Luke asked, eyes scanning every inch of the collage.

Jonathan ducked his head. "I'm not very artistic when it comes to drawing or painting, but I like to put things like this together. I used to do it with folders and stuff when I was younger, but I decided to do something larger one day. I started with only part of the door, but the design has since spread to the whole thing."

"This is impressive, Daniels." Luke's use of his last name continued to fill Jonathan's stomach with warmth, and he couldn't stop himself from smiling, even as he took a step back.

"It's not that big a deal." Jonathan walked over to sit on his bed while Luke finished examining his creation.

Luke, however, turned to face him. "Why do you do that? Why do you avoid compliments and praise from other people? Hell, you don't even let people flirt with you without trying to shut it down."

"I don't shut it down!" Jonathan protested, though he knew he had done that before.

"Oh, no?" Luke took a step toward him, eyes gleaming with mischief and something else Jonathan couldn't pinpoint.

"No." Jonathan shook his head and tried not to laugh as Luke continued advancing on him.

"Then you would be fine if I told you I think you're adorable and you have a nice butt? And with you sitting there like that, it's taking everything in my power not to just push you back on your bed, hold you in my arms, and kiss you . . . ?" Luke let the words fade into silence as he slowly invaded Jonathan's personal bubble.

Jonathan was practically bursting with nerves, and his forehead broke out in a sweat, but he tried to respond with a sarcastic and superior denial. The only thing that came out of his mouth, though, was a high-pitched squeak that broke the tension. They dissolved into laughter.

As they calmed down, Luke took a seat next to Jonathan on his bed. "You also have a cute laugh."

"Oh, whatever," Jonathan waved the words away without thinking.

Luke raised his eyebrows. "See! You just did it!" He squeezed Jonathan's leg right above the knee, eliciting a laugh and a wriggle. Grinning, Luke reached for his other leg and squeezed it purposely. "I'm going to keep complimenting you until you accept it!"

Luke continued to tickle Jonathan and call him cute until Jonathan reached out with both hands and grabbed Luke's head. They were both breathing heavily, and Luke's eyes were crinkled at the corners. Blood pounded in Jonathan's ears as he concentrated on breathing and looked directly into Luke's shining eyes. Without thinking, Jonathan pulled Luke's face closer and pressed their lips firmly together.

Leaning into the kiss, Luke slowly lowered Jonathan onto his back and lay beside him. The press of Luke's body against his sent ripples of electricity through Jonathan. This was the moment he'd been waiting for his whole life, and it was with Luke *freaking* Martin! Their tongues chased each other back and forth between their mouths in an endless pursuit that Jonathan very much felt like he was winning.

Pulling away briefly, Luke propped himself up on his elbows, his eyes locked on Jonathan's. "Is this okay?"

Jonathan was so surprised by the question, he could do little more than fervently nod as he reached for Luke again. Luke switched positions, leaning over Jonathan rather than lying next to him, and kissed a trail along Jonathan's chin to his neck, where he alternated between light kissing, biting, and the tiniest bit of suction.

"Luke Martin, I swear to god, if you give me a hickey—"

Luke laughed into Jonathan's neck, causing Jonathan to squirm. But he didn't stop what he was doing, and Jonathan didn't care enough to push him away.

They continued kissing until Luke finally lifted himself off Jonathan, whose lips felt slightly bruised from the force of their kissing. They were both once again breathless, but this time for a very different reason.

"I stand corrected," Luke said, taking a few deep breaths. "Maybe you can take a compliment."

Twenty-Seven

Jonathan and Luke spent the next hour lying on Jonathan's bed, talking as if nothing unusual had happened. They didn't kiss again, though Jonathan desperately wanted to, but he was still reeling from the first one.

I kissed Luke. I grabbed Luke's face and just kissed him. I didn't even think about it—just acted on instinct.

"I'd better get going," Luke said eventually. "I still have practice, and if we're late, Coach makes us run laps around the outfield." Climbing to his feet, Luke held out a hand to help Jonathan up.

"Running? On purpose?" Jonathan laughed. "That sounds terrible. Count me out."

"It's not the highlight of practice, but getting to kiss you would make it worth the extra laps." Luke's eyes dropped to Jonathan's lips.

Heat crawled up Jonathan's neck and face. "I guess I'd better make it worth your time, then."

Taking Luke's outstretched hand, Jonathan pulled

himself to his feet and pressed his body into Luke's. Neither of them moved as they stared into each other's eyes.

Just as Luke closed his eyes and wrapped his arms around Jonathan's back, his cell phone rang, and Jonathan pulled away. Grabbing his phone, Luke silenced it without checking to see who was calling, but he did catch sight of the time and groaned. Jonathan's stomach sank.

"I'm sorry to do this," Luke said, backing toward the bedroom door. "It's later than I realized, and I really do need to go now."

"Of course, no worries," Jonathan said numbly. "I'll walk you out." He led Luke to the front door and walked with him to the end of the driveway. "I hope you have a good practice," he offered weakly.

"Thanks," Luke replied in a similar tone. "Sorry again about this." Turning, he ran down the street toward the school.

Dejected, Jonathan went back inside, plopped down on the couch, and aimlessly scrolled through options on the TV. Eventually, he selected a random episode of *The Great British Baking Show*, primarily for background noise while he replayed everything that had happened with Luke, starting with the kiss and how it had felt. When he remembered what Luke had been doing to his neck, he ran to the bathroom to check for marks. Fortunately, he was hickey-free and surprisingly disappointed that he had no physical proof of what had transpired that afternoon.

He wondered how it had affected Luke. How was he feeling after their kiss? According to him, it wasn't his first same-sex kiss, but had the first one felt the way this one had? How could anyone question their feelings after something like that? Jonathan also thought about the rest of the afternoon. What they had talked about, how it had felt having Luke in his bedroom with him, and how empty the house felt now that he was gone. Had he always felt this way and never realized it before, or was he somehow missing someone who had left minutes ago?

As if in reply, Jonathan's stomach rumbled, and he realized he'd never eaten lunch since he'd gotten distracted by Luke, and now he was starving. Getting up, he went to the kitchen and browsed the contents of the refrigerator and freezer. Nothing looked appetizing, so he turned to the pantry and grabbed some chips and a loaf of bread.

Opening the refrigerator again, he pulled out mayonnaise, mustard, cheese, turkey, and a can of Coke, before closing the door again and getting to work. Once satisfied with the sandwich he'd made, he smashed it down, breaking up the chips. He then carried the finished product back to the couch, where he watched contestants struggle to make intricate bread towers.

The show helped take his mind off what had happened a little. However, when it showed one of the contestants at home baking for his husband and their kids, Jonathan was right back where he'd started, imagining what his future would look like and if he would ever be able to share something like this with his future husband.

When the episode ended, Jonathan decided he'd done enough lying about. He sent a message to Billy, asking what his availability might be for getting together later that afternoon. A few minutes later, he got a reply.

Billy: *Hey, I'll be free in a little while, but I can't make it out to see you today, if that's what you were hoping for. I told one of the guys he could use my car, so I'm stuck close to home for the rest of the day.*

Jonathan: If I could somehow figure out a ride, could I come see you?

Billy: Yeah, for sure!

Jonathan: Okay, let me work on that, and I'll get back to you in a bit.

Billy: Sounds good. Just keep me posted.

Jonathan had no idea how to make that work, but he had to at least try. His mom was at work until later that evening, so she was out. Destiny's mom was also working, which left only one person who might be able to give him a ride if they weren't already busy.

Jonathan: Hey, would you be willing to drive me to see Billy later?

Chance: Maybe. What time are you thinking?

Jonathan: I dunno, soonish?

Chance: Yeah, that should work. I have stuff tonight, but I'm free until 5:30.

Jonathan: Perfect, I'm ready whenever you are.

Chance: Okay, I'll head over in a bit.

Jonathan texted Billy back to get the address and let him know he should be there within an hour.

"So, where are we headed?" Chance asked.

Jonathan smiled. "Dunlap. Just go like you're heading to Peoria, and I'll give you directions along the way."

Chance nodded and took off down the road, heading toward the highway. "And what are we going to do once we get to Dunlap?"

"*We* aren't going to do anything. *I* am going to try to

figure out what the heck I'm going to do about the dance," Jonathan said, his legs nervously bouncing.

"Still don't know what to do, huh?" Chance asked, eyes on the road. Jonathan just shook his head. "I say you just say yes to everyone and see what happens at the end of the night. Maybe all three of you could—"

"Ew! No!" Jonathan objected quickly. "I'm not trying to have a three-way in high school, okay? With my luck, they would probably be more into each other than me, and I'd get squeezed out of the whole situation completely while they left together."

Chance laughed but quickly smothered the sound before Jonathan got too upset. "You worry too much. That would not happen to you. You're a tall, blond, blue-eyed, all-American-looking good guy. People like that. Maybe not everybody, but many people do."

"I don't even like that," Jonathan offered, finally joining Chance in making light of his distress.

"Yeah, but you've proven that you have bad taste, so you can't always trust yourself. You haven't once tried to get in my pants, and I'm literally a Greek god." Chance winked.

"And so humble as well," Jonathan replied with a laugh.

Chance laughed, too, and changed the subject. "So, what's your plan when we get there?"

"I'm not sure yet. I'm just going to wing it, I guess . . ." He didn't sound confident even to himself, but he hadn't had time to make a real plan. He was just going on instinct for now.

"That is perhaps the best thing I have heard you say during this whole mess!" Chance slapped his hand onto

Jonathan's leg and squeezed. Jonathan's leg twitched, and he jumped in his seat.

Laughing, Jonathan swatted Chance's hand away. "Cut it out! You're gonna make me kick a hole through the floorboard!"

"I doubt it, though you're putting in the work all on your own over there," Chance said, indicating Jonathan's nervous bouncing.

Jonathan stared out the windshield, concentrating on the road in front of them. "I can't help it. I'm trying not to talk myself out of this plan altogether."

Cranking up the music, Chance started singing along as loudly and poorly as possible, until Jonathan couldn't ignore him anymore and finally joined in. The two of them sang and laughed together for the rest of the drive.

They were a few minutes away from the apartment complex when Jonathan sent Billy a text message to let him know they would be there soon. Billy let him know he would meet them so they wouldn't have to try to find their way. A few minutes later, he did just that, and Jonathan and Chance followed him into the building. He led them up a flight of stairs to the second floor and then down the hallway a bit before stopping at the door with a colorful doormat that read, *No, I can't turn the music down.*

"This is it." Billy opened the door and stepped inside to hold it open for the other two. "Come on in."

The apartment was small but surprisingly clean for a couple of guys in their late teens. The kitchen was off to the right of the door, and there was a collection of water bottles on top of the refrigerator. Straight ahead was the living room, where a giant beanbag and small loveseat surrounded what appeared to be a welcome mat on top of two ice chests—a makeshift coffee table. A TV remote and a lit candle sat on top. There was a door to the left and a small hallway to the right with another door, which Jonathan assumed were the two bedrooms.

While Jonathan took the place in, Chance walked inside, took off his shoes, and sat on the giant beanbag, making himself comfortable. "Do you have anything to drink?" Stretching out, he put his arms behind his head.

"Oh, sure. Do you want some water?" Billy walked into the kitchen and opened a cabinet door.

"Sure," Jonathan and Chance said together.

Nodding, Billy went to work filling glasses with water before handing them to his guests.

"You two have fun." Chance pulled some headphones from his jacket pocket. "I'm just going to hang out here. Don't mind me."

"Sorry about him," Jonathan said, gesturing to the now-singing Chance.

"That's okay." Billy took Jonathan's hand. "He got us the gig at your school. Letting him hang out here is the least I can do."

He pulled Jonathan toward the door on the right next to the kitchen and opened it. Following Billy in, Jonathan glanced back at Chance, who was still singing but watched the two of them closely. Before Jonathan closed the door completely, Chance winked.

The only piece of furniture in Billy's bedroom was a bed, which stood in one corner of the room. The rest of the room was unfurnished, leaving space for amps, his guitar, and other equipment no doubt used by the band.

Sitting down on the bed, Billy patted the space beside him invitingly. "Not that I'm unhappy to see you, but what brought you all the way out here?"

Jonathan took the few steps required to get to the bed

and sat down next to Billy. "I just wanted to see you before classes started again."

Taking Jonathan's hand, Billy intertwined their fingers, and Jonathan felt like he would melt. Slowly, Billy leaned closer, eyes locked on Jonathan's. Jonathan could feel the heat of their mingled breath on his face, and he closed his eyes.

Closing the remaining distance between them, Billy kissed Jonathan softly on the lips. "I'm glad you did."

Twenty-Eight

The kiss only lasted a few seconds, but Jonathan's palms grew sweaty as his pulse raced. It ended almost as quickly as it had begun, and he felt like he was falling forward from lack of balance. Reaching out, he put his hand on the bed to steady himself and looked up into Billy's eyes, which watched him carefully.

"How was that?" Billy asked.

"It was . . . nice—I mean, great—I mean, I enjoyed it."

Billy laughed softly. "I'll take your rambling half-answer as a compliment," he teased gently. "I'm sorry if that was unexpected. I've wanted to do that since the party, but I was never sure how you felt or if you were ready for something like that. But having you here, in my room, on my bed, well . . . I couldn't help myself."

Jonathan's head spun upon hearing that Billy wished they had kissed earlier. "I've been wishing you would kiss me since the party, but I'd never kissed another guy before, so I didn't know what to do."

Billy's lips spread wide. "That was your first kiss with a guy?"

Jonathan started to say yes but then realized it wasn't. "Mm-hmm," he said instead, unable to form the lie but also unwilling to admit he'd kissed someone else since the last time they'd seen each other.

"No wonder you don't know what to say." Billy chuckled. "The first time I kissed a guy was at the end of our first date. He asked if he could kiss me, and I said yes. I couldn't feel my face afterward. I ended up calling a friend and yelling into the phone for five minutes as I drove away. I'm impressed you kept any semblance of composure."

"That must have been some kiss."

"Honestly, I don't even think it was that great. It was just the first time a guy had kissed me. Needless to say, I liked it." He leaned forward but didn't try to kiss Jonathan again. "How do you feel?"

"I feel like I'm floating, sort of, but also falling. Disoriented, but in a good way." Jonathan laughed, and Billy joined in as he leaned away again.

"I like that!" Billy said and then pulled Jonathan farther onto his bed.

Jonathan froze up, unsure what Billy was planning, but he relaxed when Billy just pulled off his shoes and told Jonathan to get comfortable before lying back and patting his chest. Kicking off his boots, Jonathan cuddled up to Billy, who wrapped an arm around his shoulder.

"As much as I'd like to believe a first kiss was worth the drive out here, I'm guessing you came for some other reason," Billy said once they'd lain there for a few minutes. He'd started playing music on his phone, but it was soft and faded into the background.

Trying to laugh away his discomfort, Jonathan buried

his face in Billy's side for a moment. "I was hoping to talk about the dance a little bit."

"What about it?" Billy's hand drew slow circles on Jonathan's back.

"Well, I know you'll be busy playing most of the night, of course, and I'm super excited to see you play. I mean, obviously. But I was wondering if—when you weren't playing, I mean—you might dance with me?" Jonathan said the last part so softly, he wasn't sure it was even audible over the soft music. He waited for a response, hoping he wouldn't have to repeat himself.

"Jonathan," Billy began, "you know I like you, and I like hanging out with you and everything, and this is amazing." He gestured with his free hand to indicate the two of them. "But I don't think I can do that."

Jonathan's stomach tightened; it felt like he'd been hit in the diaphragm, but he tried to speak around the pain. "I know you said the band is trying to make moves right now, but I just thought that . . . maybe we could . . . I dunno, that one dance wouldn't be that big of a deal?" His voice caught in his throat, but he was determined not to cry, especially not where Billy could see.

"I'm sorry if you feel like I led you on, but this is important to me. Music is important to me."

"I know it is; I just thought—especially now that we've kissed and you told me you'd wanted to do that for a while—that you might be willing to try it." Jonathan's forehead prickled with sweat despite the room's coolness.

"Jonathan, I'm not sure what to tell you." Billy pulled away so he could look Jonathan in the eye. "I like you, and it was a nice kiss, but this is my potential career. I can't throw it away before I've given it a chance to begin. I hope you can understand that."

Jonathan just nodded because there was nothing else he could say. "I understand." He wiped his forehead and sat up, scooting to the edge of Billy's bed. There, he reached down and began putting on his boots.

Billy sat up and followed Jonathan's lead, putting his shoes back on. Standing, he waited for Jonathan to finish and then led him out of the room.

Jonathan followed Billy with his head down, so he didn't notice when Billy stopped short upon exiting the room. When he ran into Billy's back, Jonathan looked up to find Chance on the loveseat, making out with Alonzo, the Tacos' bass guitarist.

"You've got to be shitting me right now!" Confusion, hurt, and anger made Jonathan's voice much louder than he intended.

Startled, Alonzo jumped back, away from Chance, and turned to face them. Lifting a hand, he began scrubbing his mouth guiltily.

Sitting up more slowly, Chance smoothed his shirt down a little with fake modesty. "So, how did it go?" Looking past Billy, he met Jonathan gaze. "Oh, not well, I see." Grabbing his keys, he turned to the bassist. "Alonzo, always a pleasure to see you, but I think we have to go now."

Chance stood up and walked toward the door, and Billy started walking again. Jonathan followed behind him silently, refusing to look at anyone.

"I'll be right back," Billy said to his roommate before following Chance and Jonathan out into the hallway.

The three of them walked silently to the staircase and descended it quickly before heading toward the door to the parking lot where Chance's car was waiting.

"I'm sorry about this, Jonathan," Billy said as they stepped out into the late-afternoon sun.

"Everything's fine, don't worry about it." Jonathan refused to turn and look at Billy, afraid his emotions would overwhelm him if he did. "It's my fault for thinking something might happen between us. You were very clear that your music was all that mattered." Before Billy could respond, Jonathan stepped off the sidewalk and into the parking lot, Chance following close behind.

"Jonathan." Before he could open the car door, Billy touched him gently on the shoulder. Jonathan glanced back at him. "I'm sorry to have to ask this, but can you please not tell anyone about us? I can't afford for people to know I'm gay, not when we're so close to a big break." His eyes were pleading, and his lips pressed together so tightly, they practically disappeared.

The hope that had flared within Jonathan's chest when Billy touched him—that he might apologize or beg for a second chance—extinguished. He laughed humorlessly. "You don't have to worry about that with me. I'm not going to out you. I would never do that."

Refusing to let Billy know how much he was hurting, Jonathan turned away and bit the insides of his cheeks to keep from crying.

"Thank you!" Billy said, clearly relieved, as Jonathan climbed into Chance's car. "Text me later if you want to."

Jonathan closed the door without responding. Fixing his gaze straight ahead on some distant point, he said to Chance, "Can we please get out of here?"

"You got it."

As Chance turned on the car and pulled out of the apartment complex, Jonathan gave in to the pain, and fat tears rolled silently down his face.

The drive home was quiet, only the music breaking the silence. Jonathan refused to speak, and Chance didn't try to lighten the mood with his terrible singing. Instead, he followed the random paths that opened for him to get back to Eureka as quickly as possible.

Only after he had turned onto Main Street did Chance finally speak up again.

"Are you going to be okay?"

Jonathan released a short, humorless laugh. "Oh yes, I'll be fine. I love getting told I'm not as important as a potential career. Rejection is my favorite thing!"

Chance scrunched up his nose as he tried to absorb the anger and embarrassment coming from Jonathan. "Is that something multiple people have told you?"

Jonathan looked like he was going to respond, but he hesitated. Then he laughed, this time with some humor. "Well, no, this was the first. But in movies, people are always giving up their big-city jobs for their small-town love. I guess I assumed that would happen to me as well."

Jonathan covered his face with his hands and laughed, tears once again streaming down his face. Chance could feel that his emotions were all over the place, something he had never been able to sense before.

"Why am I so stupid?"

"What do you mean? You're not stupid!" Chance replied honestly. "You're emotional, you can occasionally be crazy, and you refuse to take my advice, which is sometimes really good . . . but none of those things make you stupid." Reaching over, he grabbed Jonathan's hand and gave it a squeeze—partially to provide comfort and partially to see if the physical connection would allow him to alter Jonathan's feelings.

It didn't.

Jonathan wiped away the last of his tears as they pulled up to his house. "Thank you for saying that. I appreciate it."

Chance parked his car and turned toward Jonathan, who made no move to get out. "I know it may take a little time, but are you going to be okay?"

"Eventually, yes. But I'm honestly not sure how I'm going to get there." He gave Chance a sad smile and leaned over to hug him. Pulling back, he opened the door. "I'll see you later." He climbed out.

"See you later," Chance said with a slight wave as Jonathan closed the door behind him and walked up the driveway to his front door.

Once he was safely inside, Chance pulled away from the curb and headed home, but not before sending Destiny a text to let her know what had happened. Even if it meant he might lose the bet, he wanted to ensure that Jonathan was okay.

The bit about his powers increasing he kept to himself. No reason to give away everything.

Twenty-Nine

The rest of spring break passed by quickly. Well, for some people. For Jonathan, it was a mixture of sleeping as much as possible and only getting out of bed to use the bathroom or eat the occasional meal that his mother refused to let him skip. He ignored Destiny, Chance, and Billy whenever they called or sent him messages. Luke sent a message on Friday night inviting Jonathan to hang out with him and some friends, but Jonathan lied and said he and his mom had taken a last-minute trip out of town and they wouldn't return until Monday. Destiny stopped by on Friday and Saturday, but Jonathan's mother told her he wasn't feeling well and that he didn't want any visitors, so she didn't try again until Monday morning.

When Jonathan walked outside on Monday morning to head to school, he had already decided he would get down the street a little way before texting Destiny that he was running ahead of schedule and was going to get a head start on the walk. But after locking the door, he turned around to find her standing at the end of his driveway, ready to go and holding a pink-topped concha in her extended hand.

Once he'd turned around, she extended the Mexican pastry further. "Peace offering."

He walked toward her, took the pastry, and hugged her. "You know you didn't have to get me anything. I'm not mad at you."

"I know, but clearly you're not having a great time of things. A little sugar and dough never made any problem I've ever had worse, so I figured it couldn't hurt." She looped her free arm through his, and they walked in companionable silence, eating their breakfast pastries.

"I have to see Chance today," Jonathan said quietly.

"Did he do something to you I don't know about?" Destiny asked, her voice rough.

"No, he's fine. He didn't do anything wrong. I'm just embarrassed that he was there for my—" Jonathan stopped, realizing he hadn't told Destiny what had happened yet.

"It's okay. Chance told me what happened with Billy," Destiny said, sparing him from recounting the incident. "But it would be just like him to leave something out," she added before focusing on Jonathan again. "So Billy's not going to share that dream dance with you at prom that you were hoping for?"

"I know I was stupid to get my hopes up, but he was being so sweet. And he told me he wanted to kiss me at the party, so I just assumed he didn't because we didn't have a moment for that to happen. I hadn't realized the actual reason was that he never plans to be out publicly as gay!" Even as he ranted, Jonathan was careful to keep his voice down, as other students were walking to school around them. "I feel so stupid for putting myself out there for someone who never planned to publicly reciprocate those feelings."

When he finally stopped speaking long enough for Destiny to respond, she unlinked her arm from Jonathan's and pulled him around to face her. "Listen to me, you put yourself out there and asked for what you wanted. That's brave, not stupid. His inability or unwillingness to give you what you asked for has nothing to do with you, and I'm certain, in this case, also has nothing to do with his lack of interest in you. He likes you. That much is clear."

Having gotten her point across, she looped her arm back through Jonathan's, and they continued their walk to school.

"Then why do I feel the way I do?" Jonathan asked genuinely.

"Oh, that *is* because you're being stupid."

Jonathan snapped his head around and gaped at her.

She broke, quickly apologizing, even as she laughed. "I'm sorry, I'm just kidding . . . it was just too easy. You feel the way you do because you're an emotional person who feels things deeply, but even this feeling will pass." Eyes darting to the corner they were quickly approaching, she grinned knowingly. "I also recall that Billy wasn't your only option for prom, and you still haven't told me what you plan to do with Luke."

When they turned the corner, Jonathan's eyes locked on Luke, who stood off in the distance with a few of his friends. He noticed Jonathan as well, though his attention drifted back to his group of friends before too long.

"Yeah." Jonathan sighed. "I'm not sure what to do about that. Admittedly, I don't want to go with his friends, even if he is the reason I'd be going. I don't want my memory of prom to be hanging out quietly on the sidelines of some big group of people I barely know because a guy I like asked me to."

In the past, he and Destiny would have crossed the street to avoid the group of jocks, but today, Destiny held Jonathan on their current course. Once they were close enough that the guys with Luke noticed them, Jonathan braced for the inevitable teasing.

To his surprise, they didn't say anything, and a couple of them even moved aside so Jonathan and Destiny could pass comfortably on the sidewalk. Jonathan couldn't be entirely sure, but it also felt like Luke might have reached out his hand and run it across Jonathan's arm and backpack as he passed. Jonathan didn't turn around to look back, but when his cell phone notification went off a few minutes later, he knew who it would be from before checking.

Luke: *GM, you look really good in that shirt.*

When he and Destiny walked through the front doors at school, he felt like all eyes were on him, as if everyone knew what had happened with him and Billy. He did his best to ignore the looks, but he soon realized it was just his imagination, as someone ran into him because they didn't see him.

He managed to avoid Chance until first period. He was waiting outside the classroom, and he followed Jonathan in. He took the desk immediately to Jonathan's right, forcing the kid who normally sat there to switch to Jonathan's left, where Chance usually sat.

"You can't avoid me forever," Chance said after a long moment of him staring at Jonathan and Jonathan refusing to look at him.

"I'm not avoiding you," Jonathan responded shortly. "I'm choosing not to look at you at the moment."

At that point, Luke walked in and looked at Jonathan briefly on his way to his seat.

Chance left Jonathan alone until class began and Jonathan still refused to look at him. "You didn't respond to me all weekend, and now you're facing away from Ms. Halpern, which you never do."

Jonathan had sat with his body turned to the left to avoid looking at Chance, but that also meant he was turned away from their teacher. Not wanting to be called out by Ms. Halpern, he finally turned in his chair to face her, but he continued to ignore Chance until the bell rang for the end of the period.

"I wasn't avoiding you," he finally said to Chance as they left the classroom. "I was avoiding everyone. You just happened to be included in that. But so was Destiny, so don't take it too personally."

Chance laughed. "I've already told you, I don't take anything personally. But I'm glad you're talking to me again; I have some news about Billy and the Tacos."

Luke walked by just as Chance mentioned Billy, and Jonathan turned on his heel to glare at Chance. Moving closer to avoid being overheard in the crowded hallway, he said, "I don't want to know anything about Billy, okay? Unless some tragic event happened for which I should mourn, I don't want to hear about him or the rest of the band."

"It's just that—"

"Chance! I'm serious. I'm not in the mood to hear anything that has to do with them right now. I'm sure whatever you have to share is great, and I'm sure you think the news is important, but please keep it to yourself, for my sake."

Spinning away, Jonathan stalked off down the hall alone.

Destiny was waiting for Jonathan at his locker. "Hey, how was English?"

Jonathan spun the dial on his lock, and once he had it open, he turned to her and blew a raspberry with his tongue out.

"That bad, huh?" She leaned against her locker while he switched out his books.

"Chance was bugging me and then tried to tell me something about Billy, but I told him I didn't want to know. I just need to get through the rest of this week, and then everything will be fine. Once all this prom stuff is over, I'm hoping we can just return to how things used to be." He shut his locker with a little more force than he intended, but the sound was swallowed immediately by the noise of the hallway.

"I'll talk to him and tell him you want to be left alone." She smiled wickedly. "He knows if he messes with you, he's gotta answer to me."

Laughing, Jonathan felt better than he had all morning, which was good since the next time he saw Chance would be in math, at which point the week without Mr. Davies would also come to an unfortunate end.

He and Destiny talked the rest of the way to second period, and his mood continued to improve. When he walked into math an hour later, he learned that Mr. Davies had actually gone home sick an hour into the day. How fortuitous!

Jonathan's day improved further at lunch when he received an unexpected treat in the form of the last of a batch of cookies donated by the PTA. Destiny suspected his sudden windfall had more to do with Chance than luck, but she let it slide since it lifted Jonathan's mood. She did note that his ability to change things that impacted Jonathan had improved, so maybe they both were keeping secrets regarding their growing powers.

By the time chemistry started, Jonathan was downright happy again. Unfortunately, as they walked into class, Destiny noticed something was off. Paths she had seen earlier in the day had been altered, and the lab group that should have included Luke, her, and Jonathan now included two girls on the cheer team instead. Luke was across the room with a different lab group, but he kept glancing at them. Destiny was now certain that Chance had altered too many things to make Jonathan's day better; as a result, other events had shifted to bring things back in balance.

Halfway through class, the two girls started talking about prom. Jonathan tensed, but he remained focused on the lab, and his mood didn't darken.

That changed, however, when one of them mentioned that she intended to go to prom with Luke. Jonathan's hand slipped, cracking the prepared microscope slide he'd been trying to bring into focus. The two girls didn't notice the mistake, having decided not to participate in the lab other than writing down what Destiny wrote on her paper. But Destiny knew Jonathan wouldn't be able to finish his work, and at this rate, he'd barely make it through the rest of class.

"Mrs. Saunders, we've had an accident at our station," Destiny sputtered. "Jonathan needs to go to the restroom to clean himself up."

Meeting her gaze, Jonathan mouthed, *Thank you,* before standing up and slipping out of the room. Luke stood up to follow him, but she caught his eye and shook her head until he sat back down.

As expected, Jonathan didn't return to class, so Destiny gathered up his stuff and met him in the hall afterward.

"I'm sorry you had to hear that," she said. "If it helps at all, they kept talking after you left, and she admitted he hadn't asked her."

"You know what? I don't care if he asks her. I'm fine. Luke can go with whomever he wants, and they can spend the night dancing to the Telepathic Tacos and doing whatever the hell they want to do. It won't matter to me because I'm not going." His anger carried him through the crowd of students.

"I don't think that's the answer," Destiny interjected as Chance joined them. She cast him a look so ferocious, he kept his mouth shut and just walked with them.

"Sorry to be rude, but I don't care what you think," Jonathan snapped. "I can't do it anymore. I feel dumb for getting so worked up over one stupid dance that I didn't care about a few weeks ago. You two should go, though. Please don't let me stop you. I just don't think I can do it, and frankly, I don't want to try."

"What about Luke?" Destiny asked. "He didn't ask her to the dance. He asked you."

"He asked me to go with him and his friends," Jonathan replied. "That's not exactly the kind of invitation I was looking for. Anyway, he'll be fine. He probably did it to be nice." She knew he didn't truly believe that, but he wasn't giving himself time to think about it. "I'd better get to class. I'll see you guys later." Turning, he walked away.

"Okay, what did I miss?" Chance asked.

Destiny spun around and jammed her finger into his chest. "You never know when to quit, do you?"

"Ouch! What did I do?"

"What did you do? What did you do? Why don't you tell me what you did?" Her voice was quiet and fierce, and her eyes had no doubt begun to glow.

"Okay, fine! I may have manipulated a few things into going his way so he wouldn't be so upset."

"And in doing so, you changed things for the worse. Luke was going to sit with us in chemistry and eventually get around to asking Jonathan about prom again! But you can't stand to lose, so you messed everything up, and then we had to sit with Bianca and Vivienne, and Bianca said she was hoping to go with Luke, which set Jonathan off. Now he's not going to the dance at all, and it's all. Your. Fault!" She slapped his arm with each of the last three words to punctuate them.

He crossed his arms. "How do you even know Jonathan would have said yes?"

"I don't. But thanks to you and your influence, things had to balance themselves out, and Luke didn't get his moment with Jonathan."

"Shit." Chance rubbed his forehead with his thumb and forefinger. "What can we do?"

" *We* are not going to do anything, okay? You're done. I'm going to see what I can do to fix this, and you're going to stay out of the way, or so help me, I will make you wish you were never reborn!" With that, Destiny walked away, leaving Chance on his own in the rapidly clearing hallway.

$\mathcal{J}$onathan successfully avoided all conversations about prom for the next few days, and Destiny and Chance didn't bring it up, which he appreciated. But he couldn't avoid the daily announcements about tickets or the signs in the hallways with the theme and colors posted all over the school. As the week went on, he became increasingly withdrawn until finally, on Thursday, when he'd somehow gone the entire day without speaking, Luke tracked him down after seventh period.

He was so shocked that Luke was speaking to him at school in plain view of everyone that it took him thirty seconds to realize Luke had asked him a question. "I'm sorry, I missed what you said."

"I asked if you were planning to come to the game tomorrow."

"Oh, um, I had honestly forgotten about it. What time did you say it was?" Jonathan looked around for Destiny or Chance to provide an excuse to decline politely, but they were nowhere in sight.

"It starts at four thirty and usually lasts a couple of hours. I'd really like it if you could come." Reaching out, he put a hand on Jonathan's shoulder and gently squeezed. When one of the other players walked up, Luke dropped his hand but didn't step away from Jonathan.

"Hey, Martin, do you have that extra glove you said I could borrow for practice?" He looked back and forth between Jonathan and Luke but didn't comment on how close they were standing.

"I've gotta get going," Jonathan said quickly, using Luke's teammate as a distraction.

"What about the game?" Luke asked again, taking a step to follow him.

"I'll try," Jonathan called back without stopping.

"Hope to see you there!" Luke called after him, before turning and walking toward the locker room with his teammate.

Jonathan moved as quickly as possible toward the school's side doors, where he and Destiny typically met after school. When he got there, she was already waiting, and so was Chance. The two of them had their heads together and seemed to be talking about something serious, but when they saw Jonathan approaching, they backed away from each other and waited for him to join them.

Jonathan eyed them suspiciously. "What's going on?"

"Chance was telling me that he heard there was a baseball game tomorrow, and we were just talking about going since he's never been," Destiny said with an expression that betrayed nothing.

"I don't want to go," Jonathan replied flatly. "Besides, we've never seen a single baseball game or any other sporting event. Ever. Why start now?" He crossed his arms and eyed them, but neither squirmed under his scrutiny.

"That's my point. We've never been to a high-school sporting event. We should change that! Plus, hello, boys in baseball pants. What's not to love?" Destiny said slyly, nearly eliciting a laugh from Jonathan, but he managed to hang on to his serious expression until Chance chimed in.

"If you wanted to see someone in tight pants, that's all you had to say." To Jonathan and Destiny's shock and horror, he unbuttoned his jeans and pulled them down. Their shock and horror was quickly replaced by peals of laughter when they realized he was wearing tight stretch pants underneath the jeans.

"What are you wearing?" Jonathan asked when he finally caught his breath.

"Yoga pants," he replied, as if that explained everything. "What? They make my butt look good."

"Please, pull your pants up." When Chance pulled at the waistband of the yoga pants, Destiny hurried to correct herself. "Pull up the jeans."

Chance did as requested, but not before making a big show of turning away from them and bending over to give them a clear view of his assets. Jonathan looked away, but to his surprise, Destiny did not. Though she didn't look impressed.

After dropping Jonathan off at home, Destiny and Chance spent the next two hours talking through their plan for the weekend and how to make sure things went the way they intended. Once satisfied that they had accounted for everything that could happen in response to the amount of influence and change they were about to exert, they finally called it a night, and Chance went home.

The next school day went by quickly, as most teachers

realized the juniors and seniors would be impossible to handle with the dance the next day. Fortunately for Destiny, Jonathan was in a better mood than he had been all week and didn't seem to mind the prom talk taking place in every class that day. He smiled politely, nodded, or shook his head at appropriate times, but she could tell he was otherwise distracted. While she noticed the change, she decided not to say anything in case mentioning it ruined whatever magic was keeping him happy. She did talk to Chance early in the day to make sure he wasn't doing something, but he swore it wasn't him, so she let it go.

By the time the final bell rang, Destiny had met Jonathan early and kept him so distracted that when Luke stepped in front of him on his way out the door wearing his uniform, she could tell he'd completely forgotten about the game.

"Are you going to come watch me play this afternoon?" Luke asked, his left thumb hooked in the waistband of his pants.

"The game!" Jonathan's eyes grew wide. "Um, I'm not sure if I—"

His text message tone interrupted him, and he pulled his phone out of his pocket. With a glance, Destiny saw that the text was from his mom, letting him know she was staying late at work and that he'd be on his own for dinner.

When he looked up from his phone, Luke's eyes had dropped a little, and his bottom lip jutted out in a tiny pout.

"Yeah, I can make it."

Luke's eyes lit up. "You can? That's awesome! The game is at four thirty on the baseball field." When Jonathan didn't reply, he added, "The baseball field is behind the—"

"I know where the baseball field is!" Jonathan said

with enough faux attitude that Luke stopped talking and laughed.

"Well, you looked like you might be a little confused. I didn't want you to get lost."

"I'm sure we'll be able to find our way there, don't worry." Laughing, Jonathan reached for Luke's arm, but he dropped his arm before he made contact, his eyes darting toward the other students still in the area.

Luke's grin faltered a little, but he nodded. "I hope you enjoy the game. I'll look for you when it starts." Slowly backing toward the school, he eventually walked inside.

"What was that all about?" Chance asked as he joined them.

"He asked me to go to the game again, and we said yes," Jonathan replied, his voice betraying his excitement.

"We?" Destiny said, her eyebrows shooting up.

"Yes, I volunteered us all to be there, so *we* will be there."

Chance looked at Destiny, who shook her head but smiled. "That was unexpected," he said. "What time do we have to be there?"

"It starts in two hours," Jonathan said, "so we have time to—"

"Go make signs?" Destiny offered.

"Ooh, yes, we should make signs!" Chance grabbed Jonathan's hand, and they led him toward Chance's car. "What number is he?"

"I have no idea," Jonathan admitted. "Fourteen?"

Destiny knew it was a complete guess, but it felt right.

"That's okay. I'm not looking at his number when his back is to me either," Chance teased.

"Shut up!" Jonathan said with a laugh, his face taking on a pink hue.

"Mm-hmm," Destiny agreed. "Let's go get something to eat before the game. I'm not paying for melted cheese from a pump."

Neither Chance nor Jonathan disagreed, so they all piled into Chance's car and drove to Manny's for the sampler platter. When Chance ate more than half of it on his own and ordered a second one, Destiny shook her head. "You really are an unending pit where food just disappears, aren't you?"

Chance waggled his eyebrows. "I'm just showing you what this mouth can do."

"Unhinge at the jaw and swallow food whole?" Jonathan offered.

They all laughed. Chance wiped his mouth with a napkin and replied, "Exactly."

Once they'd finished the second platter, they climbed back into Chance's car and drove to a local gas station to get drinks for the game. When they pulled up around four, the team was warming up on the field, and the bus from Heyworth was already in the parking lot. People had slowly begun to arrive, but most of the Eureka High parents had brought lawn chairs or blankets to sit on since the metal bleachers were uncomfortable.

Luke walked out a few minutes later. He didn't seem to notice them at first, but when he glanced up in their direction, he made his way over to the fence behind home plate to talk to them.

"What, no sign?" Luke asked when Jonathan met him at the fence.

Jonathan's mouth dropped open in surprise, and Destiny spoke up before he could recover. "I told you we should have made signs!"

Luke held his hands out placatingly. "I'm just messing

with you! That would have been a little too much for this game."

"Show us your number!" Chance called from the stands, having stayed behind to ensure no one took their seats at the top.

Luke looked at Jonathan and Destiny curiously but turned around as requested. "Okay . . ."

"Fourteen!" Chance said with a laugh. "You were right!"

Luke turned back around. "You knew my number?" He reached his fingers through the fence, curling them around the thin wire.

"I guessed," Jonathan admitted. "I just got lucky."

"Not yet," Chance called down. Destiny was surprised he'd even heard Jonathan's response.

When the meaning of his words hit them, they all started laughing.

Luke looked into Jonathan's eyes for a moment before finally backing away from the fence. "I'd better get back to warming up. Coach doesn't like us to get distracted before the game. Come find me after, okay?"

"Yeah, okay," Jonathan agreed, though he seemed disappointed they couldn't keep talking until the game began.

Ten minutes before the game started, the bleachers had finally filled, and the additional parent seating had spread from behind the dugout to halfway back in the outfield on both sides. Heyworth wasn't their primary rival school, but it brought out a lot of support.

Destiny watched Jonathan, who watched Luke warming up with keen interest.

"He looks so strong, doesn't he?" Jonathan asked quietly.

"Definitely strong enough to pin you down," Chance offered.

Destiny hit him in the stomach. "Why are you like this?" she demanded. "Though I do agree; he does look strong, and those pants are definitely working for him." Glancing back at Jonathan, she noticed a flush of pink crawling up his neck and face.

Finally, both teams cleared the field, and the umpires took their positions. Heyworth batted first and managed to score one run before the inning changed over.

Mike started the bottom of the inning with a leadoff double, followed by a base hit from another player and a foul ball caught for the first out. By the time Luke was up, they had scored one run and had two outs.

Luke hit the first pitch, which went foul but fortunately wasn't caught, and then waited while the next two pitches went wide. The fourth pitch was a fastball right down the middle, which Luke connected with, sending the ball soaring into the outfield. Jonathan jumped up with excitement, but the ball was caught by the center fielder, ending the inning.

Sitting back down, Jonathan chuckled a little nervously, ducking his head to hide from the stares that both students and parents from Eureka were throwing his way. "Whoops!"

By the middle of the fourth inning, the teams were tied at two runs each. Mike was batting again and ended up hitting a home run, which caused everyone on the Eureka sidelines except Jonathan, Destiny, and Chance to cheer.

When he made it back to the dugout, Mike reached into a large bag and pulled out a rolled-up piece of poster board, which he unfurled and held up to the fence where his recently on-again girlfriend, Kelly, was sitting. A few seconds later, she stood up, screamed, "YES!" and ran to the fence to kiss him through it. He passed the poster board to someone to give to Kelly so she could have it.

Chance pointed. "Looks like those two are back together again."

When Jonathan looked over, his face dropped. "I'm ready to go now," he said, looking around and gathering up his belongings.

"What? Why? The game isn't over yet," Chance said, his eyes still on the field.

Destiny elbowed him in the ribs, and he read the sign Kelly was holding: *Better late but with a date—PROM?*

"That's not very good at all," Chance said, still not realizing what had happened.

Destiny gestured toward the visibly upset Jonathan before grabbing her drink and standing up. Despite Jonathan's seemingly good mood earlier, Destiny had been careful to avoid talking about the dance the whole day, but the sign seemed to have put Jonathan right back into his negative headspace.

Finally understanding, Chance stood up. They made their way down the side of the bleachers and walked quickly to Chance's car, before climbing inside and driving away. Jonathan didn't say anything for the few minutes it took to drive to his house, and then he just thanked Chance for the ride and told them he would see them on Monday. Climbing out of the car, he went inside.

"What the hell are we going to do now?" Chanced asked.

"I'm honestly not sure," Destiny replied. "I can't figure out why this keeps happening."

 Thirty-One

Saturday morning came and went. Jonathan had shut his phone off the night before and slept well into the day, finally waking up around 11:45 a.m., when his mom checked on him.

"Are you planning to get out of bed at all today?" She took a seat on the edge of his bed and softly ran her hand over his forehead, brushing hair out of his face. "I don't know what happened, and you don't have to tell me, but avoiding the world and your friends all weekend isn't the solution."

Rolling onto his back, he blinked up at her, trying to get his eyes to adjust to the late-morning light streaming through the blinds. "I know, I'm getting up. I just need a minute." He stretched.

She kissed his forehead, then walked out of his bedroom and closed the door behind her, humming as she walked down the hall toward the family room.

Grabbing his phone off the bedside table, he turned it on and headed to the bathroom. Once he'd completed his immediate bathroom needs, he scrolled through his notifications. Chance had sent him a random GIF of hot, shirtless men dancing, along with a message that read, *It us.* He also had a voicemail from Destiny asking him to call her when he was feeling up to talking. She'd sent a text of the same thing with the prayer emoji and another with three hearts.

Surprisingly, he also had a text message from Luke asking what had happened to him during the game. He explained that he had looked up at one point and realized they were gone. He was bummed they hadn't had a chance to talk after the game, but he hoped to see him later tomorrow. Jonathan checked the time of the message and realized Luke was talking about today, which meant he hoped to see Jonathan at the dance.

Jonathan looked at himself in the mirror. His eyes were red, which made his blue irises stand out more than usual, almost scarily so. And he had deep wrinkles on his face from where the pillow had been bunched up under his head. He examined his arms, which looked too skinny to him, but with Luke's previous compliments floating around in his mind, they somehow looked bigger than they had in the past.

His stomach rumbled a little as he realized he hadn't eaten anything since yesterday afternoon, almost twenty-one hours ago. Before doing anything else, though, he decided to take a long shower. He didn't know why, but he spent longer than usual cleaning everything, including exfoliating his face and washing between his toes, which he rarely did. Once he was completely scrubbed, buffed, and polished—or as well as he would be—he turned off the water and grabbed his towel to dry off.

He decided not to do his hair since he wasn't planning

to see anyone for the rest of the weekend, so he threw on some clean clothes and walked to the kitchen to see what was in the refrigerator for lunch. Walking out of the hallway and turning toward the kitchen, he stopped short when he saw Chance and Destiny sitting in the family room with his mother, chatting quietly as they waited for him. When they noticed him, his two friends stood and walked toward him, their hands held out to their sides as if he were some wild animal that might spook and run away at any moment.

"Honey, your friends have been waiting for you for fifteen minutes. They said they want to take you out for the day, and I've already agreed to let them, so why don't you go put on some socks and shoes," his mother suggested, still sitting. "And maybe put on a hat while you're at it." The last bit earned her a laugh from Chance.

Once the three of them were in his room, Jonathan turned and looked at the other two carefully. "What are you doing here?"

"We knew today wasn't going to be a great day for you, so we decided to kidnap you to keep your mind off everything." Destiny rummaged through his dresser for a pair of socks and threw them at him.

"I said we should all play strip twister and see what happens, but Destiny said she wouldn't do it. This was our second option. But I'm sure you could make her if you wanted to . . ."

Jonathan shuddered. "Lady parts? No, thank you!"

Destiny huffed. "It's not like there's a—" Realizing Jonathan had been joking, she picked up a shoe and threw it at him. "Don't flatter yourselves. It's not like I'm dying to see your bits and pieces either!"

Jonathan laughed as he caught the shoe and slipped it on, before grabbing the other one and putting it on. He then looked through his closet until he found an acceptable hat, pulling it on over his mess of hair before turning and facing his friends again. "Okay, I'm ready."

Destiny and Chance grabbed his hands and pulled him down the hallway toward the front door.

"Bye, Mom!" Jonathan called as they walked through it.

"Bye, Mom!" the other two called out in unison immediately after.

His mom laughed. "Bye, kids! Have fun, and don't hurt my baby!"

"No promises." Chance shut the door and hurried Jonathan to the car waiting in the driveway.

"What's first on the list?" Jonathan asked. Before they could reply, he added, "If it isn't food, can we at least make a quick stop so I can eat something? I didn't have dinner last night after the game."

"Food first," Chance said as he backed the car out of the driveway.

"That's practically his motto," Destiny said from the back seat.

Chance laughed. "It wasn't, but it is now! Food first!"

"Food first!" the others responded in tandem.

Chance left the neighborhood, seemingly without any intentional direction, until he finally pulled into Uncle Joe's. "How about this place?" he asked, looking from Jonathan to Destiny.

Jonathan spoke up first. "This is where Billy and I went on our first . . . well, I guess our only real date."

Destiny glared at Chance, who shrugged and said, "We can go somewhere else, then."

"No, I like their food." Jonathan sat forward and put a hand on Chance's arm to stop him from putting the car in reverse. "This is my hometown, damn it! He doesn't get to ruin my favorite restaurants for me just because he doesn't want to be with me!" Jonathan locked eyes with Chance, who put his hands up in surrender.

"Are you sure?" Destiny asked, leaning forward from the back seat.

"Yes, I'm fine," he replied. "Honestly."

Chance pulled into the drive-through line. While they waited, a couple of guys from the baseball team walked past. Fortunately, Luke wasn't one of them, but Jonathan stiffened all the same. That was an altogether different problem that he wasn't going to think about right now.

Once they'd ordered their food and gotten everything, Chance suggested they get out of town and let Destiny give him directions to their next stop. The three ate quietly on the way, mainly because Jonathan was so hungry and the other two seemed unsure about what to say.

Once he had food in his system, Jonathan began to feel better and even turned up the radio to sing along with the music. The other two joined in, and that was how they spent the next fifteen minutes of the trip.

They finally pulled into the small parking lot of a strip mall, and Destiny pointed to the storefront to their left as they made the final turn. "We're getting mani-pedis!" She squeezed Jonathan's shoulders and shook him back and forth a little, before taking off her seat belt and climbing out of the car.

"Why?" Jonathan asked, confused.

She shrugged. "We're having a self-pampering day. Why not?"

"Oh, I am in!" Chance said, heading for the door.

Jonathan smiled and shook his head as his friends coaxed him into giving in to their plans, but once he was in the massage chair with his feet in warm blue water, he could feel the stress he'd been holding on to for the past week melting away.

Two hours later, all three of them had had their feet scrubbed, their toes polished, and their nails trimmed, while Destiny had gotten a full set. They climbed back into Chance's car to head to the next stop. Chance seemed particularly happy with his manicure and black nail polish.

"Food first!" Chance called out once they were on the move.

"Food first!" Jonathan and Destiny responded with a laugh.

Chance pulled into the first fast-food restaurant they encountered, and they each got a drink and a small snack before heading down the road another ten minutes.

"Turn right here!" Destiny said suddenly, surprising Jonathan, but Chance just turned the wheel smoothly as if he'd known it was coming. "Okay, park over there." She pointed to an open space in front of a small white building. "I'll be right back." She hopped out of the car as it stopped and ran to the closest door. She emerged five minutes later with a small white box and climbed back in.

"What did you do?" Jonathan asked once she was back in her seat.

"I wanted to get us a little treat." Leaning forward, she opened the box to reveal delicious-looking cookies in a variety of flavors. Once Jonathan had selected one, Chance grabbed his own and popped it in his mouth.

"Have you ever heard of taking small bites?" Destiny asked with a laugh as she took her own cookie from the box. She handed the box back to Jonathan.

"I have to keep my hands free so I can drive safely," Chance replied, his mouth still full of cookie.

He turned left out of the shopping center to head back toward Eureka. "Sorry to end the fun, but I promised my dad I'd be around for a little bit this afternoon. Maybe I can come over later and we can watch a terrible movie or something."

Jonathan shrugged, having nothing else planned and permission from his mom to do whatever, so when Destiny agreed, he did too. The drive back to Eureka was filled with more terrible singing to the radio and lots of laughter. When Chance pulled up in front of Destiny's and Jonathan's houses, Jonathan had to wipe away a few tears from laughing as hard as he had.

"Let me know when you want to get together, and I'll head over," Destiny said before quickly disappearing into her home.

Jonathan frowned. "That was weird." He turned to Chance, but Chance didn't react.

"She's always seemed weird to me. I've stopped noting specific instances at this point."

Jonathan laughed once more before climbing out of the front seat. "I'll see you later," he said before closing the door. He watched Chance drive off before heading inside and then to his room. Once there, he sent a quick text to Luke.

Jonathan: *Hey, I'm not going to make it to the dance tonight, but I wanted to say that I hope you have a good time!*

Luke: *What? Why not?*

Jonathan: *A lot on my plate. I didn't end up getting tickets or anything, plus I don't want to bring your night down by pulling you away from your friends.*

Luke: *You wouldn't ruin my night! My friends don't own me . . . we could hang out.*

Jonathan: *Sorry, I don't mean to be a downer. Take lots of pics and send me some if you think about it!*

Jonathan watched the three dots appear and disappear multiple times before a photo of Luke sitting on a couch with guys from the team finally came through.

Luke: *We won the game btw.*

Jonathan: *OMG, that's amazing. Congrats! Looking good, btw! But don't tell your friends I said that. I don't want to ruin the chill gay vibe I've worked so hard to cultivate.*

Luke: *You're ridiculous but thank you. And don't worry, your secret and your "vibe" are safe with me.*

Thirty-Two

A few hours later, Jonathan was watching TV on the couch with his mom when there was a knock at the door. He checked his phone to see if he had missed a text from Destiny or Chance, but there was nothing. Getting up, he opened the door to reveal his two friends, looking more beautiful than he'd ever seen them look before.

Destiny's hair was styled in large, soft curls that cascaded around her heart-shaped face and highlighted the golden centers of her irises, which somehow seemed to glow. The effect was enhanced by the golden heart pendant around her neck and the glittering, ruby-red dress she wore. The sleeves were gathered beautifully—as if they had been draped across her chest—and hung effortlessly. The fabric highlighted her wide hips, skimmed her midsection, and flared out in a full skirt below. A high slit on the left gave the dress an even sexier look, especially given the tall heels that glittered as they peeked out from beneath the dress and caught the light.

Chance was also a sight to behold, with his signature

tight curls conspicuously absent, replaced by a freshly buzzed head, which made Jonathan gasp. His deep-brown eyes seemed to glow in the same way Destiny's did, which Jonathan attributed to a trick of the light. His black tuxedo jacket was tailored perfectly, and he looked like he'd been born for this very outfit. The light on his face showed off his high cheekbones; Jonathan automatically touched his own cheeks without realizing it.

"Are you going to stare at us all night?" Chance finally asked with a grin.

"What? Oh! Sorry, come on in." Jonathan stepped back out of the doorway to let them in, unable to look away. "You both look amazing."

Destiny placed a hand gently on Jonathan's arm as she walked by. "Thank you."

"But aren't you a little overdressed for a movie night?" Jonathan asked, refusing to accept the reality of what was right in front of him.

"There's been a change of plans," Chance said carefully. "We're skipping movie night to go to the dance."

Jonathan's face dropped, and it felt like all the oxygen was being sucked out of the room. "Oh, okay. Well, as I said, you look great. I hope you have a nice time."

"No! Oh no! We're not ditching you to go to the dance!" Destiny took a step forward, and Jonathan suddenly noticed the large white shopping bag she carried.

He looked back and forth between them. "I don't understand what's happening, then. I can't go to the dance."

"Can't or don't want to?" Chance asked.

"Well, both, I guess. I don't have a ticket or anything else."

Destiny waved away Jonathan's objections. "Let us worry about that. You go take a shower and get ready."

"But . . ."

"Nope, I don't want to hear it," Chance said. "Go take a shower, or I will throw you over my shoulder and take you myself." Widening his stance, he squatted as if preparing to tackle Jonathan.

"Okay, weird but kinky," Jonathan said. Chance and Destiny laughed. Jonathan turned and headed down the hall. "Fine, but I'm not putting out!"

"Jonathan!" his mother called after him, shocked.

"Sorry, Mom!" he called back.

"Never say never, hon," she replied evenly.

Chance and Destiny cracked up, and Jonathan made retching noises. "I could have lived my whole life without having this conversation," he called from his bedroom.

Once his shower was over and his hair was done, Jonathan opened the bathroom door, releasing a cloud of steam that rolled out into the hallway and preceded him into the bedroom. Chance and Destiny sat on his bed, as did the bag Destiny had been holding earlier.

Destiny grinned slightly. "So, we may have done a little shopping after we dropped you off earlier, but in the grand scheme of things, I think you'll forgive us when you see what we got you." She picked the bag up by the handles and held it out to him. Taking it from her, he was surprised by just how heavy it was.

He set the bag down on his dresser and pulled out a large white box wrapped in a white ribbon. "If you got me a white tux, I cannot promise I won't spill something all over it!" His nerves were extremely high, and his hands shook with excess energy.

"I wouldn't do that to you," she said sincerely. "We've been friends our whole lives; I know how messy you are."

"Yeah, good point." Untying the ribbon and lifting the

box's lid, he revealed a stunning sapphire-blue jacket. He lifted it out of the box, touching it carefully. It had a soft satin notch lapel, which disappeared into the two buttons at the front. The color matched his eyes, and when he looked in the mirror, he realized it made his eyes shine with a light of their own.

Underneath the jacket was a matching vest so soft, it felt like he was touching air. A white button-up shirt with French cuffs was neatly folded under the vest. Slim-cut black tuxedo pants with a thin stripe down the outside of each leg and a black bow tie completed the ensemble.

"Go put them on!" Destiny said, a little teary-eyed.

Before she could do anything else, Jonathan dropped the clothing carefully on the bed, wrapped her in his arms, and squeezed her in a tight hug that had them both gasping for air by the end. When he'd finished hugging Destiny, he moved on to Chance and gave him an equally tight hug, which Chance reciprocated with a tight squeeze of his own. Jonathan felt like he'd be able to face whatever life threw at him as long as these two were by his side.

Destiny wiped away some tears and then waved at Jonathan impatiently. "Well, don't just stand there. Try everything on!"

Jonathan grabbed the tuxedo, walked back into the bathroom, and emerged a few minutes later, fully dressed except for his bow tie, socks, and shoes. The vest fit him perfectly, and the slim cut of the jacket showed off his body in every way that mattered. The pants, which were tapered and ended just above the ankles, made his thighs and butt look amazing and showed just how tall he was.

"I need help with the bow tie," he admitted, holding it up.

Taking it from him, Chance spun Jonathan around

and wrapped his arms around Jonathan's neck to ensure it was situated correctly. Once he was happy with the placement, he turned Jonathan back around to face him and tied the bow tie perfectly on the first try, then pulled the top of his collar down over the back and sides.

"You look amazing," he said sincerely, with no trace of his usual humor. "All the boys will want a piece of you tonight, and even the girls who think they might be able to change you!"

Jonathan laughed loudly. "I don't know about all that. I'll be happy even if the whole night is just the three of us dancing in a corner while everyone else does their own thing."

"Well, I'm not going out looking like this"—Destiny slid her hands down her body—"to hide in a corner."

"And I'm not going out with her looking like that to *not* try getting her into a corner," Chance said with a wicked grin, which earned him a smack on the arm.

"You're so crude sometimes, you know that?" Destiny laughed. "If anything, I'd be the one forcing you into the corner to try to stop you making a fool of yourself in public. You know you'd prefer to show off your exploits."

"You've got me on that one," he admitted. "I do love an audience when I'm doing my thing."

As Jonathan watched them jesting back and forth, he realized they'd gone from practically hating each other to having some sort of weird chemistry without him noticing. He sat back and listened as they continued to joke, fight, and give each other crap, all while laughing and having a good time.

Once he'd slipped his socks on, Jonathan went looking for an appropriate pair of shoes to wear. Behind him, Chance cleared his throat.

"I wasn't sure if you would have shoes for the getup Destiny got you since you didn't know it was coming, so I brought a pair of my dad's shoes for you to try out and see if they might work." He held out a pair of new-looking brown dress boots that Jonathan instantly fell in love with. When he attempted to slip his foot in the left shoe, it fit better than he expected. Once the right shoe was on and he stood up, he realized they were comfortable.

"These are amazing!" Jonathan said, ecstatic. Looking at himself in the mirror, he was pleased with how good he looked. "I could never have done this without you," he admitted before giving them a big hug. "Thank you so much!"

Now that Jonathan was dressed, the three of them made their way to the family room, where his mother was waiting anxiously with her phone in hand, ready to document the moment with photos. When she saw him, her eyes immediately welled up, and she put a hand over her mouth.

"Oh, Jonathan, you look amazing!" Walking forward, she gave him a gentle hug, careful not to wrinkle anything or get makeup on his shirt. "All right, you three, get together so I can take a photo." She held up her phone and waved them toward the door, where the light was best.

Chance and Destiny arranged themselves around Jonathan to ensure he looked as good as possible and then motioned to his mom when they were ready. There were a few false starts as she accidentally slid her camera to video mode and then couldn't get the flash to work correctly, but eventually, she got it to work. When the photos were done, Jonathan hugged her one more time. Then she shooed them out of the house and told them to have fun.

Hurrying to the car, Chance opened the back door for

Destiny, who ducked her head carefully to avoid messing up her hair, before sliding the rest of her body in. Once she was safely inside with the door shut, Chance opened the front door for Jonathan. Jonathan unbuttoned his jacket to make sure it wouldn't wrinkle and sat down, allowing Chance to shut the door for him.

Crossing to the other side of the car, Chance walked as if he were on a catwalk—and in his tux, he looked like he belonged on one. He held his head high, and his smirk made him look cool and aloof.

Jonathan wished he could pull off something like that but settled for his natural smile that crinkled the corners of his eyes and showed off his teeth. It may not have been "cool," but it was him, and he was starting to understand that being himself was better than anything else he could have ever hoped to be.

Thirty-Three

They pulled into the parking lot ten minutes later. The lot was already pretty full, and a line of cars waited to drop students off. Once they found a parking spot that wasn't too far away, Jonathan, Destiny, and Chance got out and did a quick once-over for one another to make sure they looked as good as possible before they made their way toward the doors.

Small groups of students clustered outside the doors, waiting for other friends or simply watching their classmates arrive. Chance pushed through the gathering crowd, ensuring their attention would be focused entirely on Destiny and Jonathan as they walked by.

Jonathan leaned in close to Destiny. "Why do you let him flirt with you when you and he both know nothing will ever come of it?"

She looked around as they passed the other students, whose eyes were glued to them. "I'd rather he flirt with me than hurt someone else," she said quietly. "I'm not going to fall for his tricks or be influenced by his . . . charm," she said carefully. "In a way, it feels like a public service."

Jonathan laughed and shook his head. "You two are so different from everyone else I know."

"You have no idea." Laughing, she threaded her arm through his and pulled him close.

Jonathan, for once, didn't feel self-conscious about the stares he was getting from everyone around him. He'd adopted the walk he'd seen Chance use earlier, with his head held high and his unique smile pasted proudly on his face, as his best friend escorted him inside. Once they caught up to Chance, Jonathan looped his left arm through Chance's. They walked together as a force much bigger than Jonathan understood.

Once they made it to the front door, Jonathan panicked for the first time since agreeing to attend the dance as he remembered he didn't have a ticket. Right before they made it to the front of the line of students, however, the teacher checking tickets turned away to answer the question of a parent who had barged in, skipping the line, and demanded answers

The three friends walked inside while the teacher was distracted.

"There's no way we'll get away with that all night." Jonathan's forehead prickled with sweat, cracking his confident facade for the first time.

"No one is going to check tickets once we're already inside," Destiny said.

Even inside, people continued to stare at the three of them as they stood just inside the doors together. They had stopped under a recessed light, which acted as a spotlight that reflected off Destiny's dress, making her whole body appear to glow. And when they moved to the side to wait in line for photos, the golden glow from the photographer's softboxes made all three of them look like they belonged in a magazine and not at a high-school dance.

They filled out the necessary forms and stood on their marks for the photos. Even though they told the photographer they were okay with group pictures, she took individual shots, mixed-couples shots, and photos of all three of them together. Eventually, Destiny gave Chance a look Jonathan didn't understand, but neither of them said anything. The photographer finally seemed to notice how long she'd been photographing them and asked them to move along.

"Okay, now that we've gotten photos out of the way, before we do anything else . . ." Chance pulled them to the side conspiratorially. "Food first!"

Laughing, Jonathan and Destiny repeated after him and followed him to a table with cups and large containers of water, lemonade, and iced tea. Next to the drinks were large platters of cookies, brownie bites, lemon squares, and small cheesecake bites in muffin liners. They each grabbed a small plate and helped themselves to a few snacks and a cup of something to drink, before they made their way to a nearby table to enjoy their refreshments. It was still early, and while music was playing, no one had begun to dance yet, so they relaxed and enjoyed each other's company.

An hour later, Jonathan's spine stiffened. Billy and the rest of the Telepathic Tacos had arrived and begun to set up their equipment for their performance later that evening. They were busy, which kept Billy's attention on the work at hand, but every once in a while, he would look out at the students standing in front of the stage. Jonathan couldn't be sure, but he assumed Billy was looking for him.

Just then, his phone vibrated in his pocket. It was a

photo from Luke, which showed the line of students standing outside the venue doors, with the message *Wish you were here* beneath it.

Jonathan considered responding, but he didn't want to leave his friends, who had gone to such great lengths to get him here, just to hang out with Luke and his friends, so he slid the phone back into his pocket without replying. If they ran into each other later, he'd deal with it then, but for now, he was focusing on his friends.

Once the room had gotten a bit fuller and people had started dancing, Destiny and Chance stood up and each extended a hand to Jonathan. Grabbing them both, he let them lead him to the dance floor, where they danced together for the next few minutes.

When the music quieted down, they stopped and turned to the stage, where Cam, lead singer of the Telepathic Tacos, had grabbed the microphone and was staring out over the crowd.

"How's everybody doing tonight?" he called out to the crowd of students. There was a smattering of positive responses, but Cam didn't seem convinced. "Sorry, I thought this was your prom night, not some random day of the week! I said, how is everybody doing tonight?" This got more of a response, but he still didn't look satisfied. He looked behind him. "Guys, I think I'm going to need your help with this one. Can you come on out?"

The other three band members walked up and took their places on the stage, and almost immediately, they began playing one of their more popular and loud songs.

The students who knew the band started to go crazy, including Jonathan and Destiny, who stood off to the right near the front of the stage, where Alonzo usually stood. The students who hadn't heard their music seemed hesitant, but the longer the song went on, the more they started to get into it, and by the time the song ended, everyone was on their feet and dancing to the music.

"That's what I want to see, Eureka High School. Now let's do this!" They launched into the next song.

Jonathan and Destiny sang along as they danced, while Chance, who still didn't know the songs, danced around, occasionally jumping up and down, which caught Alonzo's attention. Jonathan could tell when he recognized Chance; his fingers slipped off his guitar strings, but he recovered quickly.

The band played a mix of new music Jonathan and Destiny had never heard and older songs they knew and loved. After fifteen minutes, Cam got back on the microphone again.

"We're gonna slow it down for a couple songs now, so find that person you want to hold on to and don't let go."

As he finished, the lights dimmed, and they began to play a song Jonathan didn't recognize. He, Destiny, and Chance danced together, holding onto each other until it got awkward. Deciding to take a break, they walked back to their table.

"I'm going to go get a refill," Jonathan said. "Do either of you need anything while I'm gone?" The other two shook their heads, and he walked away.

As Destiny watched Jonathan make his way to the refreshment table, Chance leaned into her. "How do you think he's doing?"

"Honestly, he's doing better than I had hoped. He seems to be having a good time so far and just going with the flow."

She started to relax, but then something shifted. Stiffening, she focused on the paths and tried to figure out what had happened. Before she could, a commotion drew her attention to the refreshments table, where Jonathan was backing away from Mike Lawler as quickly as possible. From the looks of it, Jonathan had spilled a drink on Kelly Noe's dress, and now Mike was all up in his face about it.

Destiny and Chance rushed over in time to see Mike shove Jonathan, who tripped and fell to the ground. A small group was already forming around them, making it difficult for Jonathan to get back on his feet. Destiny could feel that even more things were falling out of order around them—the result of what she and Chance had done to make tonight happen for Jonathan. They couldn't stop it, not without risking even worse fallout.

"Screw it! Chance, do something, quick!"

Pushing him ahead of her, she did what she could to keep people from looking over while Chance threw his influence out in every direction possible. Suddenly, the students who had been watching the altercation seemed to find something much more interesting happening anywhere else.

"What's your problem, Mike?" Chance demanded as he approached from Jonathan's left.

"This little dick just spilled his drink all over my girlfriend, and now I'm gonna make him regret it."

"It's not little," Chance said, glancing down at Jonathan.

Mike looked confused, only to stumble backward when Chance grabbed his shoulder and pushed him.

As Destiny grabbed Jonathan's hand, helping him up and out of the way, he hurriedly explained. "I didn't mean to spill it on her. I was trying to balance three cups in case you and Chance changed your minds, but I ran into the leg of a chair and dropped one of them on her." He still held the other two cups, though they were only half full since Mike had pushed him.

Taking hold of Kelly's hand, Destiny saw that this was her last straw. She was already planning how to break up with Mike before the night ended. "Kelly," Destiny said, "are you okay? Do you need help getting your dress cleaned up? I'm happy to do whatever you need."

"It was just water," Jonathan added, trying to help.

Looking relieved, Kelly laughed. "Oh, thank god. My mom would have killed me if I had ruined this dress!"

"I am so sorry, Kelly," Jonathan continued. "I didn't see the chair leg."

"It's fine." Kelly accepted a handful of napkins from one of her nearby friends and began patting her dress down. "No stain, no foul." She giggled.

"Let's get back to our table," Destiny said now that things were de-escalating quickly. Jonathan carefully stepped around Kelly and behind Chance, who kept Mike back from the rest of them.

"We all good here?" Chance asked, even as he continued to manipulate things around him to keep everyone distracted—including Mike, who appeared to still be recovering from Chance's earlier retort.

Nodding, Kelly grabbed Mike's arm and pulled him to the side for what would no doubt be a serious conversation. By the time they made it back to the table, Destiny could see that people were returning to what they had been doing before the fight.

Well, except for one person, who still had their eyes locked on Jonathan.

"Don't look now, but Billy's looking at you."

Thirty-Four

Jonathan sighed and took a sip of water and then jumped a little as someone tapped on his shoulder. He turned around to find Luke standing there, looking as hot as ever.

"What're you doing here?" Luke asked when Jonathan stood up. "You told me you weren't going to make it." His eyes were focused on Jonathan's, and he seemed unsure how to continue now that he'd confirmed it was actually Jonathan.

Jonathan opened his mouth, but nothing came out as he caught the look of disappointment on Luke's face. "Yeah, sort of a last-minute decision," he finally said, gesturing vaguely to Destiny and Chance seated behind him. His cheeks began to heat up. "I should have said something to you. I'm sorry."

Luke looked Jonathan up and down. "You look . . . wow!"

Jonathan took a moment to look at Luke fully as well and realized that even though his tuxedo was emerald green, it was an exact match for Jonathan's in every other detail. His blue eyes, which also matched Jonathan's, were bright and full of emotion—including something that might have been desire. His hair was combed into a messy perfection that Jonathan could never hope to pull off but that looked incredible on him.

"You look pretty wow yourself."

Luke puffed out his chest. "Thanks. I'm glad you decided to come. Even if you didn't tell me about it."

They stood there awkwardly for a few seconds before Luke spoke up again. "Hey, did Mike start something with you earlier?"

"Oh, that. I accidentally spilled some water on Kelly, and he got in my face about it. Why? Did he say something?" Jonathan wondered what Luke's friends said about him when he wasn't around.

"Sort of. I went to the bathroom before it happened, and when I came out, he was in the corner with Kelly yelling at him. He left after that." Luke glanced at the door. "When I walked out to find out what happened, I found him crying in his car, and he said you made Kelly break up with him or something?" Luke seemed unsure of what to make of what he'd seen.

Jonathan opened his mouth a little as he tried to think of how to respond, but he eventually went with, "I'm not sure I can take the credit or blame for that."

Luke laughed but then got serious again. "I told him not to mess with you anymore or he'd have to answer to me, and he told me he didn't want any trouble. Then he asked something about 'how big is it?' I didn't understand that part."

Jonathan's face scrunched up in confusion, but behind him, Chance laughed. Shrugging, Jonathan shook his head. "I'm not sure I can shed any light on that either. Sorry." Then he realized what else Luke had said. He'd stuck up for Jonathan in front of his friends, including the team captain. "You didn't have to do that—stick up for me, I mean. I could have dealt with things on my own," he said, though he knew Chance and Destiny would have been there to help.

"Oh, I know; I wanted to. Besides," he added casually, "I can't have anyone else making moves on my boyfriend. It makes me look like I can't stand up for what's mine."

Jonathan's heart jumped. "I'm sorry, I think I misheard what you just said. Did you call me your . . . ?"

"My boyfriend?" Luke repeated, suddenly looking uncertain. "Is that too much too soon?"

"I'm just—I think I—I'm not sure I understand what you mean by that." Jonathan's heart was in his throat, making it difficult to swallow, let alone breathe.

"Well, we've been hanging out a lot lately and you came to the game and now you're here and you kissed me the other day . . . so I sort of assumed we were dating. Did I get that wrong?" Luke looked around as if looking for someone else to clarify the situation.

"You want to date me?" Jonathan asked, still unable to believe he was hearing Luke correctly.

"Was that not clear from what I just said?" Luke looked past him at Destiny and Chance, who were no doubt listening from the table behind them.

Jonathan turned and looked at his friends, who stared back at him blankly. Before he turned back around, though, Destiny gave him a thumbs-up.

"Maybe this will clear things up for you." Stepping closer, Luke wrapped his hand around the back of Jonathan's head and pulled him into a kiss that made everything around them seem to fade into the background. After a few seconds, Luke pulled away, and Jonathan stared at him as he attempted to regain his balance.

"I'm not sure," Jonathan finally said. "You might have to try again." He tried and failed to hide a smile.

"Oh, is that so?" Luke leaned forward again and kissed him softly.

"Still not getting it," Jonathan tried when they finally separated, but he couldn't keep a straight face.

Luke threw an arm around Jonathan's neck anyway and pulled him close. "I'll make it clear this time. Jonathan, do you want to be my boyfriend?" Luke's lips were right next to Jonathan's ear, and Jonathan could feel the warmth of his breath and smell the spearmint from his gum as he asked the question.

Jonathan had never imagined he would start dating in high school. He'd resigned himself to waiting until college, so the directness of Luke's question caught him off guard. He took a shallow breath, relieved that he could no longer feel his pulse in his throat, and responded, "Yes."

Luke pulled back. "Yes?" he asked, as if worried he had misunderstood.

Jonathan nodded. "Yes!"

Leaning in, Luke kissed his cheek. Then he reached down, grabbed Jonathan's hand, and led him out to the middle of the dance floor. As he did, everyone else moved away from them, clearing the entire center of the floor for the two of them. They swayed gently back and forth, spinning in slow circles.

"People are staring at us," Jonathan whispered in Luke's ear.

"What people? All I see is you," Luke responded as the music swelled, and he leaned in and kissed Jonathan again. As the kiss ended, he whispered, "Are they still looking?"

Jonathan held Luke closer as his heart raced. "Who?"

When the song ended, Cam announced that the band would take a quick break and return soon. As soon as Cam finished, Billy practically dropped his guitar on the stage and headed straight for Jonathan.

Seeing him coming, Jonathan backed away from Luke a little. "I'll be right back, okay?"

Following the line of Jonathan's gaze, Luke nodded. "I'll be here when you're ready." He stepped back so Jonathan and Billy could talk.

"I didn't think you'd be here," Billy said once he was close enough for Jonathan to hear him.

Jonathan averted his gaze. "Admittedly, I wasn't planning to be, but my friends talked me into it."

"I know you probably don't want to talk to me right now, especially with what just happened, but I'd like to talk to you if possible. Would that be okay?" He extended his hand.

"Yeah, okay." Taking Billy's hand, Jonathan allowed himself to be pulled in close as they danced and talked. He looked around to see if people were staring, but to his surprise, no one seemed to have noticed them yet. "What did you want to talk about?"

"I wanted to apologize for how I treated you, including refusing to see how much you wanted to spend time with me and not making myself available when I had the chance. I also wanted to apologize for not agreeing to come to this dance with you when you asked. I was dealing with a lot, including some stuff with the band, but I didn't share that with you. You didn't know what was happening, and that was my fault, not yours."

"I understood that you were busy, Billy. It was never about how much time we spent together, though I wouldn't have been upset if we had been able to spend more time together. It was the fact that you dismissed me entirely, without even considering my invitation." To Jonathan's surprise, he was no longer upset by what had happened. With Billy's arms wrapped around his waist, he had gotten what he wanted in the end. "What changed, anyway?"

"What do you mean?" Billy asked, confused.

"You said you couldn't dance with me because the band had to appear 'straight' or whatever."

"Oh, that!" Billy laughed, which surprised Jonathan, and pulled him closer. "Well, it turns out that more of us are queer than we originally realized. When I saw Alonzo making out with Chance that day you two came to our apartment, I asked him what happened, and he said he felt the sudden urge to kiss him and wasn't sure he was straight."

Jonathan couldn't believe what he was hearing. He turned to look at Chance, who glanced away when he realized Jonathan was looking in his direction. "Why did that matter?"

"Well, we ended up having a band meeting the next day to discuss our image and decided that if people didn't like us for who we were, we didn't need those people as fans in the first place. Plus,"—he shrugged one shoulder—"there aren't as many queer-leaning punk indie bands from the Midwest as straight punk indie bands, so it helps us stand out a little bit."

Jonathan laughed and shook his head in disbelief. "And did Chance know about this?"

"I don't know. I think so. I'm pretty sure Cam told him since he was the one who helped us get this gig."

"He told me he had news about the band that he thought I would want to hear, but I shut him down. This whole time, I could have had you as my date!"

Billy shrugged and laughed. "Funny how things work out, huh?" He looked beyond Jonathan—where Luke stood, giving them space but keeping a careful eye on them—and then up at the stage. Jonathan was still processing the information Billy had already shared when Billy spoke again. "When, uh . . . when you didn't call me back or return my messages, I talked to Alonzo a little bit more about things, and we ended up kinda going on a date."

Spinning around, Jonathan looked at Alonzo, who looked away when he realized he'd been caught staring. Jonathan chuckled and turned back toward Billy. "Good for you two!" he said with genuine happiness. "You make a cute couple!"

"Whoa, I'm not sure we'll go that far with things. We already live together. If we broke up, it could potentially mess up the band and our living situation." He looked up at Alonzo again and waved. "But thank you for saying that. And for what it's worth, I'm sorry again for what I did. I never meant to hurt you. I hope you don't regret letting me be your first kiss."

Guilt struck Jonathan at those words. "Since we're being honest with each other, I have to admit something to you." He looked Billy in the eyes. "You weren't the first guy I kissed."

"Oh?"

"What I meant when I said I had wanted that to be my first kiss was that, at the time, I had wanted it to be my first kiss, but by the time you kissed me, I had kissed someone else." Jonathan squeezed his eyes shut. "Earlier that same day, actually."

When Billy remained silent, Jonathan slowly opened his eyes.

Billy's eyes sparkled, and he started laughing loudly, which caused a few people to glance at them. "We are quite a pair, aren't we?" Billy poked Jonathan in the side, making him laugh and squirm a little. "That's okay. I'm not upset, and I appreciate your honesty. Who knows," he added with a shrug, "maybe things would have been different if we'd talked about things before it all went sideways."

Jonathan looked over at Luke and then up at Alonzo, who was still pretending not to watch them, before finally facing Billy again. "I dunno. I think maybe we ended up right where we were supposed to."

The song ended a moment later, and they took a step back from each other. Billy nodded at Luke, who walked over and grabbed Jonathan's hand, intertwining their fingers.

"I think you're right," Billy agreed and took another step back. "Well, I'd better grab some water before we're on again. It was nice seeing you again, Jonathan. I hope you'll still come to our shows in the future."

"You'll have to take out a restraining order to keep us away," Jonathan admitted with a laugh as he and Billy shared a quick hug. Waving goodbye to Luke, Billy walked away, and Jonathan and Luke rejoined Chance and Destiny at their table.

Destiny waited about three seconds before demanding to know what had happened. Jonathan gave her, Luke, and Chance a brief recap of the highlights. He included that Chance had helped the band realize that owning up to their queer leanings wasn't a bad thing.

"I tried to tell you about that," Chance said, "but you weren't ready to hear it yet."

"I know, and I'm sorry. But I appreciate that you respected my wishes, even if you knew I probably would have done things differently if I had had all the information."

Thirty-Five

Some of Luke's friends joined their table and congratulated Jonathan for snagging the undatable friend they'd been trying to help set up for years. He laughed and squeezed Luke's hand, which rested on his leg. "I'm not sure I can take any credit for that. I don't want to over-share, but he's pretty charming when he wants to be." He leaned into Luke.

Luke laughed and squeezed Jonathan's hand back. "I guess I just had to wait for the right person to come along so I could be the guy I've always wanted to be."

On stage, Billy walked over to Cam to say something in his ear, and Cam nodded. Once their current song ended, Cam handed Billy the microphone and stepped to the side.

"All right, everyone, we hope you've enjoyed our set tonight!" Billy called out to the crowd, who turned their attention to him now that the music had stopped. "We are the Telepathic Tacos!" The crowd broke into applause, including Jonathan and Luke. "We've got one more song to play for you tonight, dedicated to one of your own." The students looked around as if waiting for someone to own up to it, but no one did. "I hope that no matter what happens, you always choose love. Happy prom, Eureka High School!"

The students began cheering again as Billy handed the microphone back to Cam and walked back to his spot on stage. The music started up again, slowly at first and then building into something a little faster. "This one's for the new couple in the room," Cam said, and everyone looked at Jonathan and Luke. "It's called 'Floating and Falling.'"

"We've gotta dance to this one!" Luke gently pulled Jonathan out of his seat and toward the dance floor. The rest of their friends followed close behind, forming a circle around the two of them as they danced slowly to the music. By the time Cam started singing, the song had changed rhythm, and the other students had paired up again for one last slow dance of the night.

> We started as friends at first
> But quickly became strangers.
> I refused to let you quench my thirst
> In this desert full of dangers.
>
> Then I was stuck in the day in and day out,
> I wouldn't let you see the real me.
> I resigned myself to scream and shout,
> And that's all I thought I'd ever be.
>
> But I can't stop thinking about that kiss.
> You were floating; I was falling.
> No, I can't stop thinking about that kiss.
> You were floating; I was falling
>
> I told you I could never change

Because I didn't want you to see.
I'd never let my life get rearranged,
But that's exactly what you did to me.

Then I was stuck in the day in and day out,
I wouldn't let you see the real me.
I resigned myself to scream and shout,
And that's all I thought I'd ever be.

Yeah, I can't stop thinking about that kiss.
You were floating; I was falling.
No, I can't stop thinking about that kiss.
You were floating; I was falling.

Cuz I didn't wanna let you in,
So I kept shutting you out again.
No, I didn't wanna let you in,
So I kept shutting you out again.

But I can't stop thinking about that kiss.
You were floating; I was falling.
No, I can't stop thinking about that kiss.
You were floating; I was falling.

Now I can't stop thinking about that kiss.
You were floating; I was falling.
No, I can't stop thinking about that kiss.
You were floating; I was falling.

Cam's voice filled the venue, and everyone was dancing as if by magic. Jonathan made eye contact with Billy, who nodded at him as the chorus repeated. Blushing, Jonathan pulled Luke closer and nodded a thank-you to Billy before looking away again.

After everything, he couldn't believe he'd ended up here with Luke. All the drama and stress, the days spent moping around, and somehow, he had still gotten the guy.

He laughed at how lucky he had been, and Luke pulled away briefly so he could look Jonathan in the face.

"What's so funny?" he asked, looking happier than he had in a long time.

"It's nothing. I just can't believe we ended up here." Jonathan looked around at the other students dancing nearby. "Dancing. At prom. As a couple!"

"Well, you might have had some idea if you had just stuck around the game like I asked you to!" Luke squeezed Jonathan tightly in a hug.

"What do you mean?" he asked, genuinely curious.

"Mike stole my thunder when he asked Kelly to the dance at the game. Since you still hadn't responded to my invitation, I got some of the guys to wear T-shirts under their uniforms that spelled out *PROM?*, and I was going to ask you when the game ended. But when I went looking for you, you had already left. What happened to you anyway?"

Jonathan laughed and dropped his head onto Luke's shoulder. "It's a long and dumb story. Let's just pretend I stuck around and said yes."

Luke spun him around on the dance floor and kissed him once more as the song ended. "That works for me."

There was a brief pause while the music switched from the band to the prepared playlist. Once the music started up again, Chance, Destiny, and Luke's friends formed a circle that Jonathan and Luke joined. They all danced together for the rest of the night, laughing and singing along with the songs they recognized. They were pulled into one conversation after another, until the dance was nearly over, at which point, Jonathan and Luke broke off from the group to dance on their own again.

Chance and Destiny joined the other students in enjoying the last dance of the night, paying particular attention to Eureka's newest couple. Jonathan looked at his friends, and they gestured back encouragingly before Luke spun him away again.

"Well, it didn't happen the way I thought it would." Chance laughed despite losing their bet. "I really thought the new song would put Billy ahead," he admitted. "And I didn't see that twist with Alonzo coming." He shook his head, but the twinkle in his eye gave away his true feelings.

Destiny could tell he wasn't telling the truth. "You knew Alonzo was gay, didn't you?"

He shrugged but looked away from her scrutiny. "I knew he was attracted to me, but not that he had been pining after Billy for months. How was I supposed to know they would walk out right after I started kissing him and see us on the couch?" His power sparked, but he was content to leave everything alone.

"Uh-huh . . ." Destiny laughed and rested a hand on his chest. "I didn't realize you were such a softy, Chance. You did something to help someone other than yourself for once."

"I did, didn't I?" He watched Jonathan laugh as he and Luke spun each other. Jonathan's eyes had a golden ring he'd never noticed before, but somehow, it felt like it had always been part of him. "Some things are worth doing, even when they go against my better judgment. Especially if it makes someone I care about happy," he said quietly enough that only she could hear. "Don't tell anyone I said that. I don't want to ruin my reputation as a self-centered international playboy." He managed to keep a straight face until Destiny turned to him, mouth hanging open. Then he cracked a wide grin. "Got ya!" He laughed.

Destiny nudged him in the side with her elbow. "I'm not sure about that last part, but your secret is safe with me. And I should tell you, I'm surprised by how much I've enjoyed spending time with you over the past few weeks. I can't say it was always easy," she admitted, holding her hands up in front of her, "but it has never been boring."

Chance chuckled at her honesty, which he appreciated. He always knew where he stood with her. "I'll take that." They continued to dance in companionable silence for a few seconds before he voiced the question he'd been pondering since they'd walked in the doors a few hours ago. "What do you think will happen now that prom is over?"

Destiny looked at Jonathan, surrounded by Luke's friends, and sighed loudly. "Honestly, I have no idea. I'm not sure he needs us anymore. After all, he finally got what he wanted."

Chance's chest tightened. "You don't really believe that, do you?"

"I guess we'll just have to wait to see what tomorrow brings."

Chance nodded but didn't feel comforted by her reply. A sharp pain had started in his chest when Luke asked Jonathan to be his boyfriend, and now it had grown and spread. "At least it looks like everything happened the way it was supposed to this time." He gave Destiny a serious look, and she looked back at him with tears brimming.

Her eyes widened, and she grabbed her stomach but said nothing.

Chance bit down hard, his teeth grinding as his entire body filled with the same pain he'd felt all those years ago.

His muscles tightened, and his legs locked in place. A cold fire began to burn just below his diaphragm, making it difficult to speak. He made eye contact with Destiny and saw that the tears had started falling from her eyes as she hugged herself tightly.

"Oh, Chance, when will you learn?" She closed her eyes tightly, speaking slowly as if trying to prolong the inevitable for as long as possible. "This . . . was . . . always . . . meant—"

"Don't you dare!" he said, covering her mouth before she could finish her sentence. "I actually like this song. I want to stay until it ends."

Opening her eyes, she looked down at his hand and took a deep, shuddering breath.

Chance realized there was no bright light, and the cold burn and chest pain had slowly faded, making it easier for him to speak. Destiny wiped a few tears from her eyes before taking another deep breath and letting out an unexpected laugh.

"Me too."

Thirty-Six

Jonathan opened his eyes as a beam of sunlight somehow found its way through the curtains and landed on his face. Rolling over, he grabbed his phone off the charger and saw it was just before seven in the morning.

He plopped back down on the bed. "It's too fucking early for this."

"Mnnpf." The angry groan from beside him told him that Destiny was also awake. "Who are you talking to?"

"No one," he said. "Go back to bed. It's too early to think." He rolled onto his side and away from the window and the offending sun.

"Why are you both still talking?" Chance asked from the floor next to Jonathan's bed. "Some of us were still trying to enjoy a nice weekend of sleeping in even though we weren't allowed to be in bed with the rest of you."

"You know the rules," Destiny said. "Jonathan's in a relationship now, so no more flirting with you. And I'm not willing to have you breathing on me all night."

"Oh my god, will you three never stop talking?"

Jonathan snorted as the familiar, if angry, voice broke up the argument between Chance and Destiny. "Sorry, Luke," he said with a giggle.

"Sorry, Luke," Destiny added.

"Sorry," Chance grumbled, having covered his face with his pillow.

A few moments of silence followed before a particularly loud fart erupted from Chance.

"That's it." Luke sat up and threw his pillow toward the bed. "I'm getting coffee. There's no way I'll make it the whole day without caffeine, and falling back asleep isn't gonna happen now. Anyone wanna join?"

There was an immediate chorus of agreement among the other three, and Chance and Destiny hopped up and began getting ready. After a few minutes of mostly quiet scrambling, they left the room to use the bathroom, though based on the looks they sent Jonathan as they closed the door, they did it more to give him a moment of privacy with Luke.

Luke climbed into bed next to Jonathan, carefully draping his arm over him and pulling him close so they could spoon.

"Good morning," Jonathan said quietly and kissed Luke's arm.

"Mm, good morning to you too. I wouldn't mind waking up like this more often." Luke kissed Jonathan's neck, eliciting several fairly high-pitched squeals.

Jonathan spun around to face Luke. "I wish! But my mom would kill me if she walked in on this."

"You know, I don't think she ever checked last night. We missed our shot. I could have slept in the bed with you." Luke's eyes were closed, but the grin on his face and the way he grabbed Jonathan's butt communicated plenty.

Jonathan laughed and covered his mouth quickly, concerned about his morning-breath situation. Luke finally opened his eyes and leaned forward for a kiss.

"Huh. I've never noticed that ring of gold in your eyes." Grinning, Luke kissed Jonathan again before turning around and grabbing his cell phone. "All right, they're ready. Let's go!"

"What do you mean?" Jonathan asked, but Luke was already up and halfway out the bedroom door.

After brushing their teeth and putting on their shoes, they joined the other two at the front door and quietly stepped out into the early-morning light, careful not to wake Jonathan's mother. Luke grabbed Jonathan's hand and intertwined their fingers as they walked ahead of Destiny and Chance.

Jonathan took a deep breath of the cool morning air and tilted his head back. The sun was warm on his face, his sexy boyfriend had come out for him in front of everyone at the dance and was now holding his hand in public, and his two best friends were finally starting to get along. It felt like there was nothing that could touch his happiness now.

Destiny watched Jonathan and Luke walk hand in hand down the street. Jonathan practically radiated happiness, and Luke's energy had finally stabilized and was firmly attached to Jonathan. This was all she'd ever wanted for Jonathan: someone who would treat him how he deserved and, as far as she could tell, would be careful with his kind heart.

Chance nudged her shoulder gently. "You're looking pretty pleased with yourself."

"I won. Of course I do."

Chance raised his eyebrows. "We both got him to the dance. If anything, we tied."

Destiny looked at him thoughtfully. "You know what, I'm feeling good today, so I'll be generous and agree with you. We worked well together. Who knew that was possible?" She laughed.

Suddenly, a bright beam of sunlight caught her attention, and she looked back at Jonathan and Luke.

Chance stopped in place, wide-eyed and slack-jawed. "What the hell is that?"

"I have no idea." She watched the wide beam of sunlight illuminate the couple like a spotlight, following them as they kept walking. She sent her power toward Jonathan, expecting the same emptiness she was always met with, and her breath caught in her throat. "Oh my gods . . ."

"What? What is it?" Chance demanded, still enamored with the sunlight following the couple.

"It's Apollo." She gestured toward the light that continued to pace Jonathan and Luke.

Chance turned his attention to Destiny at her revelation. "The sun god? What does that mean?"

"I have no idea." As Destiny watched, row after row of deep-purple flowers sprouted behind Jonathan as he walked. "But I think I know why we can't use our powers on Jonathan."

"Why? Who is he?" Chance's eyes were squinted against the sun's brightness, which he kept trying to look at, presumably for some hint as to what was happening.

"Apollo's ex."

Acknowledgments

This story is very close to my heart for various reasons, and I have many people to thank for helping me bring it to life. Your support has been instrumental in the completion of this book.

I want to start by thanking my wonderful, supportive, and amazing husband, Cameron, for believing in me and always supporting me and my writing. He gave me the time and space to keep writing when I was close to the end of this book and, more importantly, when I needed that final push and encouragement to get through each round of edits, of which there were many. He has been the ultimate supporter of my dreams, and without him, none of them would be as far along as they are today. Thank you, I love you so much!

I also want to thank my friends and family who read, provided feedback and encouragement, asked helpful questions (some of which I didn't have good answers for at the time), and supported me as this book went from a vague idea to the final version you just read. Mom, Dad, KT, Joey, Jackie, Casey, Kelly, and Devin—thank you so much for everything you've done to help me and this book along the way. Even the smallest amount of support was appreciated! Thank you to Jess for reading and critiquing the first draft. I hope you love what the story has turned into! Thanks also to Georganna, Clay, Chase, and Monica for your continued support and interest in my stories. I appreciate you putting up with me occasionally taking over conversations with book talk.

My sincere thanks to Balance of Seven press, especially Charlene, for believing in my work from the beginning and for the invaluable feedback and support you provided throughout the process. Thank you to Tod for your editing, formatting, and other support. Your suggestions have helped this story become the best version of itself, and I couldn't have done it without you. I am truly grateful for both of you and your significant contributions to this story!

Thank you to my fellow S&S orphans, who have offered fantastic advice and support since we all became an unexpected group navigating the tumult of the publishing world! Nicole, you have been so helpful with your resources and advice! Elizabeth, your near-constant writing and editing schedule has been an inspiration over the last couple of years! I can never hope to live up to your example, but watching you push yourself keeps me motivated! Amanda, you have been so helpful when things were very much at their lowest, and your continued support with anything I have ever asked has been appreciated more than you will ever know! Zoë, Shauna, and Neal, your optimism, even in the face of rejection and disappointment, was the positivity we all needed, and I thank you for that!

To my fellow Queerkats—Caitlin, Clay, Emma, Isaac, Judah, Mazie, Milo, Nailah, and Sarah—I learned so much from you all. Our nine months together was the best writing experience of my life. I cannot wait to see all your stories out in the world! I hope you enjoy this book as much as I've enjoyed yours!

About the Author

Kenneth Creech is an award-winning author who contributed to the 2023 Independent Press Award's selection for best Anthology, *Queer for the New Year: Nine Stories of New Beginnings*. *Fate, Coincidence, and Other Curse Words* is his third full-length novel, following a queer YA paranormal fantasy duology, the Awakened series. He currently lives outside Houston, TX, with his husband and their dorkie (dachshund/Yorkie). When he's not writing, he can be found baking and trying out new cookie recipes, traveling with his family, and attempting to keep his social media updated as often as possible.

To learn more about Kenneth, his writing process, and future projects, visit him at www.kennethcreech.com.

You can also connect with Kenneth on various social media platforms here: https://linktr.ee/kbcreech_.

www.ingramcontent.com/pod-product-compliance
Lightning Source LLC
Chambersburg PA
CBHW051204220726
48293CB00014B/1879